Born in Grantham, Angela went to school i
departing for the big city when she was ei
out to be an interesting and highly vari
corporation. Majoring in IT in the 70s, sl.
managing major change programmes.

Retiring early to Stratford-upon-Avon in 2002, Angela
rediscovered her childhood love of writing. She started her first
novel, *Lakeside*, while relaxing in California's National Parks.
Completing *Lakeside*, she has since published *The Silver Sting* and
its sequel, *The Silver Dollar*, and now *The Gypsy Killer*. Her stories
draw on people she has known and places she has visited. In Angela's
own words, "The characters in my book have their own unique lives.
They represent the richness and diversity of life."

Angela loves theatre and everything theatrical and has spread
her wings into writing short and one act plays, the first of which is
due to be performed in her hometown of Stratford-upon-Avon in
2021. An active member of the Bardstown Writers group and the
Stratford Playwrights group, Angela still finds time to travel, drive
her classic car, enjoy crafting, entertain family and friends, and get
thoroughly dirty in her garden!

www.angeladandy.com

# Also by Angela Dandy

*Lakeside*
*The Silver Sting*
*The Silver Dollar*

# THE
# GYPSY
# KILLER

## ANGELA DANDY

*Sue.*
*Best Wishes*
*Angela Dandy*

**SilverWood**

Published in 2021 by SilverWood Books

SilverWood Books Ltd
14 Small Street, Bristol, BS1 1DE, United Kingdom
www.silverwoodbooks.co.uk

ISBN 978-1-80042-110-3 (paperback)
ISBN 978-1-80042-111-0 (ebook)

British Library Cataloguing in Publication Data
A CIP catalogue record for this book is available from the British Library

Page design and typesetting by SilverWood Books

# The Gypsy Killer

# One

On the fifth of December 2009, Dr Boscombe had just returned home from an early morning call-out. Slipping off his warm, navy blue wool coat, hat, scarf and gloves, he rubbed his hands together. Having been up and out at six, he was ready for his breakfast.

Eyeing the two boiled eggs in front of him with a measure of disdain, Dr Boscombe picked up his spoon and gently tapped the tops of them. He could tell by the sound whether they were cooked to his liking or not – if there was no ring to them, then they were probably overcooked and would be sent back. If they had a slightly hollow ring, then they would be soft and edible. Unusually, they were as he liked them. Carefully slicing the buttered toast on his side plate into soldiers, he smiled at his wife. Tall, and thin, with greying hair scraped back in a tight bun, she was not the sort of woman whom he would want to parade on his arm, but he had made a good choice.

"Thank you, dear," he said.

"And how was the poor man?"

"You mean my early call this morning? Beyond my help, dear, I am sorry to say. Early stages of pneumonia – it won't be long before they lay him to rest. They are all the same, you know. They smoke like chimneys all their lives, sit out in all weathers, live in filthy, dirty conditions, and then they're surprised when they get emphysema, and even more surprised when a cold turns into flu and flu turns into pneumonia. No point in blocking a hospital bed with that one – he'll be gone in a few days. Had I even suggested that he should be in hospital they would have run me out of the camp. Gypsies like to care for their own, and if the good Lord dictates, die in their own beds. No doubt they'll have stuffed him full of herbal rubbish by now. I do feel for them, I really do," he replied, as he upended the first eggshell in the egg cup and turned his attention to the second.

"It's such a shame, Dr Boscombe. They are so lucky to have someone like you to care for them and particularly at that time of the morning. Not many doctors would willingly go out and visit them at their camps. It must be a hard life for them. I do wish we could do more to help them." His wife wiped her hands on the tea towel and looked out of the window in the direction of the camp, which lay just the other side of town. She had called him Dr Boscombe ever since the first day they had met. She had been so proud to be asked to walk out with a doctor.

"God helps those who help themselves, my dear. Always remember that. There's only so much that we mere mortals can do," Dr Boscombe replied.

Dr Boscombe licked his lips; it had been quite a lucrative morning. A little more cash in the bank was always welcome. He had told them time and time again that if they paid their National Insurance like everyone else, then he would not have to charge for his visits. Little did they know. He had no intention of enlightening them.

Glancing down at the pile of notes sitting on the table – one hundred pounds for the call-out and ten pounds for the thirty-pence pack of aspirin, he thought it fair exchange for getting up and out at six o'clock in the morning. It was a pity that he couldn't charge them the same amount every time they came into the surgery, but it would never do for money to be seen changing hands. People might get the wrong idea.

Wiping his lips with his napkin, he drained his tea and picked up the telephone.

"Sebastian, I will be in a little late today…had an early call-out to the camp…pneumonia…no, too late for that…I did suggest hospital, but you know what they're like…did all I could to make him comfortable…I'll make my report when I come into the surgery."

He almost felt sorry for them – they really had had a run of bad luck in the past few months. Such a pretty girl and so young. What were they thinking about letting a fourteen-year-old child run wild? It was nothing short of criminal. Why the mother had brought her into the surgery he'd never know. It was perfectly obvious that the girl was pregnant, but according to the mother she was run down – nothing more and nothing less and needed a pick-me-up. He'd asked all the right questions. Had she been sick at all? Was she having her periods each month? "No, and yes," the girl replied. He'd even offered to examine her, but it hadn't happened – Mama knew better. In the end, he'd recommended a good regular dose of St John's Wort and plenty of exercise and sent them off in the direction of the local health shop.

It had been too late to help her by the time they had finally called him out – the baby was breech and the girl had been in labour far too long. It had been his ethical duty to tell them that the girl should be in a hospital and that a caesarean was the only thing that might save her and the baby, but he had known how they would react before he had even suggested it. He was not going to press it – if they didn't want to avail themselves of the NHS free gratis then that was their prerogative. The outcome was inevitable – and maybe not such a bad thing. The last thing that anybody needed was yet another gypsy being born into the world. On that occasion, he had graciously waived his call-out charge.

Dr Boscombe sighed contentedly and smiled.

"Is something amusing you, my dear?" his wife enquired. "You seem in very good spirits this morning. I do so love it when you're looking so happy. Everything tickety-boo as they say?"

"Tickety-boo, my dear," he replied. If she had known where his thoughts were, then she might not have been quite so happy about his good spirits.

He was remembering the long, hot summer earlier in the year when he had examined and seen more gypsy legs than he had had hot dinners. The ticks were prolific and doing their worse, and how they loved the gypsies. They were such delightful little creatures and such grand little workers, especially on warm summer days. There was no missing it – the fiery red circles that expanded outwards from the epicentre of the bites. To a man, they had all complained of runny noses and headaches – typical early symptoms of Lyme disease. They had his deepest sympathy he had told each one of them, but it was not a life-threatening problem and there was nothing that he could prescribe. The best thing they could do was to pop down to the chemist and buy a tube of antiseptic cream. What was the point of prescribing expensive antibiotics to gypsies who, the very next day, would be out and about poaching and picking up yet more of the little critters? It had crossed his mind, although never given him sleepless nights, of course, that he might have helped a few of them in meeting their maker sooner than necessary – it was well documented that the later stages of Lyme disease could be nasty and lead to all sorts of physical and mental problems. He could only hope, but he would probably never know.

He prided himself that over the years he had saved the NHS a small fortune. He had religiously kept gypsies out of hospitals. He had never offered them prescription drugs at the taxpayer's expense. He deserved a medal. Quite how many of them might still have been alive had he acted differently was not a matter that he dwelt upon. They were scroungers, the scum of the earth; they had chosen their way of life. If he had his way, they would be wiped off the face of the earth.

Dr Sebastian Fern thought that all his Christmases had come in one when Dr Boscombe first walked through the door of his surgery in

Dutton, on the outskirts of Malvern. No one could afford the price of houses in Malvern itself and so it was that Dutton had exploded with housing estates, retail outlets, and light industry. What had once been a sleepy suburb was now a vibrant community with an ever-increasing population, made even larger by the permanent Traveller site on the edge of town. After forty years of managing on his own, Sebastian desperately needed another doctor in the practice. Hoping and praying that he would not be inundated with applications from newly qualified doctors, he had advertised the vacancy in *The BMJ*. What he wanted was a good solid experienced chap who would not want to change everything the moment he walked through the door. Dr Boscombe was everything that he needed in a partner – mature, knowledgeable, travelled, kind and considerate, and a bear of a man at six foot three inches, with broad shoulders, bushy brows and a full beard. He was also softly spoken, and his kind bedside manner was soon to become legendary throughout the town. And he was an honest man – Sebastian respected him for that. Many others might have spun him yarns about their intentions, but not Dr Boscombe who told him outright that he rarely stayed in a practice for more than three years. Sebastian took to him immediately.

Sebastian had never ceased to thank the Lord for the day that Dr Boscombe had joined the practice. Uncomplaining, he took all the new patients on to his list and left Sebastian to look after his regulars, many of whom he had brought into the world. Neither had he complained about the prospect of administering to the gypsies who lived out on the authorised Traveller site nor to the transient bands of gypsies that were increasingly finding the town a lucrative and convenient stopping-off point on their travels.

Other than him being a fine doctor, Sebastian knew very little about his partner. He was fit, in his early sixties, married, and lived in a rented house on the other side of town. There were no offspring as far as he knew. Dr and Mrs Boscombe kept themselves to themselves. Which was fine by him.

# Two

Mrs Boscombe wandered around the house that they had lived in for the past three years. Rented as furnished, she had never cared much for it. On the outskirts of Dutton, the house was a box with a small garden, the nearest neighbours more than a quarter of a mile away. Dr Boscombe had chosen it for the privacy it afforded them. She completely understood; after a hard day's work, he deserved his peace and quiet. It was a small price to pay.

Mrs Boscombe was beside herself with excitement. After all the years of following Dr Boscombe around from one town to another, they would soon be moving to their very own home and staying there. She had never once thought that the day would come when he would hang up his stethoscope and retire, but that was precisely what he had said he was about to do. She could hardly believe her eyes when he showed her pictures of the house they were to buy, and a farmhouse at that. It was everything she had ever dreamed about. If she had any reservations whatsoever, it concerned the six acres of land that surrounded the house and the scores of outbuildings that littered its four corners. And it had all happened almost overnight. They would be moving, he had told her, within the month. Having rented fully furnished over the years, the removal itself would be simple. They were neither of them hoarders; their clothes could be packed in suitcases and the few knick-knacks that they had accumulated over the years would go in cardboard boxes in the back of the old four by four.

How exciting – a real old farmhouse. It would take a bit of careful thought to maintain its character and charm, but she could see it now – a lovely log fire burning in the huge inglenook fireplace, shiny brasses either side, pictures of hunting scenes on the walls, warm reds and browns in the carpets and the furnishings, and a boot scraper beside the back door for their wellington boots – his and hers – lined up on the flagstone floor. Maybe she would take up riding again and join the local hunt; it was a long time since she had been on the back of a horse. The possibilities were endless. She felt quite young again.

Mrs Boscombe poured herself a cup of tea, sat down at the kitchen table, and opened the brochure again. The kitchen was huge with a range and a huge Belfast sink. The scrubbed pine table and chairs were to be left by the sellers. All it needed was an old Welsh dresser adorned with some pretty crockery, prints on the wall, and a colourful rug over the flagstones to brighten it up. A small dining room and a study already fitted out with bookshelves led off the hall together with a downstairs toilet. Upstairs, the bathroom was old-fashioned but functional. The avocado bathroom suite would not have been her first choice, but she could live with it. The five bedrooms were all of a good size – Dr Boscombe would have his room, she would have hers, and there would be three spare bedrooms if anybody came to stay – not that they had ever had any visitors. The built-in wardrobes had seen better days but were more than adequate. She would need to buy five each of dressing tables, chests of drawers, beds, and chairs. Everything about the house was simply perfect for them.

Mrs Boscombe scanned the local papers for details of house clearance and antique sales. She knew just what she wanted, and she was sure that she could get the sales and auction houses to deliver the furniture to their new home; it was not that many miles away after all. To her utter delight, Dr Boscombe had presented her with a wad of cash and given her free rein to furnish the house as she pleased. It was so out of character that she had been left speechless for a moment. In the normal course of events, he would hum and ha over the smallest item of expenditure, and almost always suggest that it would be better to do without. Now she realised that it was just this common sense that had enabled him to save up enough money for them to buy their own property. He was such a clever man.

It would be the first house of her own. When she had first met Dr Boscombe, she had been living in Gloucester with her parents, resigned to life as a spinster with little more to look forward to than years of caring for her aged parents. He had been so kind to her when she had visited his surgery. She had explained that she was not sleeping well. He had asked endless questions about what might be troubling her. In less than ten minutes she had told him her life story. He had prescribed a nice cup of tea at the local tea shop and suggested that he might join her there. He was a well-respected man in his early fifties, she, a well-respected spinster of similar age. Everyone thought that they were the perfect match. She had never understood why he had been attracted to her, but within three months they were married. Theirs had been a comfortable existence, if nomadic. Dr Boscombe did what he did best as a doctor whilst she kept house for him. It was almost all that she had ever wanted, and it did not disappoint her that he preferred for them to keep themselves to themselves. They had been together for ten years. If there was one disappointment in her life, it was that she was still a virgin. Things had not worked out quite so well in that department as she might have hoped but overall, she considered herself to be a lucky woman.

When the time came, Mrs Boscombe was to pack the clothes and the knick-knacks; Dr Boscombe would personally deal with packing the papers in his study. And she must remember, he told her, that when they moved into their new home, she was to start calling him by his Christian name again. He would no longer be a doctor, and if they were to make a fresh start, then their past was best left behind.

The move took place a little sooner than he had planned. It was all down to a pathetic little reporter from the local press who had decided to do a little investigative reporting into the health and welfare of local and transient gypsies and Travellers.

Over the years, the frequent deaths of gypsies both explained and unexplained was a matter for the town's social conscience, the reporter had written, adding that it was strange how many accidents had befallen them and how many deaths had occurred during the past few years – far more than had ever been reported in previous years. He neither concluded anything from his investigations nor pointed a finger in any direction – but the warning signs were there, and he promised a series of articles that would make the local community sit up and think. The day following publication of the local paper, Dr Boscombe tapped on his partner's door.

"Come in," Sebastian called without looking up. "I thought that I had got to the end of today's patient list."

"You're quite right, we have. Can you give me a few minutes of your time? Some bad news, I'm afraid." Dr Boscombe poked his head around the door.

"Take a seat, old chap." Sebastian waved to the big leather armchair at the same time reaching for the bottle of whisky that he kept in the bottom drawer of his desk. "Will you join me?"

"Don't mind if I do. That's very civil of you. I'll come right to the point, Sebastian, if you don't mind. It's been a pleasure to work with you for the past three years, but it's time for me to move on. As it happens, Mrs Boscombe's mother and father are very elderly and need full-time care. We've discussed it at length. We can't afford to put them in a care home, so we've decided that we must move in with them. As a doctor, I can ensure that they get the best of care while my wife will run the house. I'm sure you understand,"

Dr Boscombe explained, between sips of whisky; a fine malt – he would miss it and of course the time he and Sebastian Fern had spent putting the world to rights. "I shall retire from practice. I need to be gone within the month."

Dr Sebastian Fern rocked back in his chair and looked across at his partner of three years. He could scarcely keep the grin from his face. On the very day that Dr Boscombe had arrived, he had made himself a promise – when Dr Boscombe decided to move on, he too would hang up his hat and take the retirement that he so richly deserved. As it happened, it would not affect the town adversely – several of his younger patients had already voted with their feet and moved to the new medical centre on the other side of town.

"I wish both you and Mrs Boscombe the very best of luck, Dr Boscombe. The end of the month it is, and thank you for everything you have done. Without you, this practice would have gone under long ago. I doubt the gypsies will find the same welcome at that new medical centre, but that's not our problem. It has been a pleasure working with you." Sebastian heaved himself out of his chair and shook his partner's hand.

It was almost time to say farewell to Dutton for good. "How can such things happen, Mrs Boscombe?" Dr Boscombe shook his head and continued reading the local paper. An almost imperceptible smile crept across his face.

It is sad that our free newspaper does not seem to have reached everybody in our community. If it had, then this tragic accident might never have happened. You will remember that I warned you all about the recent spate of problems with foxes. If not, then let me remind you. Some of you may have thought that it was an April Fool's joke, but not in September. The bones of my story were that the local foxes and their cubs seemed to have acquired a taste for brake pipes or, as some experts have speculated, the fluid within the brake pipes! As of last week, the brake pipes of five cars belonging to our residents had been damaged – gnawed through by their sharp little teeth. Thankfully at the time of writing my last feature, there had been nobody hurt or killed. Regrettably, this is no longer the case.

On Monday last five transient gypsies were killed as a result of brake failure to their vehicle. Simon O'Malley, his brother Sean O'Malley, their cousins Brian and Kevin O'Malley, and a younger friend of theirs, Ross Harding, were all killed in a road accident when their white transit van hurtled out of control whilst on the downhill slope from Hilltop down to the bypass. According to the police, it had left the road and rolled several times down into a field. All occupants were killed instantly. None of them were wearing seatbelts.

A forensic examination of their campground, on the corner of Hilltop and at the junction with Foggy Lane, uncovered a large patch of oil on the grass adjacent to their caravan and tire tracks which indicated that a vehicle similar to a transit van had been parked there just hours before the accident. The fluid found was brake oil together with tiny fragments of brake pipe almost too small to be seen by the human eye. The brake pipes on the transit van were examined and found to have been eaten away.

Mrs Boscombe wandered proudly around their new home, stopping in the kitchen to admire the tall oak dresser on which she had placed an array of willow-pattern plates and bowls. A blue-and-white tablecloth covered the scrubbed oak table on which stood a small bowl of cornflowers that she had picked that very morning. Hopefully, Dr Boscombe – Peter, she corrected herself – would be pleased with the transformation. He was a changed man – she simply couldn't understand it. In all the years that she had known him, and as far as she was aware, he had never stepped foot in a supermarket, but that day he had insisted – absolutely insisted – that he would go out and do the shopping. It was all part of their new life, he had said, and it was high time that he took his share of the household tasks. There were times when she wondered where the man she had married had gone; this one was so entirely different – so considerate and generous – she really couldn't find fault with the new model, but it was nonetheless curious.

Mrs Boscombe finished her coffee and for the first time after a week of non-stop organising found herself at a loose end. There must be something else that needed doing, she thought – the devil makes work for idle hands as her mother always used to tell her. The only unpacking that had yet to be done was the boxes containing papers from her husband's study at the old house. She was not at all sure that she should touch them – he had been quite insistent on packing them himself, but he had said nothing about unpacking them. How could he be anything but delighted if he returned home to find most everything neatly filed in the new desk, which she had found for him? It would pass a couple of hours, and then when he arrived home, she could leave him to finish off whilst she unpacked the shopping and started on supper.

Mrs Boscombe sat on the floor surrounded by papers. She didn't hear the car draw up outside the front door. She didn't hear the front door opening. She didn't hear her husband calling out to ask her if she would help unload the shopping. When he came into the room and his eyes met hers, she knew that she had married a monster.

Dr Boscombe stared down at his wife. Such a pity, he thought.

# Three

Born in 1991, the youngest of three, Jess Walmsley had just reached her seventeenth birthday. She looked forward to Wednesdays, market day in Daylesbury, a busy market town nestled in the lower reaches of the Peak District. Reaching out, she stroked the velvety heads of the gladioli which she brought to market each week during the season. Always at their best after a wet spring followed by an abundance of early summer sunshine, this year they had been exceptional. Lovingly bunched with long, delicate grasses, no bunch was ever the same and her bouquets were extremely popular with the town's local ladies. At first, she had been embarrassed by the compliments paid to her by her customers but now she welcomed them with open arms and looked forward to them. They were the only compliments that she ever received and thus she had learned to cherish them.

Carefully arranged around her feet, the baskets were a relatively new addition to the stall and almost as sought after as her blooms. Instead of the old aluminium pails she had once used to keep her bouquets fresh, the flowers were now displayed in four tall polythene-lined willow baskets, which she had made herself. It had taken her quite by surprise when one of her customers had asked if they were for sale. Flattered, Jess had given it to the woman with her blessing. From that day on she made baskets large and small to sell on the stall on market days.

It was seven o'clock in the morning and Jess was ready for her first customers. Sitting on her stool, her ankle-length cotton skirt brushing the ground, she watched as her father shuffled miserably back and forth from the van. In his arms, he carried boxes of grotesquely misshapen carrots, trays of tomatoes that had yet to fully ripen, boxes of beetroot almost unrecognisable beneath the claggy soil that he had not bothered to remove, and trays of broad beans that had been cut from their stems far too young and would be disappointingly empty when shelled. He never learned, she thought. Did it never occur to him that there was a reason that so much of the produce ended up going back home unsold? It was not something that she would ever dare mention to him; it was more than her life was worth.

Jake Walmsley was a big man – tall and heavy-set – with wiry, sandy-brown hair, a huge nose veined red by years of alcohol abuse, and sideburns that bushed down in front of his ears and ended at the first of his multiple chins. He took no pride in his appearance and each week wore the same lumberjack shirt that stretched across his pot belly, which in turn hung low over his belt. He made no bones about the fact that he hated everything there was about his trade – the market garden was a pain in his backside. He hated the outdoors, loathed physical work of any kind, and hated customers even more, but he had been saddled with it, and by his own father at that.

In Jake's opinion, life had dealt him a raw deal. If he had had his way, he would have taken a cushy nine-to-five job working in a factory with a wage packet at the end of every week. He would not be toiling in fields all the hours God sent for a mere pittance. The elder of three brothers, Jake and his father detested one another while his two younger brothers could do no wrong. Content in the knowledge that Paul and Daniel were destined for better things miles away in the cities, the market garden had been bequeathed to

Jake while the two younger brothers waltzed away with a hundred thousand pounds apiece; the old sod had had the last word on his deathbed. If, as stated in his father's will, his lazy good-for-nothing son, Jake, wanted a roof over his head then he would have to work for it, and if he ever decided to sell the business or the house, then the proceeds would be split fifty-fifty between his younger brothers, and he would be left with nothing. There wasn't a day that passed when Jake didn't think of the old man and hope that he had burned in hell.

And then he met Lillian. And then a child was on the way. Cornered by a woman and a brat, as he described his unborn son, he had had no option but to toe the line and at least keep a roof over their heads. It hadn't helped that she hated the market garden more, if that were possible, than he and made it her business to do absolutely nothing to help in it. Begrudgingly, his new wife accepted that the small semi-detached in a nice suburb and a man who came home without stinking of onions and walking dirt throughout her house was not to be. Both wished that life had dealt them a better hand.

Two daughters and one son – how was he supposed to run a market garden with a dunce for a son, a prima-donna daughter, and yet another daughter who was less than useless?

Jess glanced at her father slumped in his chair beside the stall, head back, and snoring loudly. He had unloaded all of five boxes from the van, leaving her brother Michael to unload the remaining thirty-five. It was the same every week.

"Tea, Jess?" Michael called.

"Please," she replied quietly. They knew better than to wake their father.

Jess followed her brother's ungainly frame as he strode towards the cafe. She was very fond of him, but she didn't understand him. Heavy-set like his father, Michael was four years her senior and the first person in the world whom she remembered seeing. It was a long time ago, but she had not forgotten how she had laughed when he had tickled her nor the long conversations between them – always in baby talk, but they had understood one another perfectly. She remembered him whispering to her and warning her about the dangers outside of the playpen, but she had never really understood his words at the time. It was not long after Michael had been taken away from her and sent off to school that she began to understand those words – that very first time that her father had rubbed her tummy and poked his finger deep in her tiny belly button. From that day on she had done everything possible to keep her distance from him. He was a cruel man with a chip as big as Stonehenge on his shoulder.

Michael was a man of few words, seemingly incapable of expressing his thoughts. She heard what her father called him and what other people said about him – a half-wit, a simpleton, an idiot – but she knew that was far from the truth. Deep down there was a thinking, intelligent man trapped in that shell. It hurt that he wouldn't or couldn't share his feelings with her, but she knew in her heart that one day if she were patient enough, he would open up to her. She never doubted that there was something in his past that had made him the man he was today. He was also a private man – she knew that. He had his secrets, which he shared with no one, herself included. By chance, she had uncovered one such secret.

She had been no more than eight at the time and alone in the house. Michael had been out working with his father in the field and she was missing him. Venturing into his bedroom she had lain down on his bed and buried herself in his blankets; the very smell of his body gave her comfort and made her feel safe. Buried deep under his pillow she had found a pile of exercise books filled with mysterious numbers and words. At the time they meant little to her, but later she realised that her brother had been diligent with his homework and had often received quite glowing accolades from his teachers.

Intuitively she knew that he didn't want anybody else to know; homework was not something that was discussed in their house. It rated a poor second to school reports, which were destroyed and binned before they were read. She had never mentioned it to him nor anybody else. She knew that her brother was not a simpleton and never had been. For reasons that she did not understand he chose to let people believe that he was. She loved him deeply. He was her shadow and always there in her times of need, and there had been many.

Jess worried about his future but rarely thought about her own – she had no illusions about that. She knew that no one would ever look twice at a girl who walked lopsidedly with one leg almost two inches shorter than the other. It was just one of those things. It had happened years ago and there was nothing she could do about it but live with it. She had heard tell that with all the advances in surgical techniques, her leg could be properly repaired, but she knew that it would never happen.

Aches and pain had become part and parcel of her life and she had learned to accept and manage them rather than complain. The pain was bearable in the mornings, but by the evening after a long day toiling out in the fields it brought tears to her eyes. At such times she reminded herself that the end-of-day pain was as none compared to that which she had felt at the time it had happened. It had been her own fault. She had walked behind the tractor and not noticed that the reversing lights were on. It was Michael behind the wheel. It was Michael who heard her screams and leapt down from the tractor to help her. He had gathered her up in his arms and raced for the house. It was in that moment and in that action of moving her that the ultimate damage had been done. The tibia and fibula bones in her right leg had been shattered. Six weeks in the hospital with her leg raised high above the bed in a sling, and two months before the plaster had been taken off, her only visitor had been her brother, Michael. And then there had been the long slow process of learning how to walk with the aid of crutches followed by the even slower process of learning how to propel herself along without them. If she had expected any sympathy from her mother, she did not get it. She had been twelve years old at the time. Her father had never had time for her before the accident. After the accident, she saw nothing but disgust in his face every time he looked at her.

School held no joyous memories for Jess particularly after the accident when overnight she became the brunt of her classmates' jokes. Gradually, she had withdrawn from her friends and her schoolwork – the future looked bleak. By the age of thirteen she was chief cook and bottle washer at home and expected to have breakfast on the table at six-thirty each morning, and supper ready for the men when they came in from the fields. At the age of fifteen, she left school. She had not missed her so-called friends who had been unrelenting in their bullying. She missed her lessons although she knew that they would have led to nothing. Her mother had not minced words when she had told her that she was needed at home – that was where she belonged. She had no illusions about her mother's motivation – Lillian had no intention of dirtying her hands either outside in the market garden or in the house. Over the years, Jess's household responsibilities had grown exponentially. Now, at the age of seventeen, she was expected to work the fields during the day as well as perform all her household duties.

It was not so with Katie, her elder sister. Katie was the apple of her mother's eye. Tall and slim, with long blond hair and a perfect complexion, Katie was her mother's ticket to ride; Katie could do no wrong. What she lacked in brains she more than made up for in determination and drive, her mind set firmly on a good marriage. Intuitively Jess knew that her mother hoped that when the big day came, Katie would not forget all she had done for her.

"Thanks, Michael," Jess said, as she took the mug of steaming tea from his hands. Michael nodded, smiled, and pulled a carrier bag off the string ready to serve their first customer.

Jess checked that she had enough change in her purse for the coming morning. She knew that the rush would be between ten and eleven. Few customers would want to miss out on her gladioli or the new baskets she had brought with her that day.

Sitting comfortably on the wooden stool which Michael had made for her, Jess soaked up the sun and watched as the market came to life, and the first customers of the day scuttled up and down and in and out of the market stalls seeking out the best buys. She liked to look her best on market days; wildflowers were pinned into the band of her old straw boater, her flowery skirt reached to her ankles and she wore a pale blue, short-sleeved blouse that had been washed and pressed at least a thousand times. She knew that she didn't look fashionable; Jess and the word fashion had never been comfortable bedmates, but for those few precious hours each week, she felt pretty and comfortable in her own skin. She was just a young girl called Jess whom people treated with respect and admiration, not a cripple or a skivvy.

It was late morning that same day that Jess fell in love.

"Those baskets are magnificent. Did you make them?" A quiet voice broke into her thoughts.

Jess looked down at the two remaining hand-made willow baskets, which had yet to be sold, and then at the tall, gangly boy, or maybe he was a man, squatting down on his haunches beside the baskets and running his long fingers up and down the length of the handle of one of them. Shoulder-length blond hair that shone in the sun, neck and arms tanned the rich colour of polished oak, he had brown eyes framed by long, golden lashes. And he was speaking to her.

Jess looked around furtively to check that her father had not returned from his habitual late-morning visit to the pub where, more often than not, he squandered most of the meagre profits that they had made that morning. "Yes, I make them myself," she replied shyly. "I cut the willow shoots myself, soak them, and then weave my own designs. Each one is different – I'm so pleased you like them."

"They are beautiful. You have clever fingers, beautiful hands," the stranger replied, fingering the second basket.

Jess coloured and looked at her hands. No one had ever described them as beautiful.

The stranger reached out and took one of her hands. Jess could almost hear her own heartbeat as he gently turned her hand and studied her palm; it seemed the most natural thing in the world. "You have lucky lines," he said, lifting his eyes to hers. "What more could anybody want?"

Jess laughed. "I wish I were lucky. In my dreams, maybe."

"Dreams can come true if you believe in them."

"For some, but not for me," Jess replied wistfully.

The stranger entwined his fingers with hers. "Trust me. You will be lucky in life. What's your name?"

Her cheeks on fire, Jess blushed a crimson red. "Jess," she said.

"A pretty name for a pretty girl. They call me LJ. My mother wanted to call me Jay, which my father hated, and my father wanted to call me Leo, which my mother hated – so they compromised and called me LJ."

Jess smiled. "I like it. It suits you."

"It's fine willow, Jess. I know fine willow when I see it." The stranger transferred his gaze to the baskets. "Do you mind me asking where you find it?"

"Not far from where I live. My father has a market garden. We come into the market each Wednesday to sell vegetables and eggs, and I sell my flowers and my baskets. The willow is cut from a tree a short walk from the house. There's a stream that runs right beside it. I call it my secret place. When you walk in under the branches it's like being in another world. I feel safe there. That's where I dream."

"It sounds wonderful, Jess."

"It is." Jess looked up and into his eyes. They were kind eyes, smiling eyes that held her own. "If you like, I'll show you where it is." Listening to herself she could scarcely believe her own words, but somehow it felt right. She felt his hand in hers, his fingers entwined with hers, and knew that he would not harm her. She could trust him with her secret.

"I'd like that more than anything in the world, Jess."

"Do you know where French's Wood is?"

The stranger nodded. "The beechwood on the road to Little Reaching? I've passed by a few times."

"The willow is right down in the valley on the opposite side of the road. If you didn't know it was there, you wouldn't see it. We could meet up there one day," Jess said. "But maybe..."

"Maybe nothing, Jess. I'd be honoured to spend a little time with you and to be introduced to your willow." The stranger looked over his shoulder. "I have to go, Jess. I could sit here and talk to you all day, but time waits for no man as they say. I wish it could be sooner, but I'll be out of town for five days. Could we meet there on Tuesday next week?"

Jess nodded; Tuesday, the day before market was always a busy day for her, but she could make it work – she was going to make it work. "I could be there at about four, but I'd have to be back home before they missed me – or, should I say, missed their supper on the table. If you can't make it then don't worry."

"I'll be there, trust me. And wear that blouse and skirt again – you're as pretty as a picture." Letting go of her hand, he stood up and walked away, his smile lighting up the day.

Jess watched as the stranger, LJ as she now knew him, disappeared into the crowd.

A tear slid slowly down her cheek as she gazed down at her skirt. What would he say when he saw what she was really like?

# Four

The sun had hardly poked her nose above the horizon when Jess slipped on her jumper, jeans, and trainers and made her way quietly downstairs. The house was quiet. It would be six before her father or Michael stirred. By six-thirty they would expect to find breakfast on the table.

By five-thirty she had fed the chickens and boxed the eggs ready for market the following day. By six-fifteen, the bacon was sizzling in the pan, the toast made and on the table, and the eggs ready and waiting to be cooked at the last minute. Jess checked the table anxiously to make sure that there was nothing she had forgotten. This of all days, she did not want her father to find anything at fault.

Behind her, she heard her father's heavy footsteps as he threw open the kitchen door. "Up early this morning, weren't you, girl? Up to no good as usual? Got some plans for the day, have we?" he bellowed, scraping his chair away from the table and sitting down.

Jess knew when he was trying to provoke her and that to respond with anything other than a yes or a no would be a fatal mistake. "No, Father," she replied, setting his breakfast down in front of him.

"Good morning, Michael," she said, as her brother walked in and sat down opposite his father. "Are you ready for breakfast?"

"Thanks, Jess." Michael smiled at his sister.

"Well, young Jess," her father said, "I've got a few things planned for you that will make sure that you don't get up to any mischief for the rest of the day." Jess stared into the washing-up bowl and waited. "I've got business in town today and Michael has the stall to mend – one good gust of wind and it'll fall to pieces. I want it done today. It'll take him all day to fix it properly – isn't that right, Michael?" It was a rhetorical question, and it was also a threat.

Michael nodded, continued to eat his breakfast, and said nothing. He was surprised that his father had even noticed the state of the stall let alone decided that it had to be fixed. There was a reason that he had picked this day for it to be done; his father never did or said anything without a reason.

Jess held her breath. She knew precisely what business in town meant – meeting up with his cronies, sinking pint after pint in the pub until he was fit to burst before staggering into the bookies to part with the cash that had not gone down his throat. And then she would have to put up with his abuse over dinner.

"When I'm talking to you, you turn around and listen, not bloody well ignore me," he growled. Jess turned to see her father look up from his plate, his face like thunder. "That's better," he said. "A little respect." Jess dried her hands on a tea towel and turned to face him.

If she had had a death wish she would have told him about the egg yolk that was dripping down the stubble on his chin and then onto her freshly washed tablecloth.

"You'll be doing the picking and the digging today, girl," he said. "Four rows of strawberries to be picked. Don't just pick the red ones – white ones and pink ones at the bottom of the punnets, red ones on top. Five rows of broad beans – and use your brains this time, my girl. The flat pods at the bottom of the boxes and the plump ones on the top. Three rows of peas. When you've finished that, there are two rows of carrots to be dug and pulled. And I expect a proper meal on the table when I get home."

"But…" Jess started, her heart sinking. "I can't dig, Father. It takes me forever. My leg…" she said, without thinking.

For a big man, he was agile and moved fast. Jess gritted her teeth as she felt his hands close in a vice-like grip around the top of her arms. "Are you arguing with me, girl?" he demanded, shaking her hard. "It's about time you pulled your weight around here. There's no room in this house for those that don't. Haven't I got two of those upstairs who never lift a finger? That bloody sister of yours and her mother. What is it that I ever did to deserve the lot of you?"

Jess felt the intense pressure of his hands on her arms and the thumbs that dug deep into her flesh. She knew from experience that the more she struggled the worse it would be. "I'm sorry, Father. I'll do the picking and the digging just as you say." She knew it was what he expected to hear and that it was the only way to stop the pain. Relief flooded through her as he released his grip on her, pushed her back towards the sink, and slammed out of the kitchen.

"His time will come, Jess, but not today," Michael said quietly, as he left the table. The outside door opened and closed.

With tears clouding her vision, she cleared the table, finished the washing-up, and hung her kitchen apron on the hook behind the door. She had got off lightly. Had Michael not been in the room it would have been worse, much worse.

Jess wiped her tears away. Feeling sorry for herself would get her nowhere. If she worked nonstop then she might just be able to complete the picking and still have time to meet LJ by four. Tackling the digging was another matter altogether, but she'd cross that bridge when she got to it.

The ground was uneven and the cart heavy and it pulled on her bruised arms to push it across to the strawberry field. Crawling up and down the strawberry beds, dragging her damaged leg behind her, Jess carefully selected those strawberries that were ripe and left those that had yet to ripen resting on their straw pillows. It may have been her father's way to half fill the punnets with unripe strawberries, but it was not hers. If he noticed, he would have a great deal to say about it, but she did not care. As the sun rose higher and higher the temperature soared into the high seventies. She knew that she should be drinking water to guard against dehydration, but there was no time to go back to the house to get it. Every minute counted if she were to finish in time to meet up with LJ. From time to time she glanced up and silently measured the distance to the end of the bed that she was working on, and in her mind played guessing games about how long it might take her to get there. Times four long strawberry beds, she would not be finished with them until early afternoon, and then she would have to stack the boxes on the cart and wheel it back to the shed before setting out again towards the broad beans and then the peas. And then the carrots…

Finally, she reached the end of the last row, leaving behind her a long trail of filled punnets. As she stood up and straightened her aching back, she wiped the perspiration from her brow and mopped the tears that slid down her cheek. It was already past two in the afternoon.

With the strawberry boxes safely unloaded from the cart and packed neatly in trays in the shed ready to be loaded in the van the following day, she turned the empty cart around and trudged back out to the fields and started on the broad beans. Jess glanced down at herself; she was a mess. Her hands were raw and scratched, her clothes covered in dust and straw. Shielding her eyes from the sun, she glanced hopelessly in the direction of her willow and wondered what LJ would think when she didn't show. One more dream that would not come true. Focused on picking, she hadn't noticed Michael cross the fields.

"I'll do the rest, Jess. The stall is done. He won't be back 'til late. Mother and Katie are out for the day. You don't have to worry about any of them. Just make sure you're back by five-thirty. Go and get yourself ready," Michael said. "The rest will take me no time at all."

"How did you know?" Jess turned to see her brother already working on the row behind her, stretching and filling his hands with the pods.

"I heard you talking to him at the market. He seems a nice lad. You deserve a break, Jess. Just go."

"Can't I help you for an hour first?" she asked.

"Have you looked at yourself, Jess? You don't want him to think that he's made a date with a scarecrow, do you? Take care."

Jess shook her head. He didn't know how much it meant to her. "Thank you, Michael," she said quietly, reaching up to give him a peck on the cheek. "I don't know what I would do without you."

Michael stood for a moment and watched his little sister limp back towards the house.

Jess hauled herself up the stairs and into the bathroom relieved to find that Michael had been right – she had the house to herself. Washing the dust out of her hair before towel-drying it, she chose a blue ribbon to match her blue blouse – the one she had worn to the market. Quickly she filed and cleaned her nails and applied a blob of the hand cream that Michael had given her for Christmas. LJ had admired her hands; maybe he wouldn't notice the rest of her.

She had had it all planned in her head for the past six days – from the moment that they had agreed to meet. She would be sitting in the shade of the willow, her skirt wrapped around her ankles, long before he arrived. Then they would talk for a while, he would leave first, she would wave goodbye to him, and only then would she get to her feet.


The ground was cool and slightly damp beneath her. Jess soaked up the silence and waited. Encircled by the branches of the willow, she listened for his steps. In the near distance, she heard twigs snapping and then the gentle swish of the branches behind her. Turning, she saw the man she had met but the once, backlit by the sun. Her heart leapt.

"It's just as you described it, Jess. It's another world in here, a sanctuary created by this beautiful willow. And you, pretty as a picture again."

"You found it," Jess whispered.

"I did," he said. "And the stream as well. Just the way you painted it. Can you hear the music?"

"Music?"

"Listen to the water cascading over the stones. It's like millions of little bells tinkling away without a care in the world."

"It is a very special place, isn't it?"

"Do you mind if I sit with you?"

"I'd like you to," Jess said, pointing to the dry bare earth beside her.

"Tell me about yourself, Jess. Don't leave anything out."

Hesitantly she started. "I'm seventeen and I live with my family, my mother, father, brother, and an older sister. We have a small market garden. We sell the produce at the market each Wednesday..."

Once she had started, she found it hard to stop, the words just came pouring out – the good, of which there was little, and the not so good, which would not be held back. Listening to herself, she was surprised to find herself describing a girl whom she hardly recognised – the same girl who always told herself that she was lucky to have a roof over her head and food on the table. Pent-up emotions surfaced like flotsam on the sea, feelings she hardly recognised as her own that she would have taken to the grave had there not been somebody who wanted to listen to her. "I'm sorry...You didn't come here to listen to my tales of woe."

"Is there nothing good in your life, Jess?" His brow furrowed as he held her hand in his.

"My brother, Michael. He's my guardian angel."

"Maybe I can be another of your guardian angels, Jess. Whenever you want to talk, always remember that I'm here for you."

"Do you have a story to tell, LJ?" she asked, deliberately changing the subject away from herself. There were still many parts of her story that remained untold.

"I'm twenty-one and I spent my early years in Ireland with my mother and father, no siblings. We came to England when I was five. My father and mother are back in Ireland now. I live with my Uncle Byron and my Aunt Rosa and their three sons, Byron Jnr, Colin and David, and Byron Jnr's wife, Polly. There's Buckland and Nathan as well – both cousins. My Uncle Byron's a man to respect, a man to look up to, a second father you might say."

"That's one big family, LJ. Do you all get on with one another?"

"Yes, most of the time, but we have our moments. Uncle Byron is the head of the family and runs a tight ship. It's a hard life, but I wouldn't change it for the world," LJ replied thoughtfully. "Tell me more about your willow and how you choose which shoots to pick."

Jess held out her hand and pulled a handful of shoots towards her. "You see these shoots? These are too young now, but in a few months they will be ready and perfect for basket weaving. I only cut a few at a time – never so many as to damage the tree."

LJ nodded; he was no stranger to finding and cutting willow shoots and basket making, but in his world the willow trees were treated with a great deal less respect.

"And who taught you to make those beautiful baskets, Jess?"

"I taught myself. I work on them most evenings when I've finished my jobs and before I turn the light off to sleep. Sometimes I see them in my dreams and draw them when I wake up."

"Do you see those shoots hanging over the stream?" LJ said, pointing down towards the stream. "Would I be right in thinking that they are perfect for your baskets?"

Jess followed his eye. He was right – they would be perfect, but out of her reach, now and forever.

"Let's go down to the stream. I'll help cut some for you if you like." LJ held out his hand to help her up. Jess quickly looked away and ignored the proffered hand.

"Is it something I said? Is it something that I have done, Jess?" he asked, his voice trailing off.

She shook her head. How could she ever have thought that

she could hide the fact that she was a cripple from him? It was always a matter of time. Those precious moments when they had sat together and talked about themselves would soon be no more than a memory.

Jess looked up at him as her eyes glazed and she felt her tears starting to form. "I can't get down there. I know it's not that steep, but I'd slip and fall. There's something that I haven't been entirely honest with you about. You see, I'm a cripple."

LJ sat down beside her again. "That's not a word that I'd ever use about anybody and that's not how you should ever describe yourself. Who in God's world would ever call such a beautiful young girl by such a terrible name?"

"It's just a fact, LJ. I can't run and jump like ordinary girls. I'm not complaining – it's the way things are. It was just that when I saw you at the market and you asked me to meet you, I wanted to have a few special moments to remember. I should have told you. I shouldn't have led you on," she finished, hardly noticing that it was LJ who had pulled a handkerchief out of his pocket and was wiping the tears away from her eyes.

"Led me on, Jess?" he laughed. "I don't feel as though you have led me on. From where I'm sitting, I see a very pretty young lady with the most beautiful blue eyes and long silky hair, the colour of God's gold. I see the reflection of the water in your eyes and I hear your lovely soft voice and, I'm thinking, I can't get enough of it." LJ carefully slipped his arm around her shoulder and pulled her close. He could not help but notice that she winced as he did so. Was he so repulsive or was there something else that she was not telling him?

Jess took a deep breath, rolled over on her side, pulled herself up on to her knees, and using her good leg to support herself stood up and lifted her long skirt to show him the scars. She could not look at him. It would break her heart to see the look of sympathy that would surely be written across his face. And then he was laughing, laughing out loud. "It's a scratch, Jess. I have had worse than that myself! I knew you were pulling my leg, but maybe that's not the way I should be putting it. I promise that I'm not laughing at you. You're no more of a cripple – and promise me you'll never use that word again – than I am."

Unconvinced by his words, Jess stood up and limped around in a small circle. "Now you can see properly, LJ," she said, casting her eyes down. "My left leg is two inches shorter than the right."

"Well, Jess, you don't look one bit different to me. Next, you'll be telling me that you've grown horns. Have you never been down to the water's edge or dipped your toes in the stream?"

Jess shook her head disconsolately. Many a time she had longed to shimmy down the bank and stand in the cool water. "No, never."

"Let's go down together," LJ said, holding out his hand to her.

"I can't." Jess looked away.

"There's no such thing as can't. You can do whatever your heart desires if you set your mind to it."

Jess shook her head. "I'm sorry. Sorry for everything."

"Do you trust me?"

Jess nodded.

"Take your shoes off and tie that skirt up above your knees," he said. "I'll support you all the way – you'll not fall."

He took her weight on his arm and waited until she was ready to take the first precarious step. "You're doing fine, Jess. We've no hurry." He sensed moments when she was afraid, her gait rolling in the wrong direction. Then he stopped and waited until he felt that she was ready for the next step.

"Now, was that so bad?" he said, as he gently helped her down onto a large smooth stone so that her feet were dangling in the water. "How's that?"

Rewarded by the widest grin he had ever seen in his life, he asked, "Do you mind my arm? It seems to have a habit of finding its way around your shoulder."

Speechless, Jess wiggled her toes and let the clear water run over her feet. "I can't believe that I'm doing this. Thank you."

"We should check out those shoots, but let's not spoil the moment. How about we do that next time?"

"Next time? You mean you want to meet up again?" Jess spoke softly. Could this really be happening to her?

"You'll not keep me away that easily." LJ laughed. "It's my secret place as well now. Then that's settled. Let's say four each day. If you can't get here one day then I'll wait for you the following day until you come. And the following day if I have to. And the following day…" Was he being unkind to her? LJ tried to set aside all thoughts that before long he and the family would be moving on to pastures new.

Jess laughed. "But not on market days."

"It's good to hear you laugh, Jess. Your eyes light up when you laugh. Didn't I tell you that you would be lucky one day?"

"I could stay here forever."

"Me too, but I have to be back at the camp – home," he quickly corrected himself, "by six. It's going on that now. It's a way to go."

"I have to go now, this minute." Jess checked her watch and struggled to her feet slipping and sliding on the wet stone. "I hadn't realised the time. There'll be trouble…Help me up the slope, please."

LJ pulled the branches aside and watched as she set off fast in her lopsided gait. Not once did she look back. At that moment he wished that he had just one ounce of her courage. If he had, he would have told her that he was a gypsy and that soon he would be gone.

Michael noticed the change in his sister – she had a spring in her step. He had heard her singing quietly to herself, something that he had never before heard. He was happy for her; she deserved a friend more than anybody. The friendship of a brother would never be enough – a woman needed a man, and Jess at seventeen was almost a woman. But it troubled him that if he had noticed, the change in her would not have escaped his father's eyes. There would be hell to pay if he found out, hell for both of them.

He knew only too well what his father was capable of. He himself had had too many narrow escapes in his early life. The man was mean-spirited, violent, and capable of anything. There was nothing more he hated than to lose control of his goods and chattels, and that was what they were, he and Jess. All he could do was to stay close to her and hope that when the dam burst, he would be there to protect her. It was for that reason he had willingly given up his education and dreams for the future.

He was no longer afraid of his father – those days had long since passed. He was now of similar build, broad-shouldered and muscular and ready. He knew that the day would come.

Jake Walmsley watched his daughter like a hawk. Something was going on – he could feel it in his bones, and whatever it was he had a right to know. His eyes narrowed as he spotted her heading away from the house. Almost out of sight before he started to follow her, he had a fairly good idea where she would be going. She was a creature of habit. If she wasn't in the house or the fields then she was off to her precious willow tree – the house was filled with her bloody baskets in every shape and size, and far more than she would ever need to sell at market. If it wasn't the willow tree that was putting a smile on her face, then what was it? Whatever it was he was going to make sure that it didn't stay there for long. If there was one thing he wouldn't tolerate, it was deceit.

Jake stopped fifty yards short of the willow, ducked down behind a patch of brambles, and waited. He was not disappointed, but mildly surprised when minutes after she disappeared beneath the willow, a tall gangly youth appeared from out of the woods at the top of the hill and ran down the hill towards the tree. So that was her game. Half an hour passed, and then an hour – more than enough time for them to do their business – for whatever else could they be doing? Day after day he followed her and watched as they emerged from under the tree arm in arm, before the youth waved goodbye and she started limping her way back home. And then when the youth lifted her face to his and kissed her passionately, it made his blood boil.

It was time to put paid to her shenanigans, time to step in as every father should. Jake waited until his daughter had gone and followed the youth back to his lair.

"Nothing like a good breakfast, Jess," he said throwing his knife and fork down on the empty plate and licking his lips with gusto. "You're a good cook if nothing else."

"I'm pleased you enjoyed it, Father." Jess turned and looked at her father in surprise. If she had heard him correctly then he had just paid her a compliment – something that he never did. He was smiling at her – something that he never did. He had not moved from the table – something that he always did when he had finished his breakfast.

"So how many baskets have you made this week?" he asked.

"A few," Jess replied.

"More than a few if I'm right in thinking. You've been back and forth to that willow like a bitch on heat."

"The shoots are just right for harvesting," Jess said, knowing that his words were leading somewhere.

"Harvesting, hey? That what you've been doing? Harvesting?"

"Yes, Father."

"Harvesting, sowing seeds – all the same, isn't it? I reckon you've been sowing seeds, you and that friend of yours. That what you've been doing, Jess?"

Jess froze and looked at Michael, fear showing in her eyes. "No, Father."

"You think your father's stupid, don't you? Do well to look behind you, girl, when you head off to your precious willow. Never know who might be following you. You're a whore. Just like that sister of yours. Only difference is your sister will get paid. How many times has he laid you? How many times has he planted his gypsy seed in that belly of yours? You hear me, girl – gypsy, from the camp on the other side of town. Nothing more than a dirty gypsy."

"He has a name, father. His name is LJ, LJ Lovell. We love each other. Other than a kiss, he has never touched me," Jess said, her head reeling. Why hadn't he told her that he was a gypsy? It would have made no difference to her.

"Love! You know what gypsies do, girl? They shag their mothers, their aunts, their sisters, and their cousins. They shag the girls in the town and then they up and move on to their next victims. Filthy, dirty scum, the lot of them. You'll not see him again."

"Not LJ. He's not like that," Jess said defiantly. "You'll not insult him, Father." It was the first time in her life that she had stood up to him. He could say what he liked about most people, he could abuse her, but she would not let him get away with abusing LJ.

"I'll do what I bloody well like, girl, and it's time you were taught a lesson," he shouted, as he got up from the table and reached for his belt.

"No, Father!" Michael pushed his chair aside and grabbed his father by the arm.

"Stay back, son. This little lady needs teaching a lesson," he replied, pushing Michael away with all his weight. Michael's head struck the table, but his father did not look back.

Jess's eyes burned with terror as he tore his belt from his trousers and wound the end around his hand. Eighteen inches of leather dangled from his fingers. Cowering down by the sink, she wrapped her arms around her face. The belt struck her around the shoulders and then one arm after another, and then her chest, and then her abdomen. Pain engulfed her, her ears rang from the rhythmical thwack from the belt and her own screams. Blessedly she was gradually losing consciousness.

As darkness engulfed her, she thought she saw her brother reach for a knife from the kitchen drawer.

Michael looked down at him. It was the way he had always known it would end.

# Five

My name is Byron, Byron Lovell. Mine is one of the few remaining pure Roma bands. At least it was pure Roma until Jess and Michael joined us in June 2008, just over four years ago. It is a decision that I have never regretted. Both are hard-working and now as much family to me as my own. There are twelve of us in the band now, including Jess and Michael, and Sally. We were once a bigger family, but the winters have taken their toll.

I miss my brother, John, and his wife, Sheila. It's ten years since they went back to their native Ireland and took up residence in a council flat. I can't blame them, but I miss them. John struggled for years with chronic arthritis but never complained. It's not an uncommon complaint of those who spend most of their time on the road; ankles and hands swollen like balloons. It's a miracle that he managed for so long. He's four years younger than me. LJ, my nephew, misses his parents, but they keep in touch as best they can. Jess and Sally have yet to meet them. One day perhaps.

I have three sons: Byron Jnr, Colin and David are twenty, eighteen and sixteen. Byron Jnr is married to Polly, a lovely Roma girl and we will soon have a grandchild. Colin and David are fast growing into men. I am proud of them both. They're champing at the bit for me to find suitable partners for them so that they can start families of their own. They are both mature and sensible enough, but I'm in no hurry. I intend to wait until the right Roma girls present themselves. Until then, they will remain single. I ask no questions about what they get up to when they visit the local towns. It doesn't worry me. I have taught them consideration and respect. I trust them both.

I bless the day that LJ decided that he would not return to Ireland with John and Sheila. He travels with us in a traditional horse-drawn caravan known to the Roma as vardos. He has loved the outdoor way of life since he was a youngster, worshipped our old cob horse, and maintained the vardo in a state that his father, grandfather, and great-grandfather before him, would have been proud of. He is like a son to me.

Made in my late brother's image, Buckland and Nathan are a different kettle of fish to my own sons. Silas was one year younger than me and born with an argumentative streak. He was always the first to pick a fight and the first to complain when times were hard. He was one of those types that give the Roma a bad name. He hated hard work. It rubbed off on his two sons who believe that the world owes them a living. He died from pneumonia. It is against my nature to think ill of the dead, but the world is a better place without him. I would dearly love to see the back of Nathan and Buckland, but I have a duty of care towards them.

Fortunately, my life has been blessed with two of the kindest and most hard-working women that God ever created: Rosa, my wife of twenty-five years, and my daughter-in-law, Polly, both of whom work tirelessly for the band. I could not have managed all these years without them.

I add Jess to the list of strong women in my band, and little Sally; three years old, she knows how to wrap me around her little finger. She calls me Uncle By-By. I've never seen LJ so happy. He is a good husband and father.

It hardly seems possible that it is over four years since Michael and Jess joined our band. At the time I wondered whether I was

42

doing the right thing. I deliberated long and hard before making my decision. I knew that I was asking for trouble and the direction from which it would come. I'd forbidden my sons and my nephews to marry outside of the Roma, and then I give my consent to LJ marrying Jess. Byron Jnr, Colin, and David all respected my decision. Buckland and Nathan did not receive the news at all well. At the time I was disappointed in LJ. I had hoped to find him a good Roma wife. But that's in the past – best left. I wouldn't be without Jess and Sally.

Jess has never ceased to amaze me. With strength of mind and body that belies her size, she stands poles apart from many girls of her age. She has true grit and an ever-cheerful disposition notwithstanding her infirmity. She has slotted into the family like an old comfortable glove, or should I say a young comfortable glove? LJ could not have chosen a better wife and mother for his daughter. She has had to climb mountains to learn and adapt to our culture, but she doesn't let anything beat her. Now and again, I wonder whether her cheerfulness is not skin-deep. Her leg must give her a lot of pain. LJ worries about it as well. We've tried to talk to her about it to suggest that a house made of bricks and mortar might be better for them all, but she won't have it. She knows how much LJ loves his life on the road and she won't stand in his way.

Michael is an enigma, a big man, strong, and fiercely protective of his sister. I came so close to throwing him out of the group hours after he joined us. I shall never forget that first morning I met him. There he was standing by the gate to our camp, a girl, a limp rag, in his arms, yelling for help. He was a man of few words. "LJ, help! Jess is hurt. I stabbed him," he yelled repeatedly. His white T-shirt was stained with blood. At the time, I didn't know if it was from the girl in his arms or the man he claimed to have stabbed. I couldn't get anything else out of him, just those words. LJ was down the steps of the vardo in seconds, running towards them. They were no strangers to him, although later I understood that he had never met Michael before.

It was several hours later, while Rosa and Polly were treating Jess's wounds, that the story began to unfold, slowly and hesitantly. Michael seemed incapable of stringing sentences together, but it soon became clear that their father had attacked Jess and that Michael had taken a knife to his father. Whether he had killed his father or not, we none of us knew, but if I had been in Michael's place, I would have made sure that I finished the job off properly. I have never seen such injuries inflicted on a young innocent girl. In the world of the Roma, anyone who lays hands on a woman deserves all that they have coming to them. I am not a violent man, Roma are not violent people, we walk away from trouble. There was no doubting the truth of Michael's story. LJ knew about Jess's so-called home life. I can't say I wasn't shocked, even angry, to hear that LJ had been meeting up with the girl in secret for the past week. He is a Roma, she not so. He knew he was out of order.

LJ was besotted with Jess. In love with her. I couldn't take his happiness away from him, and besides, I had a badly injured girl on my hands and her brother who wouldn't let her out of his sight. I spoke at length to LJ and then I made my decision. Jess could stay with us, permanently, and Michael on a trial basis. LJ and Jess would be married as soon as she was fit to do so. Until such time as the wedding took place, Jess would live in the vardo. LJ and Michael would pitch camp outside of the vardo.

I gave the order to pack up camp and told everyone that we would be leaving Daylesford within the hour. If Michael's father went to the police, assuming he had lived to tell the tale, then the first place that the police would look for the perpetrator would be the gypsy camp. That Jess should not be moved so soon could not be helped. I had to go with my gut instinct.

As the sun reached its zenith, our convoy trundled away from Daylesbury. Rosa and Polly rode in the vardo with Jess. Michael rode upfront with LJ. The old cob dutifully stepped out at the front of the convoy. I tried to persuade LJ that Jess would be more comfortable in one of the caravans, but he would have none of it. He wanted Jess with him.

I brought up the rear of the five-vehicle convoy, my transit towing our caravan. My eyes never left the road in front nor the road behind, watching out for the familiar blue lights. We were lucky. By nightfall, we had put thirty miles between ourselves and Daylesbury. We had no choice but to pitch in a layby for the night and hope that we would not be moved on. I may be a Roma and we may tell fortunes from time to time, but I don't have a crystal ball. What happened then, nobody could have predicted. Least of all me.

No sooner had we come to a halt than a black BMW roared up behind us, tyres screeching, and pulled into the layby alongside the vardo at the front of the convoy. I could hear insults being hurled from the occupants of the car, and what I guessed to be Michael's voice, yelling back at them. That was when Michael found his voice. I shouldered my rifle, jumped out of the van, and raced up ahead to see what had happened. I was in the nick of time to prevent a fistfight. Red-faced and enraged by something, Michael was bodily lifting the rear seat occupant out of the car, his arms extended, fists clenched, and ready to throw a deadly punch.

It took us all our strength to pull Michael clear, LJ on one side of him and me on the other. I'd seen it all before. I can't say it ever gets any easier but being insulted is a way of life for us. If we rose to the bait each time it happened, then there would be a trail of dead bodies behind us. As I have said, Roma are not violent people; we walk away from trouble. It was not until later that Michael told me what the troublemakers were after – the women in the convoy. They had shouted that they'd take turns and pay five pounds a time and that it wouldn't take long.

I keep a rifle that I only ever use for two purposes – for poaching and to show the likes of the BMW occupants that we are not to be messed with. One look at it and they roared away into the night.

Although he didn't know it at the time, Michael had broken one of the golden rules – never let yourself be drawn into a fight. It was touch and go as to whether I would let him stay or send him on his way. Hotheads I did not need. Had his sister not been in my care then I would have not hesitated to part ways with him. Instead, I decided to give him a thorough dressing-down about his behaviour. Whatever the provocation, it had been unacceptable. I made him apologise in front of every member of the family and then I started his education in the ways of the Roma.

As I look back, I find it almost inconceivable that I now sit side by side with the same man, for hour after hour, putting the world to rights. Michael has become my confidante and has almost replaced the brother that I miss so much. As each day passes, the bond between us grows stronger. There have been times when I have had to draw deep on my memory to recall the stories that my own parents and grandparents had told me. Michael is insatiable. He thirsts for knowledge.

We spend spring, summer and early autumn on the road before making our way to one of a few permanent Traveller sites for the winter. Winters are cold and wet and only the hardiest of bands stay out on the road during those months. For three years Dutton, on the outskirts of Malvern, became our winter home. Some Travellers live there permanently, others simply spend the winter months there. We're well outnumbered at Dutton. No more than ten per cent of the residents are true Roma. The rest are Travellers. We, Roma, pitch our wagons way apart from the Travellers. We have nothing in common. In autumn 2012 we set off once more in the direction of Dutton. We arrived there in the first week of October. We were all looking forward to renewing acquaintances and forging new friendships. As Dutton came into sight, I took my place at the front of the convoy and led the family towards the winter site. My heart sank – the winter base was no more. In its place was an eight-foot fence that surrounded the land on which we and so many Travellers had passed our winters. A notice pinned high on the fence announced the arrival of a supermarket – a facility that the community could not manage without.

It was late in the day. Everyone was tired, disconsolate, and looking to me for leadership. For no good reason I decided that we would head west. We were lucky, we found rest stops, and then several days later we stumbled on a vacant, unsecured piece of ground on the edge of a village called Bartonford in south Warwickshire. So far no one has tried to move us on.

# Six

Shivering, LJ turned his collar up against the bitingly cold wind, and thought of Jess, warm and cosy, sitting beside the little wood-burning stove in the vardo, Sally at her feet, up to mischief as usual. The thought made him smile. His little family warmed his heart. Cold as it was, heavy clouds threatening to drop their load, he knew that he had a great deal to be thankful for. It was just over three months since they had arrived in Bartonford and so far it had been without incident; they had been left in peace. It was a rare occasion when they happened on such a perfect site. It was on the outskirts of the village with ample hardstanding for the vehicles and land to the rear where the old cob horse could graze. A disused garage and workshop fronted the site and to the rear was an abandoned nursery; all that remained standing were the frames of the old glasshouses. It was an even more rare occasion to come across an empathetic official who, understanding their need for running water, had organised for the water supply to the old garage to be reinstated. Running water was a luxury and they were more than happy to pay for it. No one could have accused them of entering the land illegally. There had been neither gate nor sign to warn against trespassers.

Returning to the moment, LJ sighed. One thing he was not was a natural salesman. Selling the benefits of tarmac or block-paved driveways to those who were perfectly happy with their driveways as they were did not come naturally. If he had been made in the mould of his uncle with the same maturity of years and perseverance, then he might have been more successful. Byron mostly did the selling while, to the disgust of Nathan and Buckland, LJ led the work gang. Exceptionally, he had personally managed to acquire a small job from an elderly gentleman in the village, completed just days past. Now the order book was empty. Byron was locked away suffering from a bad cold. With as much enthusiasm as he could muster, LJ had offered to walk the village to try and find more work for the family.

Bartonford church dated back to the fifteenth century. Cottages nestled in gardens close by the narrow B-road, which passed through the length of the village, while an ancient schoolhouse and manor houses, three and four stories high, stood set back from the road and almost hidden from sight. According to the Doomsday book, one or more kings had feasted in their grand halls. A community hall, the village shop, and the village pub formed the heart of the community; neither LJ nor any member of the family had so far ventured into them. Once a tiny hamlet, it had grown into a sizeable village as the local farmers happily exchanged swathes of land in return for cash. The village was now surrounded by new builds, some dating back fifteen years or more, others still rising from their foundations. This morning LJ was heading deep into the heartland of the older new builds.

Feeling the first drops of rain on his head and face, LJ pulled his duffel coat tight around his body and walked determinedly on.

Sam Hawthorne looked out of his front window and grunted. It would take more than a few drops of rain to prevent him from having his Sunday pint in the pub. As the church bells rang out in the distance, Sam smirked at the thought of the village do-gooders standing piously in the church, raising the roof with their holier-than-thou rendition of 'Onward Christian Soldiers' before, within the hour, stepping out into the pouring rain and enjoying their weekly ritual of pulling their neighbours apart. At least he was not a hypocrite. Atheist, yes, but not a hypocrite. He called a spade a spade and was proud of it as his next-door neighbour, Charlie, had found to his cost. He detested Charlie and his prissy wife. That they were both teetotal, and made no bones about their opinion of those who partook of hard liquor, had nothing to do with it. That they wiped the floor with everybody at the village flower and produce show each year had nothing to with it. That their lawns and hedgerows were manicured to within an inch of their lives had nothing to do with it. Charlie was without doubt the most boring and ineffectual little man that he ever met in his life, but one that the community had taken to their hearts. In Sam's opinion, anyone who claimed to be perfect had something to hide, but he had yet to uncover Charlie's secret.

Sam rubbed the condensation off the window with the back of his hand and peered through the glass. In the distance, a lone figure braced against the wind and rain ambled up through Faraday Close, glancing left and right as he advanced. For an instant, Sam thought it was a girl, with long blond hair streaming out over her shoulders. As the figure drew nearer and started towards his front door, Sam drew breath, exhaled slowly, and did a double take. Surely not, his eyes must be deceiving him. Hadn't he reported the man to the police less than two days ago? Why in God's name hadn't the police been down to that camp and arrested him by now? Sam shook his head in disgust – he knew why – the bloody coppers were scared stiff of going anywhere near the gypsy encampment; a waste of space the lot of them. There was no doubt in his mind that this was the same man whom his father-in-law had described to him and to the police – the right age, the same build, tall and wiry, the same long blond straggly hair, the clothes – it all fitted.

Sam hated gypsies. He could smell them a mile away. Never trust a gypsy – that was what his old man had told him, and that was what he had told his father-in-law, but had he listened? No, he knew better. But this one was not going to get away with it – his father-in-law might have gone soft in the head, but he had not.

"Call the cops, Marie. Tell them to get off their backsides and get around here pronto," he shouted to his wife. "We've got a visitor and you'll never guess who." Sam grabbed his fur-lined jacket from the hallstand and bolted for the front door. Sunday morning had suddenly taken a turn for the better.

LJ had scarcely reached for the doorbell when the front door opened. A stocky, broad-shouldered man with greying hair stood, legs apart, in the porch, and pulled the fur collar of his jacket up around his neck, and grinned. For an instant LJ relaxed and let his guard down. Maybe for once, he would receive a fair hearing. "Good morning, sir. My name is LJ Lovell," he began, brushing his already sopping wet hair away from his eyes. "Looks like we're in for a storm, snow if we are unlucky."

"Couldn't agree with you more, son. There's a storm brewing alright," Sam replied. He watched with a feeling of great satisfaction as his visitor tried to shield himself from the rain, now coming down in sheets. It would not occur to him to leave a dog standing out in the rain, but this already sodden man was lower than a dog – you didn't invite his type into your porch let alone your house. He could almost hear the man's teeth chattering as he looked up at him. "Now what is it that brings you to my door?"

"I was just passing and couldn't help but notice that your drive is the only one in the close that hasn't been block-paved. I can see that the tarmac has dropped in places – it doesn't take long for puddles to form." LJ pointed at the puddles on the drive as water ran in rivulets down his cheeks and onto his clothes.

"Observant as well, hey? And what is it precisely that you are offering me? I assume you're here to try and sell me something."

"We offer a landscaping service, sir. We could block-pave right up to the road and as far as the flower beds on both sides of the drive, and this step could be rebuilt and paved as well. It would transform the look of the place. It just so happens that we've got a consignment of block paving that would look fine here and match the paving in your neighbours' gardens at the same time. It would be a very good price. You'll not find better."

"And who is it you refer to as 'we', son? I always like to know with whom I am dealing? Just out of interest, quite where do you hail from?" Sam asked, keeping the conversation flowing. There was no way he was going to let this one run off before the police arrived.

"A long time ago from Romania and many thousands of years before that from Egypt itself." LJ managed a weak laugh. "But we've lived in the UK for several generations now."

"And getting back to my other question, who are 'we'?"

"That will be two of my cousins and me. We've done a lot of this kind of work. You'll get a good job."

"And where would I find you after you had done the job if anything went wrong with the work? Would that be on the Great North Road?" Sam asked, with a glint in his eye.

"You might be right about that. We're stopping here for the winter and then probably heading north and trying to do some honest work along the way, but I assure you, you'll have no problems with it."

"Have you done any other work in this area, son? Always like to look at the quality of work before I agree to do anything."

"Sure, just finished a job in Pettifer Close – Mr Humphries. Nice old fellow – he lives there on his own. Maybe you know him. Small patio job, but if I say so myself he seemed pleased with it. I'm sure that he would speak up for us."

"And when did you do that job, son?"

"We finished it last Thursday. It was a fine day – not like today," LJ replied, glancing up at the sky and brushing his now completely sodden hair away from his eyes. It was not the day for a long doorstep discussion, but he knew Byron would be pleased if he managed to secure another week's work. There were other houses at the other end of the village that he had yet to call on, and the prospect of walking over there in the pouring rain was less than appealing, but if he had to, then he would do so.

"I might drop around and take a look at it, but not today." Sam straightened his back – a reminder that he had spent the previous afternoon around at Pettifer Close taking up a section of the block paving and checking what lay beneath. He had been disappointed to find that even he couldn't find fault with the quality. "And what would you charge me to pave my driveway?"

LJ's eyes lit up. "We have a very special offer. We could do it for three thousand cash, labour and materials included. It would be a fixed price. We never go back on our word no matter what we find. We ask for thirty per cent upfront and the rest on completion. It would be a good five days' work by the time we've taken that old tarmac up, dug down for the hardcore to go in, and then laid the blocks. You'll not regret it."

"Mmmm," Sam muttered thoughtfully. "That's interesting, but there's just one small problem, son. I don't deal in cash. It's a cheque or a credit card if you want my business."

LJ's face dropped. It went with the territory – one day even people like them would have fancy bank accounts and credit cards. "Sure, I understand, but if it's not cash, we'd have to charge you so much more." It was too soon to admit that in his circles nothing but cash would do.

"I've told you what my terms would be." Sam shrugged. "Now let me guess – if you only do cash then am I to assume that you don't pay taxes either? And why, son, do you think that you and your mates should get away without paying taxes when the likes of everybody else have to pay their fair share?"

LJ sighed. How many times had he been through this before? All he wanted to do was to earn an honest living. Was it their fault that the system couldn't cope with those who were constantly on the road? Today was not the day for getting into an argument about the rights and wrongs of taxes or welfare – it would soon be time to walk away.

"Sorry, it's cash only," LJ said. "Maybe another time?"

"And I'm sorry too, old son. No deal. But I've got another good prospect for you. How do you fancy trying to sell your block-paved driveways to the boys in blue?" Grinning, Sam waved over LJ's shoulder.

"What's this about?" LJ asked, with a sinking feeling. "What are they doing here?"

"You'll soon see. By the way, Mr Humphries is my father-in-law," Sam said smugly. "And yes, you did do a good job on his patio. I checked it out myself. It's just a pity that you were greedy. Stealing from an old man – big mistake, son. Do I always have to do your job for you?" Sam demanded of the two policemen who stood either side of LJ.

"We came as quickly as we could, Sam. It is Sunday, you know," the older police officer replied.

"I don't understand. What's this got to do with Mr Humphries? It was a fair price. Ask him yourself if you don't believe me." LJ tried to shake his arms free of the two police officers. "I've done nothing wrong."

"LJ Lovell, I am arresting you on suspicion of theft from the property of Mr Fred Humphries on Friday twenty-second of January. You do not have to say anything, but it may harm your defence if you do not mention when questioned something that you might later rely on in court. Anything you say may be given in evidence. Do you understand? Perhaps you would like to accompany us to the station, sir?" the police officer said, and turning to his partner, "Cuff him. Let's go."

LJs hands trembled as he felt the unfamiliar cold steel of the handcuffs locked around his wrists.

# Seven

At least Sally had slept through the night. It was more than she could say of herself. It was the first time since they been married that she had gone to bed on her own and woken up on her own. The night had been endless without him. Byron had tried his best to quell her fears when he had told her about the phone call from LJ, but it was written all over his face: Byron was worried, seriously worried. When will he be back? she had asked him. Tomorrow, he had replied flatly. His answer lacked conviction. She knew LJ inside out – when he was happy and when he was troubled. She could almost read his mind, and she knew that he would never, ever steal a penny from anybody. How and why would anybody be so cruel as to put him in a cell and leave him there overnight? He was a good man but not a strong man. He was her happy-go-lucky husband who had never harmed a soul, a man who loved the outdoors and feared confinement. She could feel his terror in her every bone. Sally woke early, fractious, and demanding. "Where's my daddy? One sleep, you said."

"I said he'd be back soon, and he will, Sally. You must have patience, just like Mummy. First, I'll make breakfast for us, and after that, we'll do some colouring together or I'll read you a story," Jess replied.

"No, want my daddy. Where's my daddy?" Sally buried her head under her blankets and screamed.

"He'll be back soon," Jess said patiently, "very soon, Sally. Dry those tears. What would you like to do?"

A small head appeared out from under the blankets. "Auntie Miriam. Sweeties."

Jess frowned; it would be a bad move to say no to the child after having asked her what she wanted to do but walking down to the village to see Auntie Miriam would not have been top of her list when LJ might be home at any moment. "Okay, we can go and see if she is in," Jess replied.

Wiping her tears away with the back of her hand, Sally climbed out from underneath her blanket and clapped her hands, all thoughts of her missing father temporarily dismissed.

Jess had lost count of the number of times they had called on Miriam in the past few weeks. If Sally had had her way, they would all have moved in with her, but a promise was a promise. Sally jumped up and down in excitement as Jess pushed her arms into her warm coat and stuck a knitted hat on her head. "Okay, let's go," she said. "We'll have breakfast later. Not long now – we have to be back soon."

Miriam Turner heard the garden gate open and rushed out to the door. "Come in, come in, you two. Too cold to stand on the doorstep on a day like this. Never known such a long cold spell. At least it's not snowing – yet. Take your boots off in the hall, Sally," Miriam gushed. "I heard the gate latch and saw you both coming up the garden path. Don't know why but I had an inkling you might stop by today. Call it second sight if you like. It's lovely and warm in the cottage."

"Thank you," Jess said. "We were at a bit of a loose end and Sally insisted that we walk down to see you. Isn't that right, Sally?"

"Yes," Sally said, racing away from them into the small, cosy sitting room.

"So, no new baskets for me today, Jess? I've probably got more than enough of them anyway, but I do so love seeing your new creations. Such a talented girl you are."

It had quite taken her aback when Miriam had invited them into her house that first time; it was not unheard of, but rare. At the time she was almost overwhelmed by Miriam's praise of her baskets and quite amazed when she had bought every single one of them. A heart of gold. Miriam chatted incessantly about subjects far beyond her own knowledge but rarely about herself. To this day Jess knew little or nothing about Miriam's circumstances, nor had she enquired.

"No, no baskets today, Miriam. Besides, I doubt that you will have room for any more in your new house," Jess replied, taking off her coat and her boots.

"It's not a new house, dear. It's quite old actually. It's an old farmhouse that belonged to my parents. I haven't been there for years. They called it their summer home. It's been let out to visitors for the past five years. Like us all – in need of a bit of tender, loving care. I'm going to stay there for three months and then decide if I shall keep it or sell it. But you're right, of course, I won't have enough room for many more baskets." Miriam closed the front door behind them and led the way to the sitting room. "It's lovely to see you both. I'm almost ready to start loading up the car. I really can't believe where the time has gone. I'll be off late tomorrow. I just hope and pray that the sun is shining in the Algarve when I eventually get there. It's a long way to go if it isn't."

"I am sure it will be, Miriam," Jess said, thinking how much Sally would miss her Auntie Miriam. Going off to the Algarve meant nothing more to Sally than going off to the market for the day. She knew differently; the Algarve was in Portugal and if Miriam was going for three months, it would be the last time that they saw her. The family would have moved on by the time she returned, if she returned.

"I'm so pleased that you've dropped in. I wanted to say goodbye before leaving, but I didn't like to come down to the camp. You know how it is. I mean, I wouldn't want to intrude."

Jess nodded, feeling relieved. So far, she hadn't told anyone in the family about her regular trips down to see Miriam. Even Sally had been sworn to secrecy. "Our secret," Jess had said. Bless her heart, Sally hadn't breathed a word. At the back of Jess's mind was always the thought that they would not approve of her mixing outside of the family. And Miriam had that moment reminded her of other reasons why it was unwise to make friends outside of the family; the reputation of the gypsies, whatever their ancestry and however unfounded, went before them. Nobody visited the campsites by choice.

"What are you up to, little one?" Miriam asked. Sally sat on the rug in front of the hearth, a basket full of beads upturned all over the floor. "You can take those home with you if you like. I haven't got room to take them with me. Would you like that? You can make Mummy some necklaces."

"Sweeties?" No sooner had Miriam sat down than Sally jumped up into her lap and put her arms around her neck.

"You know, little one, that you remind me of somebody I knew an awfully long time ago. She was much younger than you, just a baby..." Miriam reached for her handbag, pulled out a bag of sweets, and handed them to Sally.

"Thank you. Where pictures, Auntie Miriam?" Sally asked, looking around the room at the bare windowsill and sideboard.

"They're packed, ready to go with me."

Jess pictured the last time that they had visited Miriam. Sally was right, the photographs in their silver frames had all gone – photographs of what she had presumed to be Miriam's family had covered every square inch of space on the sideboards, the tiny windowsills, the TV, and the side tables. Most of them, she remembered, were of Miriam from the time she was a toddler through to her teens, almost unrecognisable in the drab, utilitarian clothes that she then wore. They were so unlike the clothes she wore today – multi-coloured flowing garments with matching bandanas complemented by beads around her neck and her wrists. Tall and slim, Miriam would look good in almost anything. She had hardly a wrinkle on her face – Jess guessed that she was in her late thirties.

"When you back?" Sally asked innocently.

"I really don't know when I am coming back. If I like it there, I might well stay there for a long time," Miriam replied.

"Me come too?"

"Someday, maybe. It's a long way away, Sally. It's in a different country called Portugal, in an area called the Algarve. It's down by the seaside."

"What's the seaside?" Sally frowned and pouted her lips.

"It's where the land meets the sea, and the sea goes on as far as the eye can see. People swim in the sea and play on the sandy beach. Lots of people go there for their holidays," Miriam explained.

"Seaside!" Sally's face lit up. Jess felt a lump in her throat; maybe Sally would never go to the seaside. "Jocklin take me there?" she asked.

"Jocklin's your horse, isn't he?" Miriam asked.

"Cob and old. He walks a long way," Sally said hopefully.

"Oh, a cob, is he? I should have known better, shouldn't I? No, Sally. It's too far away for Jocklin. I'm going to drive my car all the way there. It is going to take at least three days," Miriam replied, stroking Sally's hair. "Do you want to see some pictures of my house in the Algarve?"

Sally nodded.

"It's going to take a long time to make it pretty, Sally, but one day maybe you will see it. I've got some photographs in my handbag. Here, let's look at these together. These photographs are quite old, but I doubt that it's changed that much. Look. There's a big family room with a huge kitchen at one end and then there's a dining room that can seat at least ten for dinner. There's a big terrace where I can sit out in the sun. You can see the sea from there. And upstairs there are four bedrooms and two bathrooms, each with their own bath and shower."

Jess watched; the child hardly knew what a bedroom was let alone a proper bathroom with a bath or a shower. Momentarily she yearned for the comfort of a proper home with a proper kitchen with a full-sized cooker, fridge and washing machine, bedrooms with soft springy beds, a bathroom with hot running water, and a little garden that Sally could play in.

"There are shops and cafes and restaurants and schools just a few miles away," Miriam said.

"Schools?" Sally frowned.

"For the children, yes. I guess that you'll be thinking about school here for Sally in a year's time," she said, turning back to Jess. "She's such a bright little thing, she'll do so well."

"Yes, of course. It's difficult when you move from place to place, but I shall try to make sure that she has a good home education," Jess replied quickly. The very thought of Sally being singled out to spend her school days with no more than a colouring book made her blood run cold. That was how, so she had been told, gypsy children were treated in schools.

Miriam stroked Sally's hair again. "You have such lovely hair little one."

"Want it red, like you." Sally said.

"Maybe when you grow up…" Miriam started.

"When I'm old?" Sally chuckled.

"I'm old, am I, young lady?" Miriam laughed. "I'll have you know, young lady, that I'm only thirty-six – plenty of life in this old dog yet."

"That's old," Sally said.

"That's rude, Sally. You know that it's rude to pass personal remarks. Apologise to Auntie Miriam."

"She's just a child. No apologies are needed. And no tears now, Sally."

Jess laughed half-heartedly and wondered whether Miriam had ever had any children of her own. If the photographs were to be believed then the answer was, no, she had not.

Jess's thoughts were miles away as she wondered what was happening back at the camp. "Are you alright, Jess? You're looking a bit peaky today. Is there anything wrong?" Miriam asked.

Jess shook her head. How she would have loved to tell Miriam all about her worries and let the older woman wrap her arms around her as she had with Sally, and tell her that everything was going to be okay. Would Miriam believe her if she told her that LJ was innocent, or would she assume that because he was a gypsy, he would be guilty? "No," Jess said, putting on a brave face, "everything is fine. We'll miss your friendship, that's all. We must go now and let you get on with your packing. I can't thank you enough for your kindness towards me, and to Sally. I hope you have a safe trip."

"And you stay safe too, and I do so hope that the villagers see the light. In my opinion, you are none of you doing any harm up at that site."

"I'm sorry," Jess said, "I don't understand."

"The notices, Jess. Haven't you seen them? Pinned to every lamp post and telegraph pole in the village. Oh, dear, I thought you would know."

"What notices?"

"There's an extraordinary general meeting in the Village Hall tonight to discuss the camp at the old garage and workshop. They want to see you moved on. They really are a small-minded lot around here. They hate change. Anyone would think that they're going to be murdered in their beds."

"We don't murder, Miriam. We're a peace-loving community," Jess snapped.

"It was just a turn of phrase, Jess. I know that and you know that. Try telling them. I'll be glad to get a break away from them.

I'm going to try and get to the meeting this evening, Jess. I'll do my best to put your case to them."

"That's kind," Jess said. "Sorry, I snapped. It's over three months since we arrived in Bartonford now. We all thought that we'd be okay staying here for the next few months. We're not harming anybody. The site was derelict. If anything, it's tidier than it was when we arrived."

"As I say, I know that, and you know that. It's not about the site at all. It's property prices that they're concerned about. Having a group of Travellers – sorry, gypsies – on the edge of town won't do the property market any good. It's criminal really. If you were any other ethnic minority then they'd jolly well have to put up and shut up. It makes me cross."

"Maybe it will come to nothing, but thank you for telling me." Jess shrugged her shoulders. What will be, will be, she thought, making a mental note to mention it to Michael when she got back to the camp. "We really must be going now."

Jess knelt and put the beads back in the basket as Miriam watched. "Take the beads and the basket, Jess. Sally will enjoy playing with them."

"Don't want to go." Sally whined.

"We have to go, Sally. Auntie Miriam has to finish her packing and we have to get back to Daddy. You want to see Daddy, don't you?"

"Yes, s'pose," Sally whispered.

"Give me a big goodbye kiss, Sally. You really are the most gorgeous little girl."

"Boots on, Sally," Jess interrupted. "Goodbye Miriam, thank you and good luck."

"Going to see Daddy now." Sally called as Jess opened the garden gate.

# Eight

Glancing out of the window of his caravan, Byron saw the police car draw to a halt on the other side of the barrier. It was late afternoon. All morning he had paced back and forth, waiting, waiting. The longer he waited, the surer he was that the news would not be good. He cursed himself for listening to LJ in the first place; he should have known better. For all his years, the boy was naïve when it came to dealing with the police. Michael had been right – they should have been down at that police station first thing that morning demanding answers. But LJ had insisted – it was under control, he was innocent of the theft he had been accused of, they had no evidence, they couldn't charge him with anything, and they would have to release him eventually. Byron and Michael, he said, were to stay put at the camp, look after Jess and Sally and wait it out. Against his better judgement, Byron had acceded to his nephew's wishes.

Jess dropped the plates she was washing into the water as her mouth flew open. There were voices outside, loud: Byron and Michael. A car engine died, and doors slammed. Heaving a sigh of relief, she thanked God for small mercies. She had her husband back.

"Stay where you are, Sally," she said, wiping her hands on her apron. "It'll be Daddy." A cold blast of wind hit her as she opened the stable door, put one hand on the rail, and started gingerly down the steps.

"Go back in, Jess. Close the door," Byron shouted.

"But..." Jess stuttered.

"Do it, Jess." Byron looked right up at her. Jess retreated into the vardo and closed the door. Byron was not a man to be disobeyed.

Byron stared at the police car, locked eyes on its occupants, and strode purposefully towards the barrier. Michael, in Byron's wake, glanced over his shoulder as, out of the corner of his eye, he noticed two shadowy figures slink away from the campsite.

"Where's my nephew, constable?" Byron demanded.

"Sergeant, sir," he said pompously, pointing at the three stripes on the arm of his uniform. "Sergeant Brockett, and with me, I have Constable Mayhew." A pasty-faced, plump youth stood well back from the barrier. "And your name, sir?" Sergeant Brockett asked, emphasizing the 'sir'. It stuck in his gullet to call a gypsy 'sir', but nobody could accuse Sergeant Brockett of being politically incorrect.

"Byron, Byron Lovell. LJ – the man you have in custody – is my nephew. No doubt you know that already. I asked you a question, Sergeant. Where is he? I don't want to get angry with you." Arms folded across his chest, feet apart, a face like thunder, Byron had a formidable presence.

"Your nephew is currently helping us out with our enquiries down at the station in Aubrey." Sergeant Brockett ignored the thinly disguised threat, slowly reached into his pocket, and pulled out his notebook. "There are just a few things we need to clear up."

"Enquiries into what?"

"Theft of property from one Mr Frederick Humphries of Pettifer Close, Bartonford."

"Rubbish."

"A theft that took place last Friday afternoon, the very same afternoon that your nephew visited Mr Humphries." Sergeant Brockett flipped open his notebook and read the contents of the first page. "Items taken include Mr Humphries' pension money – three hundred pounds to be precise, a pair of gold cufflinks that were given to him by his grandfather on his twenty-first birthday and three solid silver photograph frames, the latter of more sentimental value to Mr Humphries than monetary – photographs of his late wife. Who'd do such a thing?" The question hung in the air. "Estimated total value, five hundred pounds."

"Not LJ in answer to your question. He's an honest man. You won't find a more honest man. We earn money honestly." Byron's eyes blazed.

"If I may continue, sir?" The sergeant eyed Byron and turned the page of his notebook. "I understand that Mr Lovell and two of his cousins recently completed a job for Mr Humphries – block paving of his front garden. Is that correct?"

"It is," Byron barked, struggling to control his temper.

"And that the charge for the job was one thousand pounds. Mr Humphries paid three hundred pounds deposit and the remaining seven hundred pounds was to be paid on completion of the job. Is that correct?"

"Yes." Byron felt a steadying hand on his arm and glanced sideways at Michael.

"And I gather that you, sir, believed that your nephew, Mr Lovell, had underpriced the job by five hundred pounds. Is that also correct? Coincidence, I'm sure…"

Byron ground his teeth. What the hell else had LJ told them? "What do you mean by that?"

"Nothing, nothing at all, sir, but you must see how it might be interpreted," Sergeant Brockett said smugly. "Your nephew, if I might call him that, tells us – I quote – that he hit it off with Mr Humphries, that it was not unusual for them to spend time together chatting. According to your nephew, it was a fine winter's afternoon – his words not mine – so on that Friday afternoon they sat outside and talked about plants and shrubs that Mr Humphries might acquire to complement the new patio. Mr Lovell apparently suggested, amongst other things, that Mr Humphries might buy himself a white heather plant – for luck." Sergeant Brockett laughed. "Does your nephew happen to be a horticulturist as well?"

"He's interested in plants. Always has been." Byron clenched his fists. "What in hell's name has this got to do with any theft?"

"I'm coming to that. According to your nephew, he spent about an hour with Mr Humphries and during that time entered his house to go to the toilet. Did you see your nephew return to the camp that afternoon?"

"No."

"I did," Michael interrupted. "I was chopping wood when he came back."

"And who might you be, sir?"

"His brother-in-law. Michael, Michael Trebold." It was not his given surname, but he was taking no chances.

"And did you happen to see if your brother-in-law was carrying anything about his person when he returned?"

"He was empty-handed apart from the seven hundred pounds final payment that he handed over to Byron about an hour later. No bulges in his pockets. No bulges in his coat if that helps at all," Michael stated. "I don't like what you are suggesting."

"I'm not suggesting anything," Sergeant Brockett spoke slowly. "There is a witness who claims he saw two men in the vicinity of Pettifer Close at about the same time. Unfortunately, it was from a distance, but he describes them as medium height, broad-shouldered, dark hair, and wearing grey hoodies and black jeans. You wouldn't happen to know anybody who fits that description?"

Byron hesitated for an instant. "No."

Michael could read Byron like a book. "No," he affirmed. Whatever had or hadn't happened, Byron would get to the bottom of it and deal with it in his own way, the Roma way.

"Search the camp if it will satisfy you. You'll find nothing here," Byron shouted, gesticulating towards the vehicles.

"That won't be necessary, sir. I'll take your word for it." Sergeant Brockett glanced sideways at his colleague and pointed back towards the car. The last thing he had any intention of doing was to step into the lion's den. He had heard what had happened to those who had tried in the past. "There are plenty of places where he could have hidden the items between here and the village. We'll find them, mark my words. Right now, we need to have another little chat with your nephew and then we'll see what happens. We'll bid you good day."

"I want my nephew released right now. You have no right to keep him. I'm coming down to the station right now. I want to see him." Byron yelled as the two police officers climbed back in the car.

"All circumstantial, Byron." Michael put his arm around Byron's shoulders. "They've got nothing on him. They can't charge him with anything. LJ is right. We'll only make matters worse if we go down there shouting the odds. That's what they want. We have to sit this one out."

Michael watched as the police car drew away. Byron swore and hammered his fist into the palm of his other hand. Michael had never seen him so angry. The volcano was about to erupt. "Take it easy, Byron," he said, as he watched Byron stride off in the direction of one of the caravans.

Jess opened the stable door to the vardo and stood on the top step. "Michael, where is he?"

Michael looked up at his sister. "He'll be back soon, Jess. Don't fret."

"Where's my daddy?" Sally screeched. "You promised…"

Michael walked towards the vardo. If nothing else he could try to comfort Jess and Sally. He knew better than to interfere with whatever Byron was about to do.

# Nine

"Come out, both of you. You useless pieces of shit. I want answers," Byron bellowed as he hammered on the door with his fists.

Michael heard the commotion and glanced at Jess. Nathan and Buckland had legged it the moment the police car had arrived. Byron wasn't going to find them at home.

Doors to caravans were pulled closed, blinds dropped around the campground. They all knew it was safest to stay well out of the way. When Byron's temper flared, nobody was safe. It didn't happen often, but when it did, it was never without reason and God help those who got in his way.

Wrenching open the door, he marched in. The caravan was empty. Byron wrinkled his nose. The place stank. Dirty clothes lay strewn across the floor, there were pots and pans stacked in the sink where they had been for days, empty cans lined up like soldiers covered a small table, ashtrays overflowed onto the threadbare, filthy carpet. It was a pigsty. Byron's thoughts turned back to Silas, his younger brother. Hadn't he been just the same, slovenly, lazy and innately dishonest? It was no wonder that Buckland and Nathan had turned out as they had.

Crawling on his hands and knees, Byron searched under the benches, under the beds and under the table. Then in the drawers, in the kitchen, in the small toilet and shower room, and then finally in the narrow vertical cupboard that served as a place to hang the few decent clothes that they might have had. His eyes alighted on four hangers from which hung clean, pressed clothes. Buckland and Nathan never wore clean clothes; to have clothes that were pressed and as new was unheard of. Pulling out the hangers, he fingered the garments. They were quality, unworn, with labels still attached. The temperature in the caravan soared as he read the labels and saw the price that had been paid for them. There was no doubt in his mind that they were responsible, and they would pay for it.

Sweeping the beer cans onto the floor with one arm, he placed the two pairs of jeans and two designer T-shirts on the table. On top of the pile, he added two pairs of designer trainers and sat back on the bench, arms folded across his chest, his face like thunder.

Like a leopard waiting to pounce, he waited. As the light of day started to fade, he sat on, unmoving, in the sure knowledge that they would have to come back, sooner or later. If it took all evening and all night, he would be there. No one would disturb him until it was over.

It was six o'clock when he heard footsteps outside the caravan and whispered voices.

"No one about." Byron heard Buckland's voice.

"Looks like he's cooled down a bit and turned in," Nathan said.

"The old man ain't happy. Uncle Byron's golden boy got himself in a bit of trouble. Couldn't happen to a nicer boy," Buckland said, as he opened the door.

Byron fixed his eyes on the door. "You're right, boys, the old man ain't happy."

Grabbing his nephew by the collar of his jacket he threw him back down the steps. Landing on his back, he took Nathan down with him.

"What's this about, Uncle Byron? We ain't done nothing." Buckland edged backward on his bottom as Byron towered over him.

"Nothing, hey? Not man enough to admit it now that you've been caught out?" Byron shouted as he turned to Nathan. "Don't move, boy. Don't move an inch if you know what's good for you."

Nathan looked around. His instinct told him to run and keep running but maybe they could blag their way out of it. "Buck's right, Uncle Byron. We ain't done nothing. What's this about?"

"You insult my intelligence, the both of you." Byron's words carried around the camp. "You disgust me. You are a disgrace to the Roma," he yelled, pulling back his arm ready to let his fist fly for the first time. "Steal would you, and see your own cousin arrested for it, would you? Since when did you two little bastards have the money to buy designer gear? Where were you this morning? In town spending your dirty money?"

Nathan and Buckland exchanged worried glances. "We did a few jobs on the side if you want to know. Nothing illegal. Just didn't hand the money over to you, that's all. It's not a crime."

"Liar," Byron yelled as he landed the first blow on Buckland's nose. Nathan scrambled to his feet and started backing away. Byron swung around. "You'll take your punishment now, Nathan, or I swear I'll kill you both."

"You got it wrong, Uncle Byron. You've really got it wrong this time," Nathan screamed, trying to pull Byron away from his brother. "Let him go."

Byron landed the second punch to Buckland's face and then to his shoulder and then to his chest. Buckland screamed and squirmed and tried to protect his body with his arms and hands. Blood trailed from his nose and his mouth and his front teeth hung loose where Byron's ring had inflicted the most damage.

"He's my brother. Look what you've done – you've killed him," Nathan yelled.

"Your turn now." Byron's eyes glowed in the dark like a hungry tiger sensing his prey nearby.

As Nathan turned to run, Byron reached out and caught him.

He was on him in a flash, landing blow after blow. Finally, exhausted, Byron let him fall to the ground and looked at the battlefield. He had taught them a lesson, one that they would never forget.

It was eerily quiet after the screaming and yelling. The campsite was in silence. Slowly the blinds to the caravans were lifted, and the occupants spilled out on to the steps. "Get them inside and clean them up," he ordered. "They'll live."

Hands under their armpits, the women slowly lifted the two men to their feet and helped them back into the caravan. It was the Roma way.

Michael held them both close to his body. He had known what was coming and he had known it would be ugly. Jess watched as Sally finally stopped shaking until, exhausted, she closed her big blue eyes and went to sleep. It was the first time that the child had ever known fear. The sound of men shrieking and crying had terrified her. It had terrified Jess as well. She had just seen the other side of Byron.

Jess looked up at her brother. "What was all that about, Michael? It sounded like he was going to kill them."

"Close call," Michael said. "They got what they deserved, Jess, believe me. Don't blame Byron. He did what he had to do. Are you okay if I leave you for a couple of hours? There's someplace I need to be."

# Ten

Chair of Bartonford Parish Council since before any of them could remember, Wanda was in her late sixties and a spinster of the parish. She filled her lonely days with parish matters. Dog poo had been her latest crusade before the crisis had occurred. She was the world-leading expert in matching the poo she found left on the pavement to each and every one of the dogs in the village. No one escaped. The offending matter was picked up on a shovel and deposited on the doormat outside the offending house. She rarely got it wrong.

There had been a crisis brewing for weeks. The gypsies had moved in and were living on the boundary of Wanda's beloved village. It was just over three months since they had set up camp and the villagers were up in arms about it. The local rags loved it; nothing so exciting had happened in Bartonford for years. Letters to the editor skyrocketed. What right did these travelling bands have to besmirch the countryside? Didn't the local authorities understand that if they turned a blind eye to one lot of Travellers then every Traveller within hundreds of miles would soon be heading their way? As time went by and the crisis was no nearer to being resolved, the For Sale signs started to go up in the village – a mass exodus was on the cards. Estate agents warned of the difficulty of selling properties in a village that hosted a gypsy community; property prices would be bound to fall.

Crisis was probably an exaggeration, but Wanda thrived on a good crisis. It was the one time when the villagers really appreciated how much she did for them. A few gypsy families camped near the village probably wasn't a crisis of major proportions, but the whole thing could so easily escalate out of all proportion if it wasn't nipped in the bud, and she was determined to do just that.

As chair of the Parish Council, she had called a meeting for the Monday evening to discuss the matter and made it quite clear in person, and through flyers nailed to lamp posts and telegraph poles, that everyone in the village was expected to attend.

It was the biggest turnout that she had seen since the Hathrey Development Proposal, a plan to build a thousand houses adjacent to the village for the young and unemployed from the nearby cities. Fought tooth and nail by the villagers, and usefully aided by some of the best QCs in London, the fight had been financed by one of the wealthier residents. Eventually, the plan had been thwarted. It was a few months that she would remember with fondness. Every one of the villagers had rallied behind the cause and each one of them had put aside the petty arguments and squabbles that so often were part and parcel of a small village community. It was her firm belief that in fighting the gypsy invasion a period of internal harmony and camaraderie would once more prevail.

The doors were closed on a hall full to bursting. "May I call this meeting to order, please?" she said in that high-pitched voice, which never failed to irritate. "Order! Order!" Wanda called waving her papers in the air.

The hubbub in the hall faded enough for Wanda to catch a comment from one of the 'council houses' sitting at the back. "Who does she think she is – the bloody Speaker of the House?"

Wanda ignored the comment. It was no more than she expected from the likes of the council houses. "Thank you all for coming this evening. We rarely see the village hall this busy," she said, smiling regally down at her subjects. "It's just a pity that you can't all spare one hour each month to attend the monthly Parish Council meetings.

"Ladies and gentlemen, we are here today to discuss how we can rid ourselves of – excuse me for using the term – the vermin now congregating in their hundreds up at the old garage and workshop site." She knew it was a bit of an overstatement but in her mind's eye, she could see them quite clearly beating a path towards Bartonford – traipsing along the roads from every county in the country, heading their way and in their hundreds. "Haven't we always been tolerant in the past and turned a blind eye to them stopping here overnight? It seems that we have been far too generous and now they are taking advantage of us. It is simply not to be tolerated, I am sure you will all agree. Before we know it, the whole place will be infested with rats and much more besides."

Sternly she eyeballed the live-and-let-live brigade in the hall and dared them to contradict her. A few had looked away but to a man and woman they had had the common sense to keep their mouths well shut. They'd been on the wrong side of Wanda on more than one occasion and it wasn't an experience they intended to repeat.

"Hear, hear." 'Squire' James Smytheson Hodge stood and strode purposefully to the front of the room. There was only one thing he liked more than the sound of his own voice and that was a captive audience. "The way I see it is that it's the District Council's responsibility to get rid of them. That's what they are there for. That's what we pay our taxes for and it's about time we got some value out of it. You, madam chairman," he said, turning back to face Wanda, "constantly tell us that you can twist them around your little finger, so now's the time to do just that. And I for one won't stand for it a minute longer. There was a time and not so long ago when the properties in Bartonford fetched the highest prices of any village in the country. Have you seen what's happening to the market now? I am a law-abiding citizen, but even I can be pushed too far. I say send the whole bloody lot of them back to where they came from and if

74

they won't go, then lock the whole lot of them up and throw away the keys. I don't give a toss about their rights – ethnic communities my arse. What about my rights? At this rate, they'll be here until the summer and expecting an invitation to my annual garden party."

"I am not sure that I would agree with everything you are saying, James, but I do sympathise with your view – indeed, I more than sympathise," Wanda replied, ignoring the jeers from the back of the hall from those who were not so easily taken in by her perceived influence with the District Council.

"To address one of your points, James, I've spoken to the council and the police at length and they insist that there is nothing they can, or more like, will do about it. Apparently, there's an Act of Parliament – the Criminal Justice and Public Order Act of 1994 which prevents them from doing anything," she said, heartily thankful that she had done her homework before coming to the meeting. "I too, James, am a law-abiding citizen but it seems that the law is not on our side this time. Now if I had my way... No, I really must not go down that route. I will read three short sentences to you that were indeed quoted to me by the District Council." Wanda picked up her notes. This was one bit of research that she had been determined to share.

She waited until the side chat ebbed and she had their attention again before perching her glasses on her nose and lifting her notes up in front of her face. "I quote: 'The gypsies can only be evicted if one of three conditions are breached. First, if any of those persons has caused damage to the land or property on the land.' Like it or not, they have not. They would be hard pushed to make it any worse than it has been for the past few years," she added, eyeballing Keith Ingrams. She blamed him in part. It was he who owned the land and it was common knowledge that he was keeping it for his pension pot. As a sizeable piece of land, it would one day be perfect for development and would fetch a significant sum of money.

"Second," she continued, "and I quote again: 'If they use

threatening, abusive or insulting behaviour towards the occupier, a member of his family or an employee or an agent of his.' Has any of this happened, Keith?"

"Not exactly," he replied. "But it's my bloody land. I say we run them out of town."

"Well, maybe you should have thought about that before you left the site unsecured, and in that state – manna from heaven to any passing gypsy," Wanda replied. "And the third condition that prevents them from being moved on is that they have less than six vehicles. That's the law and I've been up there and counted them. There are five precisely. Note that a van towing a caravan counts as one vehicle only. And the horse doesn't count at all. These people are no fools."

"In my book, they are damaging my land. We all know that they shit in bags and the bushes and don't clear up after them," Keith Ingrams replied, red-faced with anger at the implied accusation that it was he who was personally responsible for the gypsies occupying the site.

"If you had taken the time to go up to your land and look over the barrier that they have erected at the entrance you will see that there is a Portaloo – like those that we hire for the village fair – and I have it on good authority that it is taken away and emptied regularly. What's more, I hear tell that the water board has reconnected the water to the property and it's highly likely that the toilet at the back of the garage workshop is back in working order as well," Wanda said, beginning to show her exasperation. "So, the only way to evict them would be to take the matter to court at great expense to ourselves and with a less than fifty-fifty chance of winning. Or worst still – the gypsies win, and we are saddled with them permanently. So, let's look at the alternatives and the first is that we must make them feel as unwelcome as we can – and that means no more work for them from anybody – no buying on the doorstep, no giving them work in the gardens or on the farms. We do not serve them in the shop, and they are banned from the pub and the church. I, for one, would be most unhappy to find myself sharing a pew with any of them in the church. Bottom line, we send them to Coventry – if only we could."

"Is that the best we can do?" Oswald Billericay jumped to his feet. A small pompous little man, Oswald prided himself on owning and running the best boarding kennels in the country. "If we don't get them out of there fast then I can see my business going down the pan even faster. Who will want to board their dogs with me or come to me to breed their dogs when they know that there are gypsies around the corner just waiting for an opportunity to steal them?"

"If you have any better ideas, Oswald, I would be delighted to hear them," Wanda said patiently. He was far too self-opinionated, and she had little time for him, indeed, thoroughly disliked him. Quietly, she would be delighted if his business 'went down the pan' as he described it.

"Not right at this moment I don't, but believe you me I'm working on it. If you can't shift them then I will."

Another hand shot up from the back of the hall. "Don't you forget, Wanda, that if they settle in that spot and nobody moves them on then their children will have to be taken in at the local primary schools. I won't have my children sitting beside gypsies picking up their fleas or filthy habits. It just doesn't bear thinking about. It's alright for you – you don't have children."

"Thank you, Gillian, for reminding me of that. The issue of finding schools to take the children was one that I had not overlooked. Of course, there is insufficient space for our own children let alone the offspring of gypsies. Are there any additional ideas before I move on to a separate but related subject?"

Wanda peered around the room waiting for the next outburst from the council houses, but the hall was silent. The villagers were getting fidgety and eyes were turning towards the door.

"Ladies and gentlemen, I will turn now to another issue which is very much related to the one we have just discussed. It just might be the ace up our sleeve. I have the feeling that this might just teach them a lesson that they'll not forget in a hurry. And it would be my guess – but only a guess – that after they've been taught that lesson, they'll leave with their tails between their legs. Isn't that what we all want?" Wanda smiled broadly and waved to a heavy-set man sitting next to an elderly man in the front row. "Sam, would you care to take the floor and expand upon that to which I have alluded?"

Sam shoved his hands in his pockets and walked slowly and purposefully to the front of the hall. "They're stealing, thieving," he started, pausing for effect. "It's time to check all the locks on your doors and make sure that everything is locked up and secure before you go to bed at night. Last Friday in broad daylight they robbed my father-in-law, Fred, an old man living on his own with no more than a pension. It looks to me like one of them kept Dad talking out front whilst his mates broke in at the back. They stole the pension money that he had just collected from the post office, silver photograph frames with precious pictures of my late mother-in-law in them, and gold cufflinks that were given to him on his twenty-first birthday by his grandfather. I was straight on to the police that night, but did they do anything? Did they hell. Excuse my language, madam chairman. Some cock and bull story about staff shortages and gypsies policing their own. All I got was a promise that at some point in time they would go down to the camp and speak to the boss man. And then yesterday morning one of them – the one who kept my dad talking – had the nerve to come to my door looking for work. Talk about brass-necked. Marie rang the police while I kept him talking on the doorstep. I told the wife that she wasn't to take no for an answer from the police. I managed to keep him talking until they arrived and took him away. He's in custody right now. And I just had a call to confirm that he's pleading guilty. The one they've caught who calls himself LJ is up in front of the magistrate tomorrow. You can't get much lower than robbing a pensioner, and especially after he's just paid you cash for a job. The sooner we see the back of the whole lot of them, the better for all of us. I for one will be down at the court to see him get what he deserves, and I hope that the rest of you will be there as well."

"I happen to know the magistrate who is presiding this week," Ursula called from the floor. Ursula was well known for having a finger in every pie in the village, a network of contacts that extended the length and breadth of the county, and an opinion on everything that she never failed to voice loudly and frequently. Unfortunately, she heard only what she wanted to hear and consequently lived her life in blissful ignorance of the truth. "She's an old school chum of mine from Cheltenham and we've always kept in touch. I would be more than happy to give her a bell tonight and make sure she knows exactly what the gypsy has done. I know she takes a dim view of anyone taking advantage of the elderly and I am sure this will be no exception. She has a good reputation – always firm and never shirks her responsibilities. I think we can safely say that he will receive his just deserts. He won't walk off with a clip around the ear and a small fine."

"Thank you, Sam, and thank you, Ursula." Wanda smiled. "That all sounds very satisfactory. You have my full support and I assure you that I will be at the magistrates' court in Leamington tomorrow."

"Excuse me, madam bloody chairman."

Wanda frowned. "You have something to add, Fred? I'd have thought that your son-in-law has just said it all."

"I do indeed," he started. "It was my pension that was pinched, my photos and my cufflinks. I can't deny a theft happened, but I'm telling you all that the lad they've arrested is a good lad. His name is LJ – he's human just like the rest of us. He may be a gypsy, but he's a good boy – got a young wife and little daughter as well. Who's to say that he had anything to do with it? Could have been anybody sneaked into the back of my house. I say innocent until proven guilty and I'm ashamed to be sitting here and listening to all this. If it had been up to me then it would have been dropped, and I'd have been more careful with locking the doors properly in the future. But no, this caring son-in-law of mine marches me right down to the station to report it, and I have no choice but to land the lad right in it. You're bloodhounds the lot of you and an innocent man will end up in prison. Shame on you all."

Sam shook his head and looked at his father-in-law pityingly. "You've been watching too much TV, Dad. He's not innocent – far from it. Don't forget that Oswald saw his mates out the back as well. It's people like you that they take advantage of – there's no such thing as a good gypsy. I'm just protecting you and my good neighbours."

Fred looked around the hall at a sea of faces. There was not a shadow of doubt on any of their faces that LJ was guilty as charged; tomorrow would be a farce. "I can't take any more of this. You're a bunch of hypocrites and you can count me out. I for one won't be there to see the lad go down. You'll regret this – every one of you," he added, as he pulled on his coat, picked up his walking stick and stormed towards the door.

"That's what happens when you give gypsies work, Fred," Wanda called, as Fred opened and closed the door behind him. "Perhaps this will be a lesson to all of us. Is there anything else that anybody would like to add before we bring this meeting to a close?"

It hadn't escaped Wanda's notice that the farmers had been very quiet throughout the proceedings. She knew that they welcomed the Travellers passing through to get fences mended and ditches dug and to do all those jobs that their farmhands considered beneath them. She probably couldn't look to any of them for support at any other time of year. Had it been spring or summer when they needed casual labour, she was sure that they would have been more vociferous.

"To summarise then before we close the meeting, those who are able will be in court tomorrow to support our cause. Ursula will speak to her friend the magistrate tonight, there will be no work for the gypsies in this village, they will not be served in the shop or the pub, and neither will they be welcomed at the church. No one will buy anything from them on the doorstep and that includes you, Miriam," Wanda said, pointing towards the back of the room.

Miriam started at the sound of her name and looked up to see Wanda and the rest of the village staring at her accusingly. They were waiting for her to respond to the accusation. She had been miles away. It was the first she had heard of the theft and the arrest. Poor Jess, she thought to herself. It had to be Jess's husband they were speaking of – she remembered hearing her speak about 'LJ', although Jess hadn't said a thing about it that morning.

Miriam said, "I'll not deny that the young girl whom I presume to be this so-called thief's wife and her child have visited me on several occasions and that I have bought things from them. For the record, she is a nice young woman, and the child is delightful. I can assure you that I shall not be buying anything from them because tomorrow I shall be off to my villa in the Algarve and I don't intend to be back for quite a while. No doubt they will be gone by the time I return. For what it is worth I would ask you all to think again, to consider their plight. Theirs is not an easy life. Leave them alone. I know from a very good source that they are only staying in Bartonford for the winter and after that, they will be gone. Then is the time to seal off the site and make sure it doesn't happen again."

"It's okay for you swanning off to your villa whilst the rest of us have to live with it. I say we don't wait." Oswald jumped up from his chair and pumped his fist in the air. "We all know what they are like – man, woman, and child. Nip it in the bud is what I say. We can't afford to have vermin like that living down the road. It will kill our businesses. It will kill what's left of the property market in this village. We'll be outcasts in the county. Forget the council, the police, and all your nice little ploys, Wanda. I say we take the law into our own hands."

"Thank you, Oswald," Wanda replied. "In my humble opinion

tomorrow will be a deciding factor. I cannot for one minute see that they would wish to stop in our village with one of their own in some faraway prison. We should wait and see what happens after tomorrow at court. If needs be, we will reconvene at the same time next week. On that note, I am closing the meeting and thank you all for your attendance."

As everyone filed out of the door, Wanda looked for the young man who had expectedly turned up at the meeting. Respectably dressed and quietly spoken, he had heard about the meeting, so he told her, and with some interest in buying one of the many properties for sale in the village, had decided to come to the meeting to judge the severity of the crisis for himself. He had not spoken during the meeting but seemed to have taken an interest in everything that had been said, and now he had disappeared. He had said that his name was Michael but had not given his surname. She just hoped that it had not put him off buying a property in the village.

With a heavy heart, Michael walked back to the camp. He did not look forward to breaking the news to Byron.

# Eleven

LJ was thirteenth on the list in court five. Sessions started at ten. His appearance, they had been told, could be any time between eleven-thirty in the morning and four o'clock in the afternoon depending upon the speed of progress of the preceding cases. Michael and Byron were dressed and ready to go. Both wore jackets and ties above clean denim jeans. The family would be dropped off in Aubrey to sell their wares at the market. Jess and Sally had been told by Byron that they would remain at the camp together with Buckland and Nathan, both of whom were still nursing their wounds and had not been seen since the previous day. Dropping the family off at eight-thirty, Michael suggested, would give them ample time to drive to Leamington, park, and walk to the court building. Byron was touchy; Michael was anxious.

The traffic in Aubrey was light. Traffic on the A46 was near bumper to bumper. Byron concentrated hard on the road and Michael bided his time. A wad of notes bulged from Byron's trouser pocket. If there were costs to be paid, Byron was ready. He was in no doubt that LJ would walk away a free man before the end of the day.

"There's something you need to know, Byron." Michael picked his moment. The traffic had eased off, they were well ahead of schedule and Byron was looking more relaxed. "I went to a meeting in the village hall yesterday evening. Jess tipped me off about it. The topic of discussion was us – how to get us out of Bartonford."

"When we're ready and not before," Byron replied gruffly.

"It came up at the meeting, Byron." Michael glanced sideways at his friend. "LJ is pleading guilty today."

Michael grabbed the edges of his seat. For a split second, it looked as though they were about to run into the truck in front. Byron touched the brakes and created space, his face like thunder, struggling to control his emotions. "He's done what?" Byron shouted. "What the hell is the boy thinking about?"

"We both know that he's innocent, but he's pleading guilty. I don't understand it either, but I'm pretty sure it's a fact. That's what one of them said at the meeting last night. The police had called and told one of them. I spent half of last night googling the process. We need to prepare ourselves, Byron. What it means is that when he comes up before the bench today, they will pass sentence on him on the spot. If they go down on him hard, we may not be taking him home."

Byron thumped the steering wheel with his fist and the van shook. "Why, didn't you tell me this before?" Byron shouted angrily. "Why wait until we're nearly there?"

"There was nothing you or I could do about it," Michael replied calmly. "There was no point."

"Then you tell me why he's pleading guilty. You seem to know more about this than anybody else. Why would LJ admit to something he didn't do? We both know it was those bloody two cowards Nathan and Buckland who were responsible. I should have killed them yesterday and finished them off for good. If I'd known that LJ would do something as stupid as this then I'd have had those two down at the station last night. I'd have wrung the truth out of them. Is it some misguided sense of loyalty? The stupid man."

"I don't know, Byron." It was as much a shock and a mystery to him. "I didn't tell Jess. I wanted her to hang on to hope for as long as possible."

"They've got no bloody evidence," Byron boomed. "I may not

be the brightest in the world, Michael, but how in God's name has it come to this?"

"I've gone over and over it too. I'm guessing that they've convinced LJ that they've got a fairly strong case which is why he's pleading guilty. A guilty plea carries a lighter sentence than if he pleaded not guilty initially and then the court found him guilty as charged. If he hadn't admitted guilt, which apparently, he has, then I reckon that the whole thing would have been thrown out of court."

"You know why all this has happened, don't you, Michael?" Byron's eyes blazed.

"Someone wants us gone from Bartonford. They all want us gone from Bartonford."

"Because in their eyes we're all just dirty tinkers, pikeys – men with no morals, thieves, and scoundrels. There is no justice for the likes of us," Byron said.

Michael remembered the words that had been spoken in the village hall meeting. Byron was right on every count.

Michael and Byron sat side by side in the waiting area. Another group had arrived and sat apart from them. Michael recognised them. The woman called Wanda glanced in his direction. Michael spotted recognition in her eyes. She remembered him from their brief exchange at the beginning of the meeting in the village hall. It seemed that she was trying to work out why she might bump into him so soon again. She had not made the connection between him and LJ. Michael leaned towards Byron and whispered in his ear. "The village has arrived. Over there."

Byron let his eyes wander across the small group. "I've seen the likes of the lot of them before. Whatever happens, Michael, we're not going anywhere. They can do their worst, but we'll leave Bartonford when we are good and ready. We're doing no harm and we have nothing to be ashamed of."

It was one in the afternoon by the time the ninth case had been heard and the court broke for lunch to resume at two. "I need a smoke, Michael," Byron said, heading for the exit. Michael followed him. He had no desire to venture anywhere near the café – the more space between them and the villagers, the better. Byron was building up a head of steam. An explosion now would be nothing short of a disaster. Byron smoked, Michael stared ahead of him, and neither of them spoke.

"All rise," the usher said, after checking those who should be were present. "Public gallery as well, please."

Byron and Michael stood as the three magistrates filed in through a door at the back of the courtroom, took their seats on the bench, and arranged their papers. They were two men and one woman. The woman took the centre seat. Michael assumed her to be Ursula's friend. Byron shuffled about uncomfortably on his seat and fiddled with his tie. Michael wondered if it was the first time that he had been in court; it was certainly his. Ironic, he thought, when his own father had been a regular in court mostly for being drunk in a public place.

Michael felt Byron stiffen as his eyes followed LJ into the witness box. He looked as though he had slept in his clothes for days. His hair, greasy and limp, fell on his shoulders, his face was drawn and haggard. He had changed beyond all recognition in a matter of two days. He walked with his head down, the epitome of an undesirable gypsy.

"It won't help, Byron," Michael whispered, his hand firm on his friend's arm. "Stay calm."

"State your name, address, and date of birth." The clerk of the court addressed his question to LJ.

"LJ Lovell. Twenty-first of May, 1986. Presently staying on the site of the old garage and workshop Bartonford, Warwickshire."

"Your worships," the clerk of the court turned to address the magistrates, "this man is of no fixed abode. He is a Traveller, and we understand that his family is at this moment parked up on a derelict site which is the property of one Mr Keith Ingrams. They have been residing there since mid-October last year."

The magistrate looked at LJ. "I am informed that you have chosen to have no legal representation today, Mr Lovell. Is that the case?"

"Yes."

Michael put his head in his hands. The day couldn't get worse. Why on earth, he asked himself, would any sane man choose not to have representation?

"And I further understand that you are pleading guilty today," she continued. "I am obliged to remind you that this case is suitable for trial either in this room or in crown court before judge and jury. Do you understand? What is your decision?"

"I understand," LJ said. "I just want to get it over with, dealt with here."

A man wearing a grey suit stood up, fingered his notes, and looked up at the bench.

"Your worships, the defendant is charged with theft. The theft took place on Friday the twenty-second of January from number four Pettifer Close, the property of Mr Frederick Humphries. Money and goods to the value of five hundred pounds were stolen. Mr Humphries has made a written statement to the effect that the money and goods were present in his house at the time that the defendant arrived at the house to collect an outstanding payment for work that he had recently completed on the premises. The money and goods were found to be missing immediately after the defendant departed the property. The defendant admits that he entered the property during that time to go to the toilet. There is a witness who describes seeing two other men lurking around the property at the time the defendant was with Mr Humphries. The witness states that he had a rear view of them only but describes them as of medium height, black shoulder-length air, and wearing black jeans and grey hoodies. In the witnesses' own words, they looked like gypsies. The defendant claims that he was on his own, that he knows of no other presence in the vicinity at the time. In normal circumstances the Crown Prosecution Service would not be presenting this case at court – there is insufficient evidence that the defendant committed the crime for which he stands accused. At first, the defendant vehemently denied any part in the theft, and then later, changed his plea of not guilty to guilty and has since made a full admission of his guilt including naming the property that he stole, which incidentally, has not yet been recovered. In the light of this change of heart, the Crown Prosecution Service has no choice but to bring this case up in front of the court. I should add, your worships, that the victim of this crime is eighty years old, and, I am informed, has been unable to leave the house since the incident occurred. He remains in shock and may need care for some time to come. Fortunately, he has a loving daughter and a son-in-law who live nearby. The prosecution cost, your worship, is two hundred pounds, and I would ask that the victim surcharge be set at one thousand pounds to repay the value of the goods and to be put towards Mr Humphries' rehabilitation costs."

Michael glanced sideways at Byron. Byron sat tight-lipped and stony-faced.

"Thank you, prosecuting counsel. Is that all?" the chief magistrate asked. The grey suit nodded. "Mr Lovell, is there anything you would like to say in your defence since you have chosen to speak up for yourself?"

LJ lifted his head and cleared his throat. The prosecutor's words had cut through him like a knife. If he had not admitted guilt, then he would probably have had no case to answer. It was too late now. If he tried to explain and rescind his statement, then it would only make matters worse further down the line. This way his sentence might not be so severe. That's what the police had told him. This way he would get back to Jess and Sally and the family soonest. "Only that I liked Mr Humphries a lot. He was kind to me, and I am sorry that he has suffered as a result of this. I have a wife and a three-year-old child who need me. I need to be there for them. I'm sorry." Tears rolled down his cheeks. The usher plucked tissues out of a box and handed them to him.

"All rise," the usher announced, as the magistrates filed out of the door at the back of the courtroom.

The public gallery sat in silence, waiting.

"All rise," the usher announced again as the magistrates filed back into the courtroom.

Putting her spectacles on, the chief magistrate conferred firstly with her colleagues and then looked accusingly at LJ. "There is a great deal that we have had to take into consideration in this case," she started. "In passing sentence, I am not moved towards leniency. It is within my power to reduce your sentence since you have pleaded guilty, but this, I intend to withhold. I sentence you to the maximum sentence that can be passed by this court. You will serve six months in custody that will start as of this time. You will pay prosecution costs and victim costs which total twelve hundred pounds. You will be advised of your options for payment after this court hearing closes."

"All rise."

Stunned, Byron rose to his feet and watched as a policeman entered the courtroom and started to lead LJ away. For the first time, their eyes connected.

"Take care of Jess and Sally for me, Byron, and you, Michael. Tell them I love them, and I'll be back soon."

"We will, son," Byron replied flatly, shaking his head in disbelief.

Michael put his arm around his friend and watched as the villagers filed out of the public gallery – to a man and woman looking like the cat that had found the cream. Michael, speechless and incredulous, swore in that moment that he would dedicate his life to seeing justice done.

Not a word escaped their lips as they walked back to the car park. It was getting late. The family would be waiting to be picked up from the market. Jess would be waiting for them to return LJ to the family.

# Twelve

It was cold and grey but dry. Jess opened the top half of the door and saw that they had already left. After a fitful night, thankfully Sally slept on. Jess crawled back on her bed wishing fervently that she had been able to go with them. Michael and Byron would soon reach the magistrates' court. The rest of the family would already be at the market selling their wares. Buckland and Nathan, she assumed, had remained in their caravan nursing their wounds. In normal circumstances she and Sally would be there at the market with the family – she with her baskets, while Sally charmed the customers with her laughs and smiles and her incessant chatter and questions, Michael, Byron Jnr, Colin and David selling their wood carvings, Rosa and Polly selling their homemade jewellery, while Byron circuited the market looking for anything that might turn them a profit.

Byron had been resolute that Jess would not accompany them to the magistrates' court. It was no place for a child, he said. She was to trust that he and Michael would return LJ safely to her. Unusually she had argued that if she could not be at court with them then she should go to the market with the family. He would have none of it. The camp could not be left unoccupied and he could not trust Nathan and Buckland not to wander off. In her mind's eye, she pictured Michael and Byron's returning to the camp both with broad grins on their faces, LJ sitting between them upfront in the van. Early that morning Byron had sat her down and talked it through at length with her. LJ was innocent, there was no evidence to the contrary, he would be exonerated of any charges and free to continue his life.

Michael had sat up with her the previous evening long after Sally had fallen asleep. Unusually he had been distant and evasive. He told her that he had dropped into the meeting at the village hall, but that there was nothing for her to worry about. It was a lot of fuss over nothing. Jess wasn't so sure. She knew her brother too well, knew when there was something amiss, but Michael was not going to open up. She had not pressed him. He always shared things with her in his own good time.

As she lay back thinking of what the day might bring, she heard raised voices outside. "Get a move on, Buckland, I can't get the van coupled up on my own." Jess moved one of the small curtains aside and watched as Buckland and Nathan coupled their van to their caravan and rolled slowly past the vardo out on to the open road. She was not surprised that they were leaving after the previous day's episode and neither was she sad to see the back of them. Byron had been right again.

The daylight hours passed in a whisker. The vardo sparkled, the paintwork and mirrors gleamed, and the small curtains were washed and rehung. Sally, with her own little dustpan and brush clutched in her little hands, swept the floors shadowed by Jess picking up all the dust and fluff that her daughter dropped from her dustpan. They were doing it for Daddy, she had told Sally. Lunch was heated baked beans and toast, Sally's favourite, which she devoured with gusto. Occupied as she had been, Sally had had little time to be bored, but it was not long before the questions started, and she became fractious. Why had Uncle By-By and Uncle Michael gone without them? Where had they gone? When would they be back? Why couldn't she have gone to the market with everybody else? Why was it that she had to stay in the camp? What time would they be back? Her questions were relentless and tried Jess's patience.

"Cold. Go Auntie Miriam. Sit by her fire," Sally whined.

"I'll find another cardigan for you, then you won't be cold," Jess said. "We've been left in charge of the camp today, Sally. It's a very responsible job. There's nobody else here to make sure that everything is safe. We can't go wandering off and leaving it unoccupied. I'd like to go too, but we said goodbye to Auntie Miriam yesterday, didn't we? Besides, she has probably left by now. She said she was leaving today, didn't she? She'll be on her way to Portugal by now." Jess regretted the words the moment they came out of her mouth. Sally took a deep breath, looked into her mother's eyes, and unleashed the air from her lungs with one long scream that filled the vardo. "I want Auntie Miriam," she wailed, tears running down her cheeks. There was nothing Jess could do to placate her. There were times when she knew that the only thing to do was to let her get it out of her system. When she tired, she would stop. When she was exhausted, she would come to her mother for cuddles, and say sorry.

Jess blocked the noise from her head and glanced at the clock. It was almost four o'clock and the light outside was fast fading. Michael had said that the court closed at five. It would soon be over. They would be on their way home and they would be back together as a family. "Daddy will be back home soon, very soon," she said.

"Promise?"

"Promise," Jess replied. "How about you have a little rest and curl up in your bed for an hour? When you wake up, they'll all be back from the market. I'm going to do the same." Jess picked her daughter up and carried her across to her little bed. No sooner had she tucked her in than she was asleep.

Jess drew the rose-patterned curtains across the tiny windows and climbed painfully up on the raised double bed that she shared with LJ and pulled the covers around her. How she longed for the spring and summer when some of her aches and pains would be lessened by the warmth of the sun. Although she would never admit it to anybody, the steep steps up the vardo that she climbed countless times each day were becoming increasingly difficult to manage, and the descent from them more and more perilous. They were a constant reminder that her physical health was not improving and that one day she would be unable to live in the vardo. She managed a small smile as she remembered the best advice she had ever been given by LJ – never go upstairs or downstairs empty-handed. How true it was; she had avoided countless journeys by remembering those words.

Staring at the ceiling above, she remembered the very first time she had woken up in the vardo. It had been night-time and she had opened her eyes to see a million stars twinkling against a midnight blue sky. Venus, the most brilliant in the night sky, hovered alone and away from the myriad of other constellations. The Seven Sisters, her favourites, were the nearest star cluster to the earth and named after the seven daughters of Atlas. All seven sisters were depicted on the ceiling, but the seventh sister was shy and rarely seen; there was nothing that LJ did not know about the stars. Aquarius, Aquila, Aries, Canis Major, the Northern Cross, Gemini, Orion, and the Big Dipper: they were all there. The following day she had learned that LJ had painted the constellations on the ceiling. Over the years he had told her of the myths and fables that surrounded every one of them – stories that LJ had heard at his mother's knee, stories that his mother had heard at her own mother's knee, stories that had been passed down through the generations from time immemorial, and stories that they would one day share with Sally. On clear nights they crept outside and stood in awe gazing at the sky above. It was part of LJ's magic. Mostly she was comforted by the constellations, but this night they did nothing to allay her fears. In her heart she felt that they were talking to her, telling her that all was not well.

Jess pulled the blankets tight around her shoulders. She was used to the cold, they all were. It was a rare occasion when LJ lit the small wood-burning stove – that was reserved as a treat, and it was a job that was always left to the men. Warm jumpers and cardigans and blankets had all been invented to keep the cold out. It had never bothered her, and Sally had known no different since she had been born.

Jess shivered. Wrapped up under the blankets, she was not cold; she was frightened. The good spirits that had pervaded every nook and cranny of the vardo seem to have flown away, leaving in their place an empty shell. The warm, deep mahogany-brown wood that covered the walls from floor to ceiling had lost its sheen, the gold leaf that adorned the carvings in the cornices had lost its lustre, the colours in the throws and cushions had lost their vibrancy, the constellations on the ceiling twinkled uncertainly. The never-ending search for those tiny cupboards hidden in the woodwork and carved by LJ's own hand, which sent her to sleep each night, seemed banal and futile. Even the rainbows that she knew would bounce off the bevelled mirrors the moment she drew the curtains back to let in the morning sun, failed to lift her spirits. LJ was in everything, everywhere. He had spent the best part of ten years crafting every detail of the vardo's interior. It was a pure work of art; it was his pride and joy. He called it their very own cathedral. Fleetingly she remembered her thoughts of the previous day when Miriam had spoken of her house with the bedrooms and the bathrooms and felt ashamed. Had it really crossed her mind that life in a permanent home with bedrooms and bathrooms would be preferable to life in their precious vardo, life on the road? Had she been tempting providence?

Their furniture was meagre but functional and had been crafted with love. Her eyes drifted unseeing in the darkness to the small hand-carved table and the fold-up seats beside the small wood-burning stove. It was there that they took their meals and there that Sally had her own three-legged stool. It was there that they sat with

Michael as a family and whiled away many winter evenings.

Never had she thought of the vardo as anything other than home but at that very moment, it felt as if the walls were closing in around her, as though there was a malevolent presence, and it frightened her.

She lay back on her pillow and listened as the silence engulfed her. Other than the whisper of Sally's gentle breathing there was nothing. Nothing stirred in the camp – it was four-thirty in the afternoon, but it felt like midnight. She needed to rest – to sleep – so that she would feel refreshed when Byron and Michael eventually returned with LJ.

Finally, she closed her eyes and she fell into a deep sleep and her dreams engulfed her. It was a warm sunny day. Sally sat on her lap. Michael sat beside her on one side and LJ on the other. They sang folk songs as Jocklin clip-clopped along at a steady pace in front of them. They reached a clearing, the grass as green as emeralds and saw their willow tree. The stream at the foot of the bank ran as clear as she remembered, the water tinkled as it ran over the rocks. Sally loved it just as much as she ever had. It was a safe place, a magic place. They laughed and joked and told stories to each other and when they were satiated, lay back in the grass and soaked up the sun.

Dreams were often cruel places, one minute caressing the dreamer and the next inflicting endless pain. Black clouds scudded across the sky, day turned to night, icy particles of snow bombarded them from above, the stream stopped and froze before their eyes. They shivered with the piercing cold. The thin clothes they wore were hopeless against the elements. They huddled together in the igloo of ice. And then the sky brightened, the sun bore down on them and warmed them, the stream crackled as the ice melted and the water set off once more down its rocky path. Soon, the grass turned to brown before their eyes, the willow tree started to shrivel, steam rose from the cold waters. The willow tree embraced them in its fiery death throes. Jocklin lay down and breathed his last breath.

They tried to run, to break out, but they were all pinned to the spot by an unseen presence, and none of them could move a muscle. They knew that it was the end.

Tossing and turning in her nightmare, Jess threw the quilt away from her, and opened her eyes – as one nightmare had finished, the next had just begun. Her eyes smarted; the smell of burning wood and cloth was intense. The quilt that she had thrown off her shoulders lay at the foot of the bed and was alight. In split seconds, the flames leapt from the quilt to the curtains which framed the tiny windows and then to the cushions that sizzled with the heat and then to the once-pretty mauve valence that framed the bed and then to the sheets upon which she lay. Wide-eyed, screaming, Jess backed up into the corner and watched as the flames leapt closer and closer until there was no escape. She could hardly breathe.

The flames were without mercy devouring the mattress upon which she lay, terrified, in agony and with no escape. Her hair was on fire – shrivelling before her very eyes, eyes that were burning, eyes that could no longer focus.

Through her pain and the veil of smoke in front of her eyes, she watched petrified as the devil flames licked at everything within reach and criss-crossed the floor in the direction of her daughter's bed. She could not see her – the smoke was too dense. "Sally," she screamed hysterically. "Sally, get out!" but she knew that it was too late.

Hurting beyond anything that she had ever experienced in her life, Jess prayed for death to come quickly. The stars were no longer twinkling in the sky, the ceiling was a murderous combination of black shot with streaks of lightning. The panelling around the vardo was burnt through, leaving it exposed to the elements. The wind whipped the flames into an even greater frenzy.

What had once been Jess's very own cathedral was now her coffin.

# Thirteen

Fred Humphries slammed the front door, leaned against it, and heaved a sigh of relief. He had seen more than enough of his son-in-law for one day. Grinning from ear to ear, he had described the proceedings with undisguised relish. The icing on the cake, so he reported, was that one Mr LJ Lovell had been given the maximum sentence – six months in custody; nothing less than he deserved. According to Sam, they had had an excellent day. It had been a triumph for the village, he said, predicting that the gypsies would be gone by the morning.

There was nothing that would have given him more satisfaction than to wipe that smug look off his son-in-law's face. He had stupidly let himself be bullied into making a statement to the police, but Sam had given him little option. Once his son-in-law had the bit between his teeth there was no stopping him and woe betide anybody who got in his way. The kangaroo court, it seemed, had had its way. It troubled him to think that the lad was back in a cell awaiting transfer to prison while the bigoted, small-minded people who lived in the village sat curled up in front of their fires without a care in the world. There was no justice.

The man was a monster. What his daughter had ever seen in him he would never know. "Don't I even get a whisky for bringing you the good news?" he had laughed.

"Goodnight," Fred said, slamming the door after him.

He blamed himself and it weighed heavily on his shoulders. The house stank of Sam's cigarette smoke and his body odour. It was cold and dark, and he needed fresh air, somewhere to clear his head and think. Fred wrapped himself up in a warm anorak, wrapped a scarf around his neck, and put on his thermal gloves. As he closed the front door behind him, he smiled. Even in the dark he knew that his new patio looked good; LJ had done a good job. He had been so looking forward to the spring and summer when he could while away the hours sitting on his new bench contemplating his navel, but his mean-spirited son-in-law had even managed to take the shine off that. Sitting out front would forever remind him of LJ and how he had been singled out and pilloried by the villagers. Already he missed the hours he had shared with LJ, missed putting the world to rights with the lad.

He was dog-tired. He had slept only fitfully the previous night worrying about the court case and the part he had inadvertently played in getting LJ arrested. He didn't like himself one little bit – too scared to stand up to his son-in-law and too weak to go to court to follow the proceedings. If he could have sat apart from the villagers, he might have gone, but he would not be part of a lynch party. Sam's words had come as no surprise, but it pained him to think that such a small matter of a few pounds and a few worthless items should result in a boy's life being ruined. He had many more photographs of his Susan in the cupboard and he had never liked his grandfather let alone the cufflinks, which had remained in the same box on the sideboard for almost sixty years. And neither did he doubt LJ's innocence, but it was too late to do anything about it now.

The church clock struck five o'clock; it had been dark for an hour already. Roll on the spring equinox, he thought to himself. The cold damp January days were almost as depressing as the fourteen hours of darkness day in, day out.

Fred zipped his anorak up to his neck, sat down, and patted the wooden slats beside him. "Well LJ, it's a sad old world, isn't it?" he said. "I didn't want to make that statement but it's a fat lot of good telling you that now, isn't it? They had it in for you boy. I loathe the lot of them and myself as well right now. I'll make one promise to you – just between you and me – we'll get even one day."

Stretching out, he rested his head on the back of the bench. It was hard and made ruts in the back of his balding head, but he didn't care. Shutting out the events of the day as much as he could, he closed his eyes and turned his thoughts to better days. He'd been twenty-one when he had got married, the same age as LJ, with his life before him. It had had its ups and downs but, on balance, he had been lucky. Neither he nor Susan, his lovely bride, had had great expectations of anything and consequently, they had never been disappointed or discontent. That was another thing that he had had in common with LJ. If he'd had the choice, he would have swapped LJ and his little wife, even though he had never met her, for Sam and Marie any day. Quietly he'd hoped that LJ would bring the family down to see him one day but now that would never happen.

Suddenly the noise of sirens broke into his thoughts. Sitting bolt upright, his head on a swivel, his eyes darting near and far, Fred strained to pinpoint the direction of the racket. Whichever emergency vehicles he had heard had stopped not far short of the village. He sniffed the air. Narrowing his eyes, he saw black smoke billowing into the night sky and drifting on the wind towards the village. It was coming from the direction of the land owned by Keith Ingrams, the land occupied by the gypsies.

His heart pounding, he headed indoors, grabbed the first walking stick that came to hand, locked the door as he left, and walked as fast as his legs would carry him in the direction of the smoke. As he reached the end of the close, he could almost feel the heat coming from the distant flames that now leapt and bounced towards the sky. As he turned onto the road that ran through the village, he was blinded first by blue flashing lights and then by a torch being shone into his eyes. A young policeman stepped out, telling him that the road had been sealed off and no one would be allowed to go further. "What's happened? Is anyone hurt?" Fred asked anxiously.

"A fire up at the gypsy camp," the policeman said, shrugging his shoulders and rubbing his hands together. "Saves on the heating bills I suppose. Seems it started about fifteen minutes ago. Someone called the fire brigade but maybe a bit too late. There's just one vehicle on fire. A bloody miracle that they haven't all gone up in smoke."

"Anyone hurt?" Fred asked.

"Sounds like it. A whole load of gypsies trundled up just after the fire had taken hold. A woman and a girl missing, they said. No sign of them so we might as well assume the worst. Sounds like it will be a job for fire forensics. Just my luck to get called out on a night like this." The policeman blew on his hands. "Least they'll not be cold down there," he chortled. "Neither will they be sitting around a campfire tonight, at least not one of their own makings. The place is cordoned off. They won't be getting back in there for a few days. Why we bother, I don't know. Waste of police time, if you want my opinion."

"Now you mention it, son," Fred glowered at the constable and poked him hard in his chest. "I didn't ask for your opinion and I don't welcome it. You show some respect. You've got a lot to learn, son, a lot to learn, and if I weren't eighty years old, I'd start that lesson right now."

"Calm down, old man. What's it to you anyway?" he replied, removing Fred's forefinger from his chest. "I suggest you go home and make yourself a nice mug of cocoa and tuck yourself up in bed. You'll give yourself a heart attack getting worked up like that."

"If it was your wife and girl you wouldn't be half so cocky," Fred snapped.

"I'm not married, sir."

100

"Then some lady has had a lucky escape, very lucky. How long before you open the road?"

"Couple of hours at most. It's not like it's the Houses of Parliament burning down, is it?"

Fred turned on his heel and strode back towards the house, his heart in his boots. A woman and a girl? Hadn't LJ told him that his daughter was the only little girl on the campsite?

Standing by the window of his cottage, his eyes glazed over as he watched the smoke drifting upwards until, an hour later, it could be seen no more. He couldn't stand by and do nothing. He owed it to those gypsies to do anything he could to help them. There was little he could do to help those departed, God bless them, but maybe he could be of help to those left behind. If the camp were cordoned off as that young bastard had said, then those poor devils would have no place to sleep for the night, if indeed any of them might sleep at all after what had happened.

Fred picked the telephone, and the vicar answered at the first ring. The Reverend Jerry Linton was one of the few decent people in the village who had made it quite clear that he had no intention of turning anyone away from his church, gypsies or not. After a brief conversation, the Reverend agreed to open the church as a refuge for the gypsies. He would be there in person, he said, to receive the bereaved. He would see to it that there were blankets, hot drinks, and food. By seven, the church would be warm.

At seven o'clock, Fred put on his anorak again, grabbed his walking stick and a powerful torch, and left the house. The police car had gone, and the road was open. Torch in hand, he picked his away along the dark road, avoiding potholes and the perilous soft verges that beckoned him whenever a vehicle approached. He did not expect to be welcomed with open arms, especially after the episode at the court, but he just hoped that they would not be too proud to accept an offer of help.

As he drew nearer, he pointed the torch in the direction of the camp. In the distance, he could just make out that there was a transit van parked up roadside outside the old garages and workshop. Hazard tape had been strung across the entrance and a police car was parked sideways barring access to the site. A dim light shone from within the van. He had no real idea how many people might be huddled in the van but from what LJ had told him there could be ten or more.

Fred edged slowly towards the transit. Windows steamed up with condensation, it was impossible to make out the faces within. Steeling himself for what might be an unwelcome reception, he tapped gently on the driver's door window and immediately took a step back to put space between him and the driver. The window was opened from within. Sitting in the driver's seat, he saw a man whom he did not recognise, and beside him a younger man whom he recognised as having attended the meeting in the village hall. Both looked stricken with pain and anguish, their foreheads deeply furrowed, their eyes red from weeping.

"What do you want?" the man in the driver's seat barked.

"There's shelter in the church and blankets, food and drink."

The man to whom he had spoken threw back his head and laughed – an ugly, desperate laugh. "So now you want to help us, do you? Well, I can tell you this – I wouldn't take charity from any of you if you were the last people on earth."

"Wait, Byron," Michael said, putting his hand on Byron's arm. "I know him. It's Fred Humphries – the man LJ did the patio for. He's on our side, Byron. I heard him standing up for us and for LJ at the village hall meeting."

"I didn't want him charged. I never believed that he had done it. It was my son-in-law who bullied me into going to the police to report the theft. I told them there and then that LJ hadn't been involved, but they didn't believe me. I can't begin to tell you how sorry I am."

"It's okay, Fred. May I call you that?" Michael leaned across

Byron. "I was there at the meeting in the village hall. I'm Michael. I heard you speaking up for my brother-in-law. Thank you for that. It's not a good time for any of us right now. We've just lost Jess and Sally, LJ's wife and little girl. It was LJ's vardo that was destroyed in the fire."

"When I saw the smoke and the flames and found out that someone had been hurt, I prayed that it wouldn't be them. I can't find the right words to say to you. Will you all accept help from me and the vicar? It'll be warm up at the church and there'll be food and drink," Fred repeated. There was nothing more he could say – it was up to them. So, the man who wouldn't take charity from them was Byron, the man whom they all respected and to whom they looked for guidance. He was their god. Fred stood quietly and waited for his reply. It would be Byron's decision and his alone.

Byron stared unseeing through the windscreen. It stuck in his gullet to have to accept help from anybody let alone people who had wished them dead anyway. "Thank you. I appreciate your offer and, yes, we need shelter. Can you squeeze in the middle between us?" Byron asked, indicating the small centre seat in the front of the cab. "It's a bit full in the back."

"I'll just tell the copper where we're going so that they'll know where to find you all if they need you." Fred nodded, walked away, and exchanged a few short words with the policeman in the police car before walking around to the other side of the van. Firm strong hands helped him up into the cab. Michael, the brother whom LJ had spoken of with such fondness, climbed in beside him. Six other family members sat huddled silently in the back of the van. No one turned to look back at the smoldering pile of ash that had once been a vardo.

# Fourteen

It was with a measure of fear and trepidation that Miriam was finally going back to the Algarve, but she had made her decision, for better, for worse. It was almost twenty years since she had last visited. She had been sixteen at the time. It was way past time that she confronted her demons. Set in two acres of garden and orchards, Villa Casa Messines, an ancient farmhouse, twelve kilometres from the ancient town of Silves, six kilometres from Messines, a five-minute walk from the beach, made for the perfect summer retreat. Bought by her parents thirty years since, it had been lovingly restored and maintained right up until the time they had passed on. Miriam had inherited it along with the tiny cottage in Bartonford. For the past five years it had been managed and let out by a local agent. Miriam had wanted nothing to do with it. It held too many painful memories, which completely surpassed the happy memories of weeks spent there during her childhood years. But it was decision time; the villa was now costing her money despite the income from letting it. According to the agent, it was in need of modernisation and it needed a swimming pool. Few weeks passed without another call from the agent informing her of work that needed to be done and how much it would cost. Her first thought had been to sell it. Her second thought had been to make it her home and sell the cottage in Bartonford. The jury was out.

After weighing up the pros and cons and changing her mind a dozen times, Miriam decided that she would go to the Algarve and live in the villa for a trial period. If she could not put the ghosts to rest, if she could not find peace there, then she would sell. There was little to keep her in Bartonford. If she so chose, she could run her modest online jewellery company from anywhere in the world. Miriam made plans for a minimum three-month stay. Hiring a car when she got there was an unnecessary expense when she had a perfectly reliable car in the UK. Thus, she decided that she would drive, crossing the channel by the Eurotunnel and then taking her time to drive down through France and Spain to Portugal.

With the car packed to the gunnels with personal effects and everything that she thought she might need for a three-month stay, she left her home in Bartonford late in the afternoon to catch the ten o'clock cross-channel train from Folkestone.

Miriam wrestled with her conscience, wrestled with the traffic, wrestled with the weather, and wrestled with time. According to Google maps, it would take her three and a half hours to reach the tunnel. In the event, it took nearer four hours. The rain came down in stair rods, the traffic was start-stop most of the way and the headlights from oncoming vehicles blinded her. Reminding herself that the Volvo was sitting well down on its springs, she maintained a steady sixty miles an hour; it was better to get there safely than not at all, she repeatedly reminded herself. Checking the clock on the dashboard at five-minute intervals, she knew she was up against time, and catching the ten o'clock departure looked increasingly unlikely. Her brain told her that it didn't matter – if she missed the ten o'clock train then there were others.

With thirty-five minutes in hand, Miriam pulled off the M20 and followed the signs for the Eurotunnel check-in. Mechanically, she passed her booking details to the check-in clerk together with her passport, answered the standard questions at the check-in desk, stuck the ticket up on her rear-view mirror, and followed the signs to the customs checkpoint.

"Cutting it a bit fine, aren't we madam?" the customs officer said, as Miriam wound down the window.

"Weather, traffic – you name it – somebody has got it in for me today," she replied, forcing a smile. "Will I make the train?"

"That, madam, depends upon what you have onboard and how long it takes me to check that all is in order," the officer replied, raising one eyebrow. "These things can't be rushed – it's for everybody's safety."

"I appreciate that, and I'm glad that you do all the checks. The car is in a bit of a mess – a bit of hasty packing, I'm afraid. I'm on my way to my holiday home in the Algarve for a long break – three months, maybe longer. That's why the car is full of boxes and blankets and suitcases. Believe you me, it's going to take me days to unpack when I get there."

Miriam watched in her mirror as the customs officer strolled around the car, glancing in the boot and the side windows, before returning to stand beside her door. "I should by rights have all this lot out, but you look honest enough to me so on this occasion we'll give you a clean bill of health. Have your passport ready for inspection at French Immigration and then proceed to the queue – they should be starting to load up any minute. Goodnight, madam, and bon voyage."

On the third day, she saw the spire of the ancient church in the centre of Messines towering above the surrounding buildings, reminding her of the carefree Sunday mornings of yesteryear when she and her parents had sat in the pews and joined in with the local worship. That had been when she was a child. There were other memories later, which she preferred to forget, but they were still there in the shadows.

With no thoughts in her head other than those jobs which would need to be done when she arrived, and those that could wait until the following morning, she allowed herself to relax and reflect on the past few days – the things she had learned, the problems she had overcome, the anxiety she had fought, and the doubts that had dogged her day and night.

As she rounded the final bend to the villa, she glanced in her rear-view mirror and saw blue lights rapidly approaching. Her heart missed a beat; so near and yet so far. To have got all this way without incident and then to be pulled up just over two kilometres from the villa would be more than she could bear, but as quickly, the vehicle overtook her and sped off into the distance, leaving her sweating profusely, her heart thumping and her ears ringing from the soon distant sirens.

The roadblock was two kilometres further on – there had been a traffic accident, and of all places on a road that was travelled by few other than those visiting Casa Messines and Casa Medina, the neighbouring property.

Miriam braked slowly and wound down the window as a man dressed in the uniform of the National Republican Guard strolled towards her, his hand firmly fixed around the Glock 19 that he wore on his belt.

"O que aconteceu?" Miriam asked him what had happened and listened silently as he told her that a car had driven at speed into a tree and that the occupants, the residents of Casa Medina, had both died instantly, but a four-year-old child had survived. She had told him how sorry she was, that she was on her way up to Casa Messines and that she was the owner of the property. The guarda glanced at her number plates and without further comment indicated that he would lead her car past the incident onto the road beyond. She had finally arrived.

# Fifteen

The escort backed the van up to the door, climbed out of his cab, and hammered on the side of it. "Won't be long, lads," he shouted cheerily. "Next stop, sunny Ranbury." It was his third and last pickup of the day. With Ranbury no more than a two-hour drive, he'd be home for tea and feet up by six. "Afternoon, officer, what have you got for me today?"

"There's just one for the charabanc today, Rex. You've got yourself a nice little gypsy boy to keep the rest company. The risk assessment is all complete and in order. This one's not going to give you any trouble, but keep an eye on him and make sure he doesn't go wandering," the custody officer winked. "You know what they're like – slippery as eels, that lot. Sign here and he's all yours."

LJ looked down at the handcuffs glinting in the sun and listened to the conversation from afar. It was as if he didn't exist; he was now nothing more than a piece of baggage. All they had told him was that he was being transferred to a prison called Ranbury. They didn't say where it was. It could have been a million miles away; he had never heard of the place.

"So, we got ourselves one of those, have we?" Rex raised his eyebrows, screwed up his nose as if there was a bad smell, and looked LJ over from top to bottom. "I rather think that there might be a few of your mates at Ranbury to keep you company," he said, turning to LJ. "You never learn. You flaunt the law and then, lo and behold, you win the lottery – a luxury break in one of our wonderful holiday camps, and we, the poor taxpayers, have to pick up the bill. Beats me. I can't for the life of me see why we don't ship you all back to where you came from and let them pay the bill. Bloody Irish. Welcome aboard, laddie."

"Roma," LJ said quietly.

"Oh, we've got a smart arse here, have we?" Rex chuckled. "And one that's got a tongue as well. We'll soon sort that one out, laddie. And don't argue with me. If I say you're Irish, then you're Irish. I don't give a toss what sort of gypsy you are. Nothing to choose between the lot of you. And if you'll take my advice, you'll not correct any of your fellow inmates when you arrive either. There are some nasty men at Ranbury – they'll eat you for breakfast. Right, let's get your little holiday started, shall we?" Rex opened the back doors to the van. "Got yourselves a gypsy for company, lads. How about that? Now no messing around, I don't want any shenanigans. Let's just have a nice quiet drive through the countryside, enjoy the scenery. Have fun." Rex locked the cage and slammed the back doors shut.

LJ exchanged glances with the two sullen-faced men sitting cross-legged on the floor inside the cage; neither of them looked up or introduced themselves. Finding a spot on the floor as far away as possible from them, and taking their lead, he sat down with his legs outstretched and his head in his arms. He was already learning that making eye contact only invited trouble.

"You tired, gypsy?" one of them called out to him. "It's all that shagging that does it, takes it out of you, doesn't it? What I wouldn't give for a bit of gypsy pussy right now...You can tell us all about it when we get to the hotel. You're a really lucky boy! Won't find any women there, but there'll be plenty of inmates for you to choose from. You'll not go short of it."

LJ put his hands over his ears to block out the sound of their voices – goading, pushing and mocking. He was not going to be provoked. Already he had been singled out as a gypsy. It would soon be general knowledge and his life would be made a misery. Keep your head down, keep your mouth shut, he reminded himself. The only thing that mattered was to keep his stay in Ranbury or any other prison as short as possible and get back to his family.

Ranbury was a closed prison housing Category B and Category C prisoners; there were no Category A, maximum security prisoners. The system had slotted him into Category C, or so he was told, and if he behaved in an 'exemplary fashion', as they described it to him, he might – just might – be re-categorised to Category D and qualify for transfer to an open prison within a month. LJ set his heart on getting that transfer. The thought of spending six months in a closed prison locked away in a cell for twelve hours each day filled him with dread.

The arrival process seemed endless. Stripped of his clothes and his dignity, and questioned time and time again, he was tired and hungry by the time he was introduced to his cellmate for the duration of his stay.

"You got yourself a gypsy for a partner, Jacky," the prison warden announced as he opened the door and physically helped LJ through it. "He says his name is Jay although that's not precisely what it says on my sheet here. It's no skin off my nose – a name's a name. If that's what he wants to be called, then so be it. Aren't Jays those big ugly birds with pink heads that don't know how to behave themselves? Good choice, I can definitely see the resemblance."

Jacky glanced up briefly and returned to a dog-eared copy of *The Sun*. "Now don't be like that. Say hello to the nice young man and behave yourself," the prison warden said, thoroughly enjoying both men's discomfort. They were oil and water – there'd be fireworks before long if he knew anything about it. "I'll leave you boys to get to know one another."

LJ glanced around the cell, taking in the bunk beds, the storage locker and wardrobe, the one solitary chair, the table, the mirror on the wall, and a small partitioned off area at the foot of the beds behind which he could just make out a toilet bowl and washbasin. For one who had spent most of his life living in the confined space of a vardo, the room did not strike him as particularly small, but it was grim and soulless.

Jacky eyed his new cellmate and tutted. "Just my effing luck. There I was thinking that I could enjoy the rest of my days here in peace with no one to bother me and now I get a dirty gypsy."

LJ picked up his bag and moved towards the storage locker. "Rule one, sonny, the storage locker is mine, as is the chair," the man barked. "Rule two, keep your fleas to yourself. Rule three, you sleep up there," he said, pointing to the top bunk. "Rule four, you shit in the toilet and nowhere else. Rule five, you touch only what's yours, and there'll be no farting right above my head."

In that moment all the injustices that he had suffered in the past few days crowded in on him: the insults, the false statement that he had been persuaded to make, the prejudice, the loss of his freedom, the enforced separation from his beloved Jess and Sally, the inhuman way in which he had been treated. For the first time in his life, LJ lost control.

Grabbing the man by the top of his arms, he hoisted him brutally to his feet. He was a big, heavy man but he had been unprepared for the attack. LJ struck out with his fist. A hollow ring sounded as the man's head thudded hard against the wooden bed post behind him. Dazed by the blow, he was not quick enough to avoid LJ's second strike. Within seconds the tables turned. The man grabbed LJ's hair, shoved him back, swung him around, and gave him a dose of his own medicine. He was barely conscious when eventually he felt the man's hands release their grip and he slumped to the ground.

The commotion had not gone unheard. "Get up," the man yelled at him.

His vision blurred; the room swam as he clambered unsteadily to his feet. He could feel the stickiness of blood on the back of his head and feel the trickle down his neck. Back on his feet, LJ saw the door to the cell open. The prison warden stood grim-faced, full square in the open door, ready for trouble. "Jacky, I warned you to behave yourself, gypsy or no gypsy, and what do I find but you banging the shit out of him? Looks like you've just earned yourself an extended stay in our little hotel and that's the end of your privileges and visiting rights, not that anybody is queueing up at the door to visit you. Come with me," he said, turning to LJ. "You'll live, gypsy. We'll get you fixed up when I've finished with this one."

"It wasn't his fault. I started it," LJ interrupted. "He was just defending himself."

The prison warden raised one eyebrow and glanced from one to the other, all the while the wheels turning in his mind. Jacky was useful – good at keeping other inmates in check, hot for tips on the horses, and a good source of information. Every prison warden needed a Jacky. It might pay to give him the benefit of the doubt.

"Well gypsy boy – sorry, a slip of the tongue – Jay's the name, isn't it?" he said. "You've just broken a prison record and got yourself into deep water in record time. If that's the way you want to play it then it looks like any chance you might have had of early parole has just gone right down the Swanee. Walk this way, son, there's someone who'll want to have words with you. The guv'nor doesn't take well to prisoners warring amongst themselves, especially when they've only just arrived. You sure you don't want to join us, Jacky?"

LJ looked back and shook his head at the man.

"No, I'll give this party a miss, but thanks for the invitation, warden."

"You had a lucky escape there, Jacky boy, but don't make a habit of it." The prison warden glanced back over his shoulder and smiled.

Jacky lay back on his bunk. If he could take those first few words back, he would. As usual, his brain connected to his mouth too late. It was the word 'gypsy' that had momentarily undone all the good work of the past few years. It brought back too many memories – bad memories. It reminded him of all his personal failings although failings didn't begin to describe what he had done. He should have known better. He was older by thirty years at least. He was wiser, at least in the way things worked at Ranbury. He had been way out of order; he hadn't given the lad a chance. He owed him an apology.

"How did it go, Jay?" he asked softly as the door opened and closed again with a bang. "I'm sorry, deeply sorry. I've got nothing against gypsies. You get shirty when you've been locked up in a prison cell for years. I'm not making excuses. Can we start again? Will you shake hands?" Jacky held out his hand. LJ took it. "Bad?" he asked.

"No visiting rights for one month. No privileges not that I ever knew what they might be anyway, and it looks like I blew any chance of time off for good behaviour or a transfer to a Cat D. Some result, hey?" LJ replied despondently. "I'm sorry too. I shouldn't have lost my temper."

"Shit, Jay, I didn't mean for that to happen. Family?" Jacky asked.

"Wife and little girl. She'll be four years old in the summer," LJ replied, as he sat down on the cold stone floor and leaned back against the wall. The only thing that would see him through was the knowledge that Sally and Jess were being cared for by Byron and Michael – he would trust them with his life; nothing else mattered.

"Get off that floor. Take the chair, Jay. They question you about that cut?" Jacky asked, looking at the plaster stuck across the back of LJs head.

LJ nodded. "I told them the truth – I had an argument with the bedpost. How's your head?"

"It's been better. You know for a gypsy you're a really decent bloke. Thanks. I didn't expect you to take the rap. You could have landed me right in it," Jacky started. "Jesus, there goes my mouth again. I didn't mean that the way it came out. Sorry, Jay. Call me Jacky – everyone else does."

LJ slowly warmed to the man. Whatever he had done to land himself in prison, he had his redeeming points. "It's what we do – take responsibility for our actions – no matter what most people think. If we make a mistake, we own up. I started the fight and you defended yourself."

"You're Roma, am I right?"

LJ nodded, surprised that a man like Jacky might even have heard of the Roma.

"Thought so, and just to put the record straight, I know that you lot believe that cleanliness is next to godliness and all that, so what I said when you walked in was way out of order. I might be an ignorant old oaf, but I have learnt a few things over the years," Jacky said, silently chastising himself for past deeds. "I probably couldn't ask for a better cellmate. There's some aspirin by the washbasin. Take a couple and then get yourself up there for a rest."

"Have you got a family?" LJ asked, climbing wearily up to his bunk.

"Once upon a time but lost them all. Drink and sloth – I reckon they're the right words – that's what did for me mostly. Old-fashioned word as it is, sloth well describes my downfall. I always expected everybody to do everything for me. I hated hard work, drank like a fish. I drove the best two of the family away and then the wife and other daughter upped and left, not that they were any great loss. No one to blame but myself. Didn't realise what I had until I lost it all." Jacky spoke thoughtfully. "I spent a couple of years looking for the two good ones. I had this wild idea that I could put things right – looked everywhere, never found them again. Probably just as well. What I did was beyond forgiveness. Finally, I gave up and went back to the bottle, the business collapsed because there was no one to do the work that I should have been doing myself, sold everything there was, ran out of money, and started robbing everyone else – small-time robberies, a hundred quid here, a hundred there. One guy wouldn't hand

114

over a few measly quid and I just lost it. I was drunk at the time and lashed out. All on CCTV and the rest is history."

"I know what you mean," LJ replied thoughtfully. It was the first time that he had ever 'lost it' and it would be the last. No good ever came of it.

Jacky's voice broke into the silence. "I owe you, Jay. Need to do something to make it right, if I can. Prison is a tough place and there are some real hard cases in this one, but they all know not to mess with me. From now on you're under my protection. We'll get your behaviour rating back up if we work at it, and if we pull a few strings here and there, then you'll get your transfer to Cat D in a few months. Might surprise you to know that the guv'nor and I are on quite good terms most of the time. Should be able to get your visitation rights reinstated as well. I'm assuming you'd prefer to be out in the open rather than banged up in here with me?"

"More than anything. Nothing personal."

"You going to be expecting visitors? I mean that wife and kiddie of yours?"

He'd thought about it long and hard. He was going to miss them more than anything in the world, but it was too far for them to travel and, besides, the last thing he would want would be for Sally to see him in a prison. He had already decided that he would write to Jess and explain. "No, I'm going to ask them not to come," he said.

"Well, in that case, let's concentrate on getting you out of here. Now listen up. This is what we're going to do…"

Jacky was as good as his word. Within days LJ had completed his induction and joined several classes. His commitment to his classwork and behaviour was regularly commented on by the wardens and the guv'nor. "He even does his homework when he's told," Jackie told the wardens at every possible opportunity.

He had kept his promise on other counts as well. Word was

out that Jacky had a new cellmate, Jay, and that if any of the other inmates called him anything other than Jay or so much as laid a finger on him, then they would have him to contend with personally. No one argued with Jacky.

# Sixteen

Fred didn't see his bed again that night. The vicar had been as good as his word. By the time the party arrived, the church was warm, blankets were stacked against the wall and the aroma of chicken soup drifted in from the small annex kitchen. Long into the night he sat side by side with Michael on one of the wooden pews listening as Michael berated himself over broken promises. He would not be consoled. Byron sat apart, lost in thoughts that no doubt mirrored those of Michael. Eventually they had all fallen asleep where they sat.

The following day, two policemen arrived at the church to take statements from each member of the family 'to eliminate them from their enquiries', as they said, and to tell them that it would be a full three days before they would be given the final verdict on the fire. Until that time the site would remain sealed off.

Other than making regular trips to the village shop to buy provisions for the families and returning home late each night to catch a few hours' sleep, Fred stationed himself in the church, ready and willing to lend a shoulder or an ear to anybody who had need of it. He had not spoken of the gypsies to anyone in the shop. No one had asked after their welfare. No one had asked him to convey their condolences. No one had offered a helping hand as he trundled back and forth with the shopping bags. Other than himself, the vicar and his wife, the villagers went about their business as though nothing had happened. Sam and his daughter were conspicuous by their absence; it did not go unnoticed. He was disgusted with, and ashamed of, the whole lot of them.

As the days passed, he grew to admire the family more and more. The women, Rosa and Polly, were steadfast. Cooking, cleaning, washing, making endless cups of tea, and watching over their men, their feet never touched the ground. Everything in the church sparkled, from the kitchen to the brass candle holders that lined the aisle between the newly polished pews. While the women worked inside the church, the men worked outside. The walls surrounding the churchyard were repaired, the grass cut, the trees, and hedges trimmed, gravestones cleaned and repaired – nothing was too much trouble and they did not wait to be asked. They gave freely of their time and labour whatever the weather.

Work was a good distraction for all of them – therapy, but at the end of the day when darkness fell and they could work no longer, there were long periods of silence. There was no joy or laughter, but a lot of prayers were said for the safe delivery of their loved ones' souls to heaven. Sometimes Byron led the prayers; at other times, the vicar led the prayers. They included him in everything; they treated him as part of their family. He knew he would sorely miss them when finally they left.

On the third day, a vehicle drew up outside the church. Sergeant Brockett climbed out of his car, put on his hat, squared his shoulders, and walked up the path towards the church.

Fred walked out to meet him. "Took your time, didn't you?"

Sergeant Brockett smiled. "These things do take time, Fred. You'll be pleased to see the back of them, after all the trouble you had with that young gypsy. Maybe we can all get back to normal soon."

"There is no normal, Brockett. Not in this village," Fred snapped. "And no, I shall not be glad to see the back of them, as you say. They are worth a hundred of the rotten devils that live in this village."

The family assembled; Brockett squared his shoulders and prepared to deliver the verdict. "Thank you for your patience," he started. "The forensics team have now completed their investigations. As you know the charred body of a young woman who went by the name of Jess Lovell was found at the scene. The body of the child known as Sally Lovell has not been found. We are therefore unable to conclude whether the child is dead or alive. However, it is more than likely that she too perished in the fire."

Fred watched on as Byron and Michael stood in stony silence and listened. "We've interviewed everyone in the village and there are no witnesses to the incident. As you have already told me, none of you were present at the time. We've also made house-to-house calls to try and establish the whereabouts of the child but without success. She, as I have already stated, is most probably dead as well, but we'll keep her on the books as a missing person – a formality in a case like this. The verdict of the coroner is accidental death. The forensics team concludes that the fire started with a spark from the wood-burning stove within the wagon and then heightened by exploding gas cylinders co-located with the wagon. There was no trace of any accelerants or anything to indicate that the fire was other than an accident. It is nothing short of a miracle that other vehicles were largely undamaged by the fire. We can release what is left of the woman's body forthwith. Finally, sir..." Sergeant Brockett turned to address Byron, "may I ask what your intentions are? Do you plan to continue holidaying in Bartonford or might you be planning to move on?"

Fred held his breath; Byron's eyes blazed, but he did not rise to the bait. "We do not stay in any place where there has been a death in the family. It is not the Roma way. Once we have put Jess to rest, we will be on our way."

"Thank you, sir. That is most satisfactory. My condolences, of course, to you all," the sergeant replied, turning on his heel and walking back to his car.

Fred watched tearfully as the coffin was carried up the aisle by Michael, Byron, and Byron Jnr. The service was short and sweet. There was no 'big fat gypsy funeral'. Respected and loved as she was, Jess was not Roma, but a Christian girl. There was nothing they could do to send Sally peacefully on her way – her body had not been recovered. The vicar conducted a moving service and waived all normal fees that would normally have been charged. Jess was laid to rest in a plot to the rear of the churchyard under a willow tree in a grave marked by a cross that had been carved by Michael's own hand. A second small cross marked the loss of Sally.

"Tell me it's not my business, but has anyone told LJ?" Fred summoned up the courage to ask the question. No one had so far spoken of it.

"No," Michael replied. "It is Byron's responsibility to do that. He will do it when he finds the right words, and not before."

Fred nodded and said no more about it. After days of listening to Michael he understood that this task was one that fell to the leader of the group and no other and that there would be no argument between them about it. "And what about you, Michael? Will you be going with the family?"

"No," he replied. "I am going to study law and then I will fight for the rights of ethnic minorities. Gypsies and the Roma will be top of my priority list."

"You can do it, son." He had heard enough in the past three days to know that the man was both intelligent and driven by his passion. "If there is anything I can do to help?" Fred said. "I haven't got much money, but what I have got I would happily give you to help you on your way. You've only got to ask."

"That's kind of you," Michael replied. "Money isn't a problem. Byron has seen to that. I have enough to get started. I'll work and study at the same time. But there is something I need you to do for me, Fred. Keep an ear to the ground. I am not convinced that the fire was started by a spark from the wood-burning stove. It was unlit when we left the camp that day. Jess was afraid of fire and would never light it herself."

"You can trust me to do that, son," Fred replied. "I'll go even further and tell you that there are going to be some big changes in this village, or my name is not Fred Humphries. Let's keep in touch, Michael. I'll not let you down, and if I get a whiff of anything, I'll let you know. Go safe, and God go with you all," Fred said, and meant it, from the bottom of his heart.

# Seventeen

LJ had been taken to Ranbury, near Retford in Nottinghamshire, so the police told him. Asked how he might apply for a visitor's permit, he had been told to look it up online. Byron had never owned or touched a computer in his life. Even the word 'online' meant nothing to him. He made his next port of call the Citizens Advice Bureau where he found the help he needed. Armed with his relative's prison number, his date of birth, and his own date of birth, he could ring the prison and organise a visit. Byron didn't know LJ's prison number but rang the prison, nonetheless. Time after time he phoned. Time after time jobsworths told him that he could do nothing without the correct details. Often his thoughts drifted back to Michael and he wished that he were still by his side. Michael would have cut through the bureaucracy; Michael would have known what to do. Byron didn't give up easily. On the tenth call, a prison officer told him that he was wasting his time; a visitation order would have been denied anyway. According to the official, the prisoner had forfeited his rights to visits until the end of February – Byron could apply for a visiting order then and no sooner.

It could not wait that long; LJ had to be told what had happened. With a heavy heart, Byron sat down and wrote a letter. It was hard work and slow. He struggled with expressing himself, he struggled with finding the right words, he struggled with how to set them down on paper. It was the first time that he appreciated the importance of a good education and vowed that his grandchildren would be better prepared for life than he. Working online, writing letters, and filling out forms would be second nature to them even if it meant that they would no longer be able to roam freely.

The letter finished, he reread it. It was woefully inadequate, but the very best that he could do. In his heart, he knew that LJ was lost to him. He would never be forgiven.

The letter arrived four weeks into LJ's sentence. He had spoken little of Jess and Sally to Jacky or anybody else; somehow, they seemed closer to him when he did not have to share them through words. He had not even spoken their names. Jacky asked few questions.

"Mail for prisoner Jay," the warden said, handing the letter to LJ. "Reckon this letter might have been sitting about for a couple of weeks, son. When you forfeit visiting rights you also forfeit rights to getting mail. That's the way it goes."

LJ glanced at the handwriting; he did not recognise it. Day after day he had waited for a letter from Jess, but it had not come.

"Somebody loves you," Jacky laughed. "Still waiting for my first letter. Who's it from anyway?"

"I don't know." LJ scanned the envelope again. "The handwriting is almost illegible. It looks like it's been written by a child."

"Your daughter?"

"She was just learning her alphabet when I came here, so, no, it can't be from her and it's not from my wife either." LJ sat down on the hardbacked chair and tore open the envelope.

*My dear LJ,*

*I don't know where to start but I've got to start somewhere. There was a fire the same day that you were in court. The vardo caught fire.*

*It happened late in the afternoon before we got back to Bartonford. I tried to come to see you, but they said you couldn't have visitors. I wanted to tell you myself*

LJ stopped reading; his face turned pale.

"What's up, Jay? Bad news?" Jacky sat up and watched as LJ read on.

*It breaks my heart to tell you that Jess died in the fire. They think it was an accident – a spark from the wood burner the fire investigators said. It was all ashes by the time we got back. We lit candles for her and said prayers. Her remains are buried in the churchyard at Bartonford. Your friend, Fred Humphries, was very kind to us and the vicar as well. He gave us a small plot of land for her grave beneath a willow tree in the grounds of the church. I remembered you telling me about the willow tree where you first met Jess. We cannot be sure what happened to Sally – her body was not found but I'm afraid that she would have perished along with Jess. We said prayers for her safety wherever she might be. I promised to look after them. I am so sorry, LJ. There is a huge hole in our family and our hearts without the three of you.*

*Michael has decided to make his own way in life. He is intent on studying law. I have done my best to give him a head start.*

*We are on the road again – we could not stay in Bartonford. I will always be waiting for you and will always be there for you. We'll be heading for one of the winter camps later in the year. I'll write and let you know. I am sorry to use these words and be so blunt. I am not good at the written word. I'm so sorry I let you down. My heart goes out to you.*

*Byron*

The world collapsed around him. LJ hauled himself up on to the top bunk, buried his head in his pillow, and sobbed until he could sob no more.

Jacky lay quietly on the bunk below and listened. Whatever news the letter had brought, it was of the worst kind. His eyes drifted to the envelope and piece of paper that had fallen from Jay's hand on to the floor below. He picked them up and looked first at the envelope.

A cold shiver ran down his spine; the envelope was addressed to LJ Lovell. "He wants to be known as Jay..." The prison warden's words reverberated in his ears. "It's no skin off my nose – a name's a name." Jacky felt his pulse race, picked up the letter, and read it.

A woman was dead. The woman was called Jess. LJ and Jess, Jess and LJ. As the reality of the words hit home, the blood drained from his face, he fell silent. Sorrow, grief, self-recriminations, guilt – it all tore at his heart. The slim chance that he had ever had to put matters right with his daughter had been snatched away from him. It was the only thing in the world that had kept him going for so long; he would gladly have gone down on his knees to beg her forgiveness. The man lying sobbing in the bunk above him was his son-in-law – the boy, now man, whom he had denied to his daughter, whom he had called a dirty gypsy. He had been wrong. She had been right. LJ was a good man.

*Michael is intent on studying law*, he read on. Jacky held his head in his hands – Michael, the son who had hated him so much that he had tried to kill him, Michael, the boy whom he had taken delight in bullying and belittling, was going off to study law. Jess had gone to her grave hating him. The child who had seemingly perished was his granddaughter whom he would never meet – Sally, her name had been Sally. Tears flooded down his cheeks. This was his punishment.

# Eighteen

Sam had had his doubts right from the outset about retiring to a village in the middle of nowhere and buying the house, but the moment his wife, Marie, had walked in the front door there was no going back. It was everything that she had always wanted – five bedrooms, three reception rooms, a fully fitted state-of-the-art kitchen, and a conservatory that encased the whole of the back of the house, with doors leading out onto a well-established garden. It wasn't as if they needed the space; by choice they had no children. It was just the two of them. Now that they had reached retirement age, they needed the space, she said. He could have his own study, she, her hobby room, and maybe her father might come to live with them one day. He wouldn't be able to manage in that little house of his forever, she had said. Over my dead body, he had thought. The possibility of spending every waking moment chewing over the good old days with Fred was his idea of hell. Fred could stay right where he was in his own cottage.

The village, on the other hand, ticked a few of the boxes close to Sam's heart. There was a golf course within minutes of the house, a pub almost across the road, with a skittles alley, and a cricket team – not the big-time stuff, but by all accounts, one that was always looking for new players, young or old, and willing volunteers.

There were a couple of things about the house that he hadn't liked so well. It had a shared access drive, and it was located in a private cul-de-sac. Try as he had to persuade Marie that it would end in tears, she was having none of it. It was her dream house; it sounded very posh to live in a private road with just five houses. They would get on with their neighbours like a house on fire, no problem. Sam had been there before; shared drives spelled trouble – just like private roads. Marie won the day. It was ten years since they had moved into Faraday Close. So far, no one had killed anyone else. He didn't much like his neighbours but like in-laws, the choice was often not your own.

As the years passed, Sam forgot about his misgivings and for the most part enjoyed living in Faraday Close, Bartonford. It was a well-known fact that it took at least five years to be accepted in the village, and ten years before he would be allowed to call himself a local; he was on the verge of being awarded his local badge. A member of the Gentlemen's Club which met for dinner monthly, a member of the local golf club, and with his very own silver tankard hanging on a hook in the bar at the local, he was fairly content with life. Dutifully he made his voluntary contribution to the community – general maintenance jobs in the village shop and at the village hall. Changing light bulbs wasn't rocket science, and it didn't get in the way of his social life.

It was early springtime when everything started to go pear-shaped. The shared access raised its ugly head and almost overnight war broke out between him and his neighbour. There had been no malice aforethought or intention of upsetting anybody when Sam had decided to relocate his wheelie bins from his back garden into the shared access area. After years of trundling the bins weekly from the back garden to the front, Sam had hit on the idea of keeping them permanently in the shared access area. Pushed right up against the wall of the house, they had been in nobody's way. There remained plenty of room for both him and Joe, the next-door neighbour, to park their cars side by side in front of the two adjacent garages. No sooner had he relocated the bins to the shared access area than Joe was standing on his doorstep waving a sheaf of papers in his face. Hadn't he read the covenant? Didn't he know that bins could only be placed in the shared access area on refuse collection days and then not before seven o'clock in the morning? Joe had stood on the doorstep ranting and raving until he was blue in the face. He had rights, he said, and if he was sufficiently provoked, then he would take this 'blatant breach of the rules' to the Residents' Association Meeting to get a ruling. And then, if necessary, to the Parish Council, and then to the District Council. Had Joe offered one please or thank you, then Sam might well have simply moved the bins there and then and left it at that. In the event, he slammed the door in Joe's face. Later that day Sam relented and returned the bins to the back garden.

It should have been the end of the matter, but events took a strange turn. The following day before Sam had even got put his socks on, Joe was hammering on the door. The wheelie bins had mysteriously reappeared in the shared access drive. Sam leaned against the door, one sock on and one sock off, and denied all knowledge of it, but Joe was not to be mollified. Sam mulled it over in his head. The previous evening, he had sunk six pints at the pub – that he did remember, and he also remembered that he had taken a pee on Joe's hedge on the way back, but he didn't remember moving the wheelie bins. But maybe he had done just that. Sam returned the bins to the back garden.

And the following morning all hell broke loose again. Pulling his coat and scarf on, Sam stepped out of the front door, slipped on the icy step, hit the deck with a thump and almost collided with two wheelie bins, their contents spread the length and breadth of the front garden. Winded by the fall, he did a double take.

From next door came Joe's whiny voice: "I warned you about those bins, pal. This is the third day that I've found them in that access. Let this be a lesson. I hope you enjoy clearing up the mess. If I find them in the shared access again then I'll set fire to them and maybe your house as well."

Sam was reminded of Marie's words of wisdom – they would get on with their neighbours like a house on fire.

Sam felt the colour rise to his cheeks and saw red as he gingerly pulled himself back up onto his feet and glared at his neighbour. If looks could kill they would have done – instantly. Joe, deciding that discretion was the better part of valour, turned and made a hasty retreat into his house. Sam moved like lightning. Sweeping two of the dustbin bags up from the lawn, he hurdled the low hedges between the front gardens and, in a manner that any cricketer would have applauded, bowled both bags overarm through Joe's front door. A trail of last week's casserole remains, potato scrapings, and rotten cabbage led right up to the front door, in through Joe's hallway, and stopped at his wife's feet.

Later that day he received a visit from the local constabulary. There had been a complaint of wilful damage made against him by his neighbour. Sam explained the background, relaying how he had been provoked by Joe. His words fell on stony ground; Sam was to expect a summons. Word spread like wildfire throughout the neighbourhood, and soon there was not a shadow of doubt in anybody's mind that Sam was the troublemaker, the guilty party.

For the first time in his life, Sam found himself up before the magistrate. It was a humiliating experience. Replacement carpets for Joe's hall cost him one thousand pounds and redecoration a further five hundred pounds. With court costs, a total of seventeen hundred pounds. Had this been the only penalty, then he might have accepted his punishment more readily, but no, the magistrate gave him community service as well. Sam huffed and puffed and fumed his way through ten hours of community service made worse by the fact that the magistrate had instructed that it was to be served in Bartonford. Picking up litter, picking up after dogs, and cleaning graffiti off walls were nothing in comparison to the humiliation of it all. What he would have given to get even with Joe was not worth mentioning, but, God help him, he had learned his lesson and was not responsible for the incident the following week.

Over a period of one week, the box hedge surrounding Joe's front garden withered and died. Joe eyed him accusingly whenever the two of them happened to be in the garden at the same time. Worthies from the village crawled around on their hands and knees day after day as the leaves turned brown and then black and then fell to the ground. It was unanimously agreed that the culprit was none other than a strong weed killer, and who was there in the village with a grudge against the quiet and well-respected Joe? Sam, of course – the neighbour from hell. The suggestion that he had been responsible had only to be made once in the village and it was God's own truth. Sam became persona non grata overnight. This time, they said, he had gone too far. His pals in the cricket club ignored him, his membership to the Gentleman's Club was rescinded, his membership of the golf club withdrawn. The village hall committee busied themselves to find somebody else to change the light bulbs – the only good thing to come out of the whole ludicrous business. The only thing left was his silver tankard hanging on its hook in the local. Things couldn't get much worse, so Sam thought, but he had been wrong.

The beginning of the end started just a few weeks after the refuse incident and the withered hedge. Returning late from town, and in need of a pint after a frustrating afternoon, he had stopped by the pub for a swift half. It was that time of day when the farm labourers stopped by for a drink on their way home. Sam enjoyed their company. One pint turned into two pints, then three and then four. Relaxed and merry and not caring that his salad would by now be in the oven, Sam returned to his car in a far more congenial mood than he had been in an hour earlier. Switching on the ignition and putting the car into gear, Sam pulled out of the pub car park. Had he looked in his mirror, he would have seen the police car pull out right behind him. The breathalyser test confirmed that he was three times over the legal limit. They threw the book at him. The fine was heavy but bearable; the loss of his licence for three years was intolerable. Nobody could survive in a rural village that had minimal public transport services without a licence to drive.

The word out on the street was that he was his own worst enemy and had only himself to blame. No one had one iota of sympathy for him. He could easily have killed someone. Sam wished he had – himself. Marie hardly spoke to him. He had ruined everything for them. The local paper, *The Courier*, carried full details of the conviction.

The For Sale sign went up within days of his conviction. The house sold quickly at a knockdown price. Within days of signing the contract, a house removal lorry was parked up outside with the ramp down. Neither Sam nor Marie noticed the small posy of white heather that lay on the doormat the morning they said their final farewell to Bartonford.

Fred stood at the end of the road in the early spring sunshine and waved goodbye to his daughter and son-in-law.

# Nineteen

Jacky knew that when Jay was ready to talk, he would, and he had no choice but to wait it out. It was two weeks after Jay had received the letter from Byron that he took the first tentative step towards sharing his pain and grief with his cellmate. For the first time, he started to talk about his family. Day after day Jacky had wanted to comfort him, but he could not admit that he had read the letter. He had replaced it and the envelope on the exact same spots where they had been dropped. There had been days when he could hardly contain his patience, he so desperately wanted to hear every single detail about his Jess and her little girl, Sally.

"Dead, both of them," LJ began as if in a daydream. "She was always stronger than me. She never let anything get in her way. She was the most beautiful girl in the world although she didn't think so. She had an accident with a tractor when she was a child and it left her with a limp. We first met at a market. And then we met again the following week. She was sitting under a big old willow tree, her skirt wrapped tightly around her legs and down to her ankles. You see, she didn't want me to see that there was anything wrong with her. I suggested we walked down the bank and paddle in the stream, but she was scared. She cried and then she lifted her skirt just to her knee, showed me the scars on her leg, and told me that she was a cripple. I laughed – I remember laughing until my sides almost split, and after a while she let me help her down to the stream. We sat on a rock and let the water run over our feet. Her smile lit up the day and would have dazzled the night. I think I must have fallen in love with her at that very moment. She was called Jess."

Jacky listened silently. He remembered the day Jess had been injured by the tractor and he also remembered that he had been furious, his only concern for himself, for the extra work that he would have to do with Jess off her feet. Even at her young age, she had already made herself indispensable. He had not given one moment's thought to the pain that his daughter might be suffering or what it might mean for her future. He could not bring himself to remember his behaviour towards her when she was a child, but it was there, lurking at the back of his mind; it would never go away.

"I didn't tell her that I was a gypsy – I didn't want to lose her as soon as I had found her," LJ continued wistfully. "Although she had a kind heart, I was afraid that she would have believed everything people would have told her about gypsies. You know the stuff – nothing more than thieves and liars, and men who took advantage of women. I didn't want her to think that of me. I could have told her that I was Roma, but it would have meant nothing to her. I'll not say that I didn't want to take her in my arms and make love to her that very first day, but that is not what we Roma do – we wait until after we are married for that most intimate moment.

"Apart from which, I couldn't love her and leave her. I knew my family would be moving on and me with them – a couple of weeks at the most before we would have to go our own separate ways. I didn't want to break her heart by getting too close. We met up in secret every day the second week – just to talk and paddle and laugh about nothing in particular. I did tell her that I loved her – the words slipped out of nowhere. Maybe it was a mistake and maybe it was fate. She said she loved me too. They were magic moments. She was kind and courageous."

"She sounds like a very special young lady," Jacky said,

swallowing a lump in his throat. He would never understand what it was in his make-up that had made him behave like an animal towards his own daughter. She had never defied him. She had worked like a Trojan and never complained about anything. Maybe if she had been defiant, had stood up to him and refused to do the things he asked of her, he would have given her more respect. It was no excuse.

"She was, the very best. Her father abused her, hit her. I saw the bruises on her arms, but she would never tell me in so many words. What kind of a man does that to his daughter? What else did he do to her, I often wondered?"

Jacky turned his head away – he could not let Jay see the shame that was written all over his face. How could he tell him that although he had hit out at her and even taken pleasure in it at the time, he had never abused her womanhood? He could not deny that it had crossed his mind, but he had never done so.

"And then one day her father beat her badly. That was when her brother turned up at our camp, Jess in his arms. We were married soon after. It wasn't an easy life for her living with the Roma, but she rose to the occasion," LJ continued from a faraway place. "There were a few in the family who resented her presence. There were others who accepted her almost from the beginning as one of our own. She had me, Sally, and her brother who was her rock, and then there was my Uncle Byron and his immediate family – we all loved her. Sally loved her Uncle Byron, or Uncle By-By as she called him." LJ took a deep breath and let it out slowly. "I'll never, ever forget the day Michael ran into our camp carrying Jess's bloodied little body in his arms. It was wicked what that man had done to her."

Jacky took a cigarette out of the packet and looked at it. He hadn't smoked for over a year, but he had kept the packet just in case. He lit the cigarette, drew deep on it, and coughed. He had never really known his daughter when she was alive, but now that she was dead there was nothing that he did not want to know about her.

"Sally was the spitting image of her mother in some respects – the same huge blue eyes and the same dimple on her chin. She was bright and intelligent and strong. She knew what she wanted, and she never had to work hard to get it. A long drawn-out 'please' from Sally and no one could say no to her. She had a love of life just like her mother. She was three and a half the last time I saw her alive. She would have been four in June. She was tall for her age with long blond hair – willowy, like me. She loved the outdoors, loved being on the road, loved riding upfront on the vardo where she sat on Jess's lap with Michael on one side and me on the other."

"Do you keep any photographs of them?" Jacky asked. "You could pin them up on the wall. It'll help to know that they are close."

LJ put his hand in his pocket and drew out a small photograph, crumpled and faded. "Just the one," he said, handing it to Jacky.

Jacky looked at the photograph and tears welled in his eyes. The child was beautiful; his daughter was beautiful.

"There was a fire the same day that I was in court. The vardo burnt with Jess inside it. They think Sally probably died with her mother although they didn't find her little body. She would have been there. Byron wrote that the police said that a spark from the wood-burning stove had caused the fire. It would have been quick. Other than the steel frame, the vardo was all wood; it would have gone up in seconds.

"If I had been there then who knows? Late afternoon, it would have been dark. Jess sometimes put Sally down for a rest late afternoon and took one herself. It was a Tuesday, market day in Aubrey. Byron and Michael were in court with me, and the rest of the family would have been at the market. For some reason Sally and Jess didn't go to the market that day. They said it was an accident. No more, no less."

Jacky looked at LJ. It would take a blind man not to see that there was something troubling him. "But you don't think it was an accident? Am I right?" Was it possible that somebody had deliberately

135

killed his daughter and his granddaughter?

LJ nodded slowly. It was the first time he had admitted it to himself let alone anyone else, but it had been on his mind. "I want to believe the truth of Byron's words, but it doesn't add up. Jess never lit the wood-burning stove herself. She always left it to me. Other than me, she let nobody near it including her brother and Byron. She was quite happy to wrap herself and Sally up in blankets when there was a chill in the air. Jess loved the three of us sitting around the fire, but never once did she light it herself. So how is it that a spark from the burner caused the fire?"

Jacky shrugged his shoulders, searching for an explanation. "Maybe somebody else lit the fire, Jay – Byron? Or maybe with you gone, she decided that she needed to start doing jobs for herself, just in case she found herself on her own for a while?"

"No," he replied, "I know Jess. The fire was never lit until the evenings."

"So, you think it might have been deliberate? Why would anybody deliberately set fire to a vardo?" Jacky asked. A shiver ran through his body. It wasn't so many years ago that he would have set fire to the whole lot of them when they were camped on the other side of Daylesbury, and he wouldn't have lost one single night's sleep over it. Many felt the same.

"The locals in the village hated us all..." LJ shook his head "But, no, even they would not have done such a thing. But I can't make sense of it. There was one good man in the village. I liked him. His name was Fred Humphries."

Jacky didn't need to ask what a vardo was; he'd seen enough of them in the year he'd spent traipsing across the countryside looking for Jess and Michael. At first, he had hated going into the gypsy camps to ask questions and then refused to believe a word they had told him. As time went by, the camps felt more familiar. He moderated his language, talked to the occupants with respect, and in turn, they told him everything they could that might help him find his son and daughter. It had been to no avail, but he had learned a lot. Much as he had been reluctant to admit it, his respect for the Roma had grown by the day – the same couldn't be said of the Irish Travellers, but that was the way it was.

"You have to let it go, Jay. Don't believe anybody who says you will get over it. You never do. Losing someone you love is forever. Take it from someone who knows," Jacky said tearfully. No one would ever know that he spoke from the heart. "But life goes on. It will always be different. Maybe you will find happiness with another woman, maybe it will be in your work. I hope it happens for you. You're out of here in a few weeks, Jay." Jacky changed the subject. "It will soon be spring, and you'll have the chance to spend time out of doors again. It'll give you a better perspective on life. I hear that Sudbury is a good place – open prison – nice class of prisoner, and decent food. I've made sure that your paperwork says your occupation is landscaper, and there's no mention of gypsy, Traveller, or Roma. It's for the best. Work hard when you get there, follow the rules and then leave with your head held high and make Jess and Sally proud of you. That's all you can do."

LJ nodded; it was the one bright spark on the horizon, and it was all thanks to Jacky. True to his word, Jacky had somehow persuaded the governor that LJ was the epitome of a model prisoner and a man who deserved a chance. What strings Jacky had pulled he would never know, but he would be eternally grateful to him.

"I'm going to apply to work in the gardens. I always had this dream that one day when we tired of the road, we would find ourselves a nice little house and I would set myself up as a landscape gardener. I think Jess would have liked that too."

"I am sure she would. So, you won't be going off to find your family after Sudbury?"

LJ hesitated; it was something that he had been thinking long and hard about. "I'm not sure. Maybe one day. It could never be the same without Jess and Sally. Michael has left to make his own way in life. Byron would tell me to follow my heart. What about you, Jacky? What will you do when you get out?"

"Me? I've another eighteen months, with good behaviour I'll be out by October next year. Then who knows? Start again."

"I'd like to stay in touch," LJ said.

"I was hoping you'd say that, Jay. Guess you don't where you'll end up and I don't know where I'll end up eventually. For the time being, I'm not going anywhere. Will you write to me here? I'll write to you at Sudbury and then, wherever you go afterward, write to me with your address. I guess neither of us is up to much in the writing stakes, but a few words will be fine."

"That is a promise, Jacky. Thanks for everything."

Jacky leaned back on his bed and went through everything in his mind. If LJ was right and someone had deliberately set fire to the vardo and killed his Jess and Sally, then they needed to be found and punished. If it took him a lifetime, he would do it. And one day, he promised himself, he would tell LJ the truth.

# Twenty

Time flew. LJ wished that his stay at HMP Sudbury could have been longer. He had hit lucky. Established solely for low-risk prisoners and classified as a Cat. D prison, it was a very different kettle of fish to Ranbury. Security was minimal, inmates came and went almost as they pleased, and everyone was encouraged to either engage in further education or participate in future job-related activities.

Soon after he had settled in, he asked if he could work in the gardens and greenhouses, explaining that he hoped to find employment in this field after his release. It was a bitter disappointment to find that there were no openings. Unbeknown to him, HMP Sudbury had won a coveted Gold Award in the Chelsea Flower Show the previous year and were entering again that year. Everybody wanted a part of it, and the head gardener had his pick of the men.

Instead, he was assigned to work in the kitchen overlooking the gardens. LJ scraped and chopped vegetables from morning until dusk and watched enviously as the preparations for the show progressed. He shared a cell with one of the lucky ones, Harry, a man no older than he, who had managed to secure one of the last openings on the project. Harry was excited by the project and more particularly the possibility that he might be one of the chosen few who would go to Chelsea to build the garden. Each night after dinner, LJ and Harry put their feet up and discussed the project. Harry recounted the events of the day, and LJ asked endless questions. If he couldn't be part of the team, then at least he could learn something from their frenetic activities.

One evening Harry didn't want to talk about it. It had been a bad day. It was looking as though they might have to go back to the drawing board, and time was running out. According to Harry, the garden designer had been far too ambitious with the hard landscaping. He had got carried away and it would be nigh on impossible to construct the garden in the time available to them before the show. The head gardener was talking about pulling out. LJ's ears pricked up. "Have you got a copy of the plan?" he asked. "How much time do we have?"

LJ listened, studied the plan, thought about it and then picked up a pen and paper. "There's an easier way," he said. "If you do it like this, you'll cut your time down by half."

Harry relayed the bones of LJ's suggestion to the head gardener the following morning. An hour later, LJ was reassigned from the kitchen to the Chelsea project as a special advisor for the hard landscaping. The head gardener congratulated him on his skills and knowledge, which had saved the day, and the team got back to work.

In late May HMP Sudbury scooped a Silver – not the Gold of the previous year – but they had been delighted when Diarmuid Gavin declared that the Sudbury Garden was his personal favourite. Spurred on by the commendation and the words of a well-known expert, the team immediately started planning the following year's garden. LJ worked with them right up until his release date. If he had been given the choice, he would have stayed.

LJ took one last look over his shoulder at HMP Sudbury, the prison that had been his home for just over the past two months. The bus to Tutbury railway station ran every thirty minutes; the next was due in ten minutes. It was the first of July. The sky was azure blue, and it promised to be a scorching hot day – far too hot for the long-sleeved fleece sweatshirt and denim jeans that he wore, but it had been Hobson's choice. Other than prison clothes, he possessed no others. In his bag, he carried a pair of pyjamas, two changes of socks and underwear, and a wash bag. In his wallet, he had the two hundred pounds that had been left in his private cash account after expenses. It was thanks to Byron that he had anything at all.

It felt strange to be standing kerbside on his own – almost as if he had escaped and was on the run. The feeling was irrational, he knew that, but it was there. From time to time he glanced back over his shoulder and wished again that he did not have to leave. It had been a safe and oddly happy place. He had had all his privileges, but he had availed himself of none.

Sudbury had been a revelation. If anybody knew of his Roma origins, they had not mentioned it. He had been treated as an equal. For the first time in his life, he learned what it was like to live a normal life and be treated as an ordinary human being. He wrote to Jacky on the day before he was released telling him that he planned to revisit Bartonford to pay his respects to Jess. He recalled there being a nurseryman in the village whom he might call upon for a temporary job until such time as he decided whether to reunite with the family or start life anew. He reiterated his promise to stay in touch.

Now he was on his own with an unfamiliar journey ahead of him – one that he dreaded. It would be the first time he had been on a bus and the first time that he had travelled on a train. He had his rail ticket to Aubrey in his pocket thanks to one of the wardens who had gone out of his way to acquire the ticket for him. He had money in his pocket for the bus fare to Tutbury and then his bus fare from Aubrey to Bartonford.

When the bus came, he climbed aboard, paid the driver, and sat down in a seat, wondering how he would know when the bus arrived at Tutbury.

"Been inside, have you, lad?" A lady tapped him on the shoulder. "Don't you worry, ducks, you're not the only one. My Bobby spent a few months in Sudbury – loved it, he did. Where are you going?"

"A long way – a place called Bartonford. It's in Warwickshire," LJ replied.

"Nice place, I hear. You'll be getting off at Tutbury then and catching the train then?"

LJ nodded. "Yes, you couldn't let me know when we get there could you? I'm not familiar with this part of the world."

"No problem, ducks. You take care now, won't you? And good luck."

The first part of his journey was blessedly uneventful. Tutbury was a small station with two platforms – trains went either east or west. The warden had told him that Derby, his first stop, was to the west. The station was deserted. He followed the signs to the westbound platform and waited for the train. It comprised of just two carriages. LJ ran towards a door that opened as if by magic and then closed by itself. If Derby and Birmingham, the next two changes, were anything like as easy then he would have nothing to worry about.

When the train arrived at Derby, LJ waited for the doors to open, but nothing happened. A boy of no more than twelve looked up at him as if he had just arrived from another planet and pressed the green button beside the door; the doors slid open. LJ followed the crowd as it climbed the staircase from the platform and, on reaching the top, veered off to the left or the right. There were platforms in every direction but nothing to tell him which direction would lead him to the right platform for the Birmingham train. Destinations and times flashed up on screens hung high above him. Barely decipherable voices boomed from speakers above. Mothers with pushchairs and screaming children, boys with bikes, suited men and women carrying leather briefcases and shoulder bags jostled one another and shouted at each other above the noise of the announcements. LJ stood stock still as crowds rushed towards him, past him, around him, and threatened to trample him underfoot. He stood in the middle of the bridge, seemingly invisible to all those around him, and felt panic setting in. In that instant, he glanced back at the platform from which he had just alighted from the Tutbury train and was sorely tempted to return to the safety of Sudbury.

A man came close to knocking him down as he shouldered his way past and sprinted across the bridge, shouting an apology as he passed, "Sorry, mate, but can't afford to miss the twelve-ten to Birmingham or I'll be out on my ear." LJ followed the man's passage across the bridge and watched as he took the steps three at a time down to platform six. At least he now knew which platform he should head for. With a sinking feeling in the pit of his stomach, he followed the man towards platform six. According to his ticket, he had forty minutes to wait for the train on which he had a reserved seat. As he descended the steps to the platform, the man who claimed he would lose his job if he missed the train, yanked open a door and, running alongside the train, heaved himself inside. Unlike the Tutbury train, the doors did not open and close automatically. The train driver shouted expletives at the man. The Birmingham man waved two fingers back at him as the train pulled out.

LJ stood on the platform and watched as trains arrived and trains departed. Some, according to a faceless voice, stopped short of Birmingham, and some veered off and went in a different direction altogether. An announcement reminded the waiting passengers one moment that smoking was not allowed on the platform and in the next, that everybody should stand behind the yellow line – a fast train was approaching. LJ stood just behind the yellow line and waited for the oncoming train to appear. In the distance, he heard a roar which grew louder and louder as the train came into view. He heard the *beep beep* of the train warning those at the station to stand clear. The lines screeched as the train approached. The noise hurt his ears and the draught as it sped through buffeted him and physically forced him to take another step back. And then it was gone – far into the distance. It was a monster of a train with two big diesel engines at the front and twelve or more carriages. LJ wondered where so many people could be going and why they wanted to get there so fast. Words spoken by Michael came back to him. "Life in the fast lane, LJ," he had said on more than one occasion when bikers, cars, and lorries had overtaken their little convoy at speeds that made the trees sway, and the birds fly high into the sky. LJ knew that whatever the future held for him, it was not life in the fast lane.

He was alone in a strange place, in a strange world that he neither recognised nor understood. Was he doing the right thing by going back to Bartonford – the last place that he had been with Jess, or was he making a fatal mistake? His heart felt heavy and his eyes glazed over as his thoughts drifted to all the people and things whom he had loved and lost, Jess most of all. He needed to talk to her, to beg her forgiveness for leaving her and Sally on their own that fateful day. He needed to hear her say that he was forgiven; only then could he move on. In that instant, more than anything, he needed to feel her hand in his.

Putting his hands over his ears, he tried to block out the screeching wheels of the trains, the never-ending raucous announcements, the screaming children, the babble of adults constantly complaining, and the teenagers who shouted non-stop into phones fixed to their ears. All around him was confusion – there was no order to anything. It was more than he could bear.

"Fast train approaching," he heard. LJ put his bag down at his feet, brushed his hair back from his face, took a deep breath, and concentrated his eyes on the approaching train. It would take no more than a split second.

# Twenty-One

It was just six months since the gypsy shenanigans and James Smytheson Hodge was heartily glad that it was all over – done and dusted, forgotten. The only reminder that remained was the girl's gravestone in the churchyard. At least the vicar had had the common sense to site it well out of the way, but in his opinion, it would have shown more respect had he been consulted about it before the deed had been done. He could not disagree with the vicar's sentiments – it was the only Christian thing to do – but he had found himself unable to resist reminding him of the possible consequences of his action. Might it not be seen as tantamount to the village admitting some kind of responsibility for the incident? It was not the sort of thing that you wanted the press to get hold of. Fortunately, so far, they had not.

Smytheson Hodge wallowed in being addressed as 'Squire', and as the major landowner in the area, he felt it only right and proper that he should be addressed as such. It pleased him that his tenant farmers had taken note of his views on the employment of casual labour. The seasonal workers now came mainly from Poland and Romania. The Irish, he had made it clear, were not welcome, and passing bands of gypsies were most definitely not to be employed.

He had no interest whatsoever in parish politics. Dealing with the petty squabbles, the village stipend, and clearing up the dog mess was best left to annoying spinsters like Wanda Turner. Neither had he any interest in local district politics. Dealing with housing applications, health and welfare, infrastructure, roads, and crime was best left to the paid bureaucrats in the Town Hall. Preferring to remain on the fringe of all things political, Smytheson Hodge made it his business to maintain good relationships with those who had influence or power. It was he to whom Keith Ingrams had turned to help expedite outline planning for the old garage and workshop and the greenhouses beyond. He had been delighted to help. The sooner the land was occupied, the better. Leaving it in its current state was inviting trouble.

James Smytheson Hodge's annual summer garden party was, he liked to believe, the social event of the year. No one was left out. Invitations went out to everybody from the wealthiest residents to the lowliest seasonal farmhands, the labourers who lived in the farm cottages, and the council house tenants whose dwellings had been discreetly erected out of sight of the main thoroughfare and centre of the village.

The downturn in the reputation of the village bothered him. And he viewed it as his personal responsibility to restore it to its former glory. There was no better way, he decided, to achieve that than to stage the best-ever Smytheson Hodge annual summer garden party. The date was set, and he had already written and posted personal invitations to local reporters, columnists and photographers. Those reporters who had bad-mouthed him and the village over the gypsy incident had been blackballed with impunity; they had a great deal to answer for. Not only had they made Bartonford the laughing stock of the county, but they had dared to accuse him, the Squire, of racial prejudice. Naturally, he had denied any such thing.

On-site preparations for the garden party started in late June. The date had been fixed for Sunday the twentieth of July. Two weeks before the event, the marquees would be delivered and erected on the lawns in front of the house from which the villagers could enjoy a commanding view of the valley below and the rolling hills in the distance.

One week in advance of the event, the floor, tables, and chairs would be delivered and stacked inside the marquee ready to be set out nearer the date. Three days in advance of the event, the caterers' lorries would form a procession up the sweeping drive with everything necessary to prepare and present a four-course luncheon to three hundred.

There was one task that he allowed nobody else to interfere with – that of the seating arrangements. There would be thirty tables, each seating ten. Table plans would be posted outside each of the entrances to the main marquee and would remain a closely guarded secret until the day of the party. With an illegally obtained copy of the village electoral roll to hand, Smytheson Hodge whiled away his evenings carefully annotating the sheet. Individuals were classified according to his own set of rules. The VIPs – those with influence – would be invited to join him and his wife at the top table at the front of the marquee raised on a dais and reached by means of four wooden steps. It was an honour that he liked to share around the village. Other worthies of the village would be allocated to one of the two tables either side of the top table – close enough so that if he wished to speak to any of them then he could, far enough away to remind them that they had yet to be chosen for the top table.

A long table immediately below the dais was always assigned to newcomers to the village. In this way, he could observe them at close quarters and assess which individuals, in the following year, should be demoted to the back of the marquee, and which might be promoted to the dais.

Other tables would be organised and positioned by wealth and social standing in the village.

The dress code was always summer frocks for the ladies and shirts and trousers for the men. Those who foolishly turned up in

147

jeans were sent home to change. Children were, of course, welcome provided they were on a lead and behaved themselves. Smytheson Hodge always made it clear that anyone who misbehaved, old or young, would go home empty-handed after the event – three long tables would be piled high with boxed gifts for the guests. For the children there would be huge tins of sweets; for the ladies, each a small bottle of French perfume, and the men, each a small box of cigars and a bottle of malt whiskey; that many of them neither smoked nor drank was irrelevant. His generosity was always remarked upon and it always gave him a warm glow.

The four-course lunch would be prepared and cooked by a team of French chefs. Smytheson Hodge would not have it any other way. This year, he believed, he had excelled himself with his choice of menu: tiny quenelles of chicken liver pâté sitting on a bed of baby spinach with Manor House caramelised onion chutney and a brioche; navarin of lamb, cooked pink, with jus and accompanied by seasonal vegetables, and finally, tarte aux pommes served with Chantilly cream. The dessert would, of course, be served after the cheeseboard in true French style. The sommelier would be flying in from Bordeaux and together with his team of waiters would explain the significance of the grapes and the character of each of the wines that would be served with the meal. It did not bother Smytheson Hodge in the least that the whole experience was wasted on eighty percent of the guests – it was part and parcel of the experience and his mission as squire to help all of them aspire to better things.

The hour was almost upon him. It was time to take a last-minute stroll around the marquee with the maître d' to check that everything was in order. Smytheson Hodge nodded with satisfaction. Starched white linen napkins, silver cutlery, crystal glasses for the wine, water glasses, and huge jugs of iced tap water had been placed on each table.

"You won't have forgotten my bottle of Evian?" he asked.

"No, sir. As always, it is on your table for you and you alone," the maître d' replied.

In Smytheson Hodge's opinion, tap water was an abomination, full of chlorine and fluoride. It assaulted his palate, but it was more than adequate for the rest of his guests.

Satisfied that all was in order, he signalled to the master of ceremonies to open the flaps to the marquee and allow their guests to enter.

That afternoon he watched with ever-increasing smugness and satisfaction – everything was going like clockwork. No trays had been dropped, no buns had been thrown, no fights had broken out, and the children had been remarkably well behaved. After the dessert plates had been cleared, he would make his traditional welcome speech. It was always an anxious time. Following his speech, he would invite his guests to accept the gifts that he had bought for them as his way of showing his appreciation for everything that each one of them had contributed to the village; it was his very own version of Maundy money.

The dessert plates cleared, Smytheson Hodge smiled, pushed back his chair, walked to the front of the dais, and stood waiting for silence to descend throughout the marquee. Wearing a cream-coloured Savile Row suit with a white shirt and red-spotted bow tie and matching pocket handkerchief, he cut quite a figure. Taking a long draught of his glass of Evian before clearing his throat, he addressed his audience.

"Ladies and gentlemen, children, my good friends one and all," he started. "It is my pleasure to see you all here today and I hope most sincerely that you are enjoying your lunch. I am sure you will agree with me that we did not have the most auspicious start to the year with our uninvited visitors. It was a diabolical shame that their visit and the whole aftermath, quite unfoundedly, brought the village into disrepute. I am delighted that we were able to commemorate the young girl who died in the fire with an everlasting memorial in the churchyard. I hope that we will always have time for those less fortunate than ourselves. I believe it is now time for us to put all that behind us and look towards a prosperous future, one in which Bartonford regains its well-deserved reputation as one of England's finest villages. I will not draw this out any longer than necessary so I would just like to thank you all for your contributions to this wonderful community of ours."

Sparked by the lead from the guests on the top table the applause slowly grew in volume until it resounded around the marquee. His heart swelled with pride as he walked slowly, head bowed in a gesture of humility, closer to the edge of the dais. Looking out at the sea of his admirers, Smytheson Hodge waved his arms in the air, graciously accepting their praise; there were tears in his eyes.

"And, to add my personal thanks I would be delighted if—" Smytheson Hodge stopped abruptly mid-sentence and clapped his hands over his mouth. The marquee started to revolve before his eyes, the crowd swayed from side to side, his mind went blank. The final words that he had planned to deliver dissipated into thin air as his vomit jettisoned and spread the width and breadth of the newcomers' tables at the foot of the dais.

He could almost have born the humiliation of it all had it not been for the infectious titter that started on one of the tables at the back of the marquee and which then spread like a Mexican wave throughout the tent. Suddenly everyone was roaring with laughter including his friends at the top table, the worthies at the two adjacent tables, and the newcomers down below. Cameras flashed left, right, and centre. His wife gave him a look of disgust, stood up, and marched out of the marquee, her head held high. Smytheson Hodge stumbled off the dais and out of the marquee.

The guests finished their coffee and brandy, picked up the gifts which they knew to be theirs, and filed out of the marquee. Everybody had witnessed the complete humiliation of Squire

Smytheson Hodge. The news spread like wildfire to the surrounding villages and in no time at all to every corner of the county. The word was out – the squire could not hold his drink. The squire made the headlines. His annual garden party was history, his reputation in tatters.

No one noticed the small sprig of white heather that had found its way into the neck of the Evian bottle.

# Twenty-Two

Looking out of the kitchen window, Peter narrowed his eyes and squinted into the distance – at the far reach of the field that sloped down towards the village, a man stood stock still staring into the distance. Reaching for his binoculars he studied the man's outline. Peter watched for several minutes.

He did not welcome strangers to his property. A few so-called do-gooders from the village had come calling not long after he had first moved in, but they had soon got the message. For the past eighteen months, there had been no other callers. What he did or did not do on his own property was nobody's business but his own. The signs at the end of the drive leading to the house and all other accesses to the property read 'Private Property, Trespassers will be Prosecuted' leaving no one in doubt about the consequences. The mailbox had been affixed to the gate at the end of the drive – not even the postman was welcome at the door to the house. A second sign pinned to the gate read 'No Hawkers' and kept cold callers at bay. If he had named the house himself, he could not have chosen a more appropriate name – Cold Comfort Farm.

A quarter of a mile distant and down a steep hill, Cold Comfort Lane adjoined the Bartonford road. The village centre lay three hundred yards up the Bartonford Road from the junction with Cold Comfort Lane. The house was perfectly positioned to be well away from prying eyes. Peter had ventured down to the village on one occasion and one occasion only. He did not use the village shop; he declined all invitations to village events including that of the annual Manor House garden party. He read only the free local papers that were regularly stuffed into the mailbox – it suited him to remain informed, but he did not need to know what was going on in the rest of the world.

Peter ventured outside of his property for essential purposes only. He fetched his weekly shop from a supermarket twenty miles away from the village. Once a fortnight, he loaded his van and made his regular deliveries of shrubs and trees to nurseries, garden centres and landscapers. When necessary he visited his suppliers. He took no deliveries at the property.

Just after he had moved in, he had purchased a rifle. If trespassers couldn't read the signs then he was more than happy to remind them by pointing the barrel in their direction. So far, he had had no reason to even pick it up, let alone load it. Taking no chances, he had done everything by the letter of the law – he had a proper licence, and the rifle was kept in a secured gun cabinet bolted to the wall in the under stairs cupboard. He had familiarised himself with the gun when he had purchased it and even gone to the lengths of watching several videos on YouTube. At times, his fingers itched.

The man in the distance standing on his property had ignored the warning signs. It made him angry.

Peter calmly unlocked the cabinet and withdrew the rifle. Standing back from the kitchen window, he raised it to his shoulder and looked down through the sight; the man was a standing target. Tall, willowy, shoulders humped, legs apart, it was impossible to tell his age, but he guessed, youngish. Fetching an old tweed jacket from the hall, he put his boots on, shouldered the gun, and walked stealthily towards the man.

"You're trespassing. Turn around and show yourself," he shouted, rifle raised, and finger closed tightly around the trigger.

*

The colour drained from LJ's face as he turned abruptly and saw a tall, broad-shouldered man levelling a rifle in his direction. He was no more than five yards away. The rifle was frightening enough but the man's appearance sent shivers down his spine. He was a huge man. It was a warm summer day, but the man wore loose heavy green cords, a roll-neck sweater beneath an ill-fitting tweed jacket and wellington boots. His dark brown eyes stared menacingly out through horn-rimmed glasses perched on an aquiline nose beneath bushy salt-and-pepper eyebrows. His beard was cut close to his face. LJ put his age at somewhere between his mid and late sixties.

"Who are you? What's your business?" Peter demanded, holding the gun steady.

LJ dropped his arms limply to his sides and returned the man's stare. "I mean no harm, sir," he replied. "My name is LJ, LJ Lovell."

Peter's eyes widened. He recalled the name, a name not easily forgotten, and vaguely recognised him. He was the gypsy whose wife and child had died in the fire; the same gypsy who had been sent down for theft. He looked different in appearance – his hair was cut short – but it was the same man. Underneath the dirt, the same gaunt face, the same height, and slight build. "You're that gypsy, aren't you, the one who got sent down for thieving in the village? Why are you standing on my land? The house is up there if you wanted to deliver a message, not down here in this field."

LJ nodded. "Yes, I'm that gypsy as you call me, but to put the record straight, I didn't steal anything," he murmured, pointing down towards the expanse of land on the opposite side of the road. "That's where they died. That's where I last saw her and Sally, my little girl. I came back to talk to them for the final time. I wanted to sit with them for the last time, but they've gone – nothing left but a mud field. I've been down to the churchyard to see Jess. There's no gravestone for Sally, nothing other than a small cross to show that she ever existed. When did they level the site?" LJ asked, looking down the hill.

154

Peter lowered the gun cautiously. A germ of an idea took root in his head. "It was three, maybe four months ago. It was a nursery once, but you probably worked that one out for yourself with all those old greenhouses. A man called Keith Ingrams owns it – a big shot developer. Never met him. I only know what I read in the local papers. It's been like that ever since, awaiting full planning permission or some such thing. It was that run-down place that first gave me the idea of growing shrubs and trees up here – wholesale only. That's what I do, over there," he said, casting his eyes back towards the house and the greenhouses. "It's mostly ornamental stuff – acers, cordyline, palms, hydrangeas, rhododendrons, datura…"

"I saw your van loaded up with shrubs when I lived here. I guessed that your business had something to do with horticulture. It's satisfying to see things growing."

"It's a business. Nothing more, nothing less," Peter replied sharply.

"I worked with the team at Sudbury to build their entry for the Chelsea Flower Show, mainly on the hard landscaping, but when they were shorthanded, I helped tend the trees and shrubs as well. We won silver."

Peter raised his eyebrows with growing interest. "When did they let you out?"

"On the first of July."

"That's a month ago. Where have you been since then?"

"Making my way back to Bartonford. I got as far as Derby by train then something happened. I couldn't get on the next train. I walked the streets and slept with the homeless for the first couple of weeks, scavenged for food like the rest of them, begged, and took all the insults that were hurled at me. I hated the city and so I left and just started walking. A Traveller in his van stopped and offered me shelter – I was too tired and hungry to refuse."

"Once a gypsy always a gypsy, hey?" Peter laughed.

"I am a gypsy, a Roma, and proud of it." LJ lifted his chin.

155

"They were Travellers – Irish Travellers. And they were thieves – taking metal out of skips didn't bother me, but when it came to stealing drain covers, garden gates, and ornaments and even copper from church roofs, I refused to be part of it. They kicked me out of their camp. I've been on the road ever since." LJ looked down at himself in disgust. Dirty from head to foot, a rank odour emanated from his body.

"Why didn't you go and find your little gypsy band again?" Peter probed.

"It's been on my mind, but it could never be the same without Jess and Sally. My home and my life were in ashes. Maybe prison has changed me. I don't know. I've become used to having a roof over my head and a bed to lie in. Jacky told me to move on," LJ said wistfully. He missed Jacky more than he cared to admit. It was Jacky who had told him to look to the future. He hadn't written to him since he had left Sudbury. He couldn't bring himself to tell his friend that he had joined the ranks of the homeless and soon after became involved with a group of Travellers. He knew Jacky would be worried. "Jacky was my cellmate at Ranbury. We wrote regularly to each other when I was moved to Sudbury. I promised I would keep in touch. I must write to him. I'll not trouble you further. I'm sorry to have trespassed on your land," he added.

"You want a bed for the night and a wash?"

LJ's face lit up and he nodded cautiously. Faced by an angry man carrying a gun, the last thing he had expected was the offer of a bed for the night. More than anything he wanted to feel clean again.

"Pick up that bag and come and get cleaned up. There's food and a bed for you and work if you want it. If you like the work, then maybe we can figure something out. There's one condition, though. Whilst you're here you do not leave the premises. I don't need the village up in arms about me providing bed and breakfast to a gypsy – and especially you. And no thieving – I've got eyes out of the back of my head and a rifle as well, and I don't mind using it."

"I'm no thief," LJ repeated.

"I know that," Peter muttered under his breath. "Call me Peter," he said, and led the way back to the house.

LJ followed warily. There was nothing about Peter that he liked but he could not fault his generosity. Peter hung his jacket on a hook high up on the wall in the hall next to a red cagoule with the badge of the Royal Mail emblazoned on the front.

# Twenty-Three

Jacky looked forward to Jay's letters. It was January 2014. He had not received a letter from him for almost six months and he was worried. However short, they had arrived regularly each fortnight. They comprised little more than a few sentences, but he valued them, religiously marking the date of their arrival on his calendar. It was always gratifying to hear that the boy was fit and active. He remembered whooping out loud when Jay had written to tell him that he was involved in the HMP Sudbury Chelsea project. He stayed glued to the Chelsea Flower Show broadcast each evening for a week, and no one dared change the TV channel until he had seen the last of the credits roll. There were plenty of raised eyebrows amongst the inmates as Jacky praised the young gypsy as though he was his own son. He would have liked for Jay to have written more about himself – how he now felt about what had happened, whether it was getting any easier, whether he slept at night, and how he felt about his future, but he wrote little of a personal nature. Each letter always ended the same: 'I try not to think about them.'

Jacky tried not to think about them either, but the photograph of Jess and Sally that Jay had shown him was ingrained in his mind. They were the first faces he saw when he woke with the dawn, the same faces that hovered by his side by day, the last faces he saw before sleep enveloped him, and the only faces he saw in his dreams.

No one would ever know how much he wished that Jay had left the photograph behind, or that he had even considered stealing it from him. Jess would be forever on his conscience and thinking about Sally took him to the darkest of places.

Michael had been on his conscience as well. His son had done nothing to deserve the way he had been treated. He too had deserved a good education and a good start in life, but he had got neither from his father. Katie, his first daughter, was the only one of the three who had escaped unscathed. Her mother's daughter in manner and appearance, she had inherited the worst of both her mother's and father's genes. When His wife and Katie had packed their bags and left, Jacky had not missed them. Where they were now, he neither knew nor cared.

In his more sombre moments, Jacky listed everything he knew about Michael in his mind; it was a short list. There were far more questions than answers. Had he gone to school when he set out in the mornings? Had he been bright or intelligent? Had he been bullied at school? Had he dreams for his future? Had he friends? It mortified him to realise too late how selfish and uncaring he had been. He had used his son as a workhorse. Was it any wonder that the boy had been withdrawn throughout his childhood and his teenage years? Was it any wonder that his son had eventually turned on him so viciously?

He would take the memory of his last encounter with Michael to his grave – that fateful morning when he had attacked Jess for going with the gypsy, and Michael had taken a knife to him. It was the first time that he had ever seen real hate in a man's eyes – his own son's eyes. In that split second he had realised that he was no longer looking at a boy but a fully grown man with a will of his own.

The knife had missed his vital organs. The wound had been deep and left a scar on his chest, but it was nothing in comparison to the scar it had left in his heart. He had crawled from the kitchen to the phone and called an ambulance. He had plenty of time to think about it in the hospital. He had been too ashamed to admit that his own son had inflicted the wound; to this day, he had never shared the secret. The wound had healed; his heart did not.

The months had slipped by surprisingly fast. Jay had posted his last letter from HMP Sudbury on the thirtieth of June the previous year. He had sounded anxious and at the same time hopeful and had written to say that the first thing he planned to do was to revisit Bartonford and pay his respects to Jess and Sally. He had promised to stay in touch. He had promised to write with an address as soon as he reached his 'destination' as he had called it.

It was not long after Jay had left for Sudbury that Jacky made up his mind to do whatever it might take to get early release. He wanted out, by October at the latest. There were things that he needed to do, not least find out what had become of Jay. He would need some cash behind him. He would need to be a whole lot fitter. He would need to learn some basic skills. Packing goods for external contractors, he worked eight-hour shifts, seven days a week. After four months he had shed two stone in weight and for the first time in his life felt fit and healthy. The pay was inconsequential, but he saved every penny. Instead of slouching in front of the television in the evenings, he attended reading and writing courses. He no longer glanced at the headlines and the pictures in the newspaper but absorbed every word. He didn't believe in miracles, but he had every intention of walking out of prison a better man than when he had arrived.

Mentally, he set his mind on achieving three goals. First, to find Jay. Second, to find out if the fire had been an accident. Jay needed to know; there would be no closure until he did. Third, to build bridges with his son, Michael. For months and years he had dismissed the possibility of any sort of reconciliation with his son. And then a chance conversation with one of the prison wardens had given him reason to rethink. The warden's story had touched him deeply. His son had been killed instantly in a car crash. His one regret was that he had been robbed of the opportunity to tell his son how much he loved him. Michael was alive, somewhere; he, Jacky, had the chance.

It was now January and over six months since he had last heard from Jay. His heart sank at the prospect of not hearing from him or ever seeing him again. He had promised himself that the next time they came face to face he would tell him the truth about the past and beg to be forgiven. In quiet moments it crossed his mind that perhaps the relationship between the two of them had been more one-sided than he had thought and that Jay, having now started a new life, had left the past, including his old cellmate, behind.

It was when he least expected it that the name Fred Humphries popped up in his mind – the old man whom Jay was supposed to have robbed, the man whom Jay had spoken of as the only decent person in Bartonford, and who lived in a road called Pettifer Close. Why he remembered Jay telling him the man's name and even the name of the road was quite bizarre, but nonetheless he had, and it had stuck. Was it remotely possible that when Jay had returned to Bartonford he had taken time out to visit the old man? It was the sort of thing he would do – he would want to apologise in person, even if he had not been responsible for the theft. It was a long shot – an exceedingly long shot – but maybe the old man might lead him to Jay. And was it just possible that Jay might have spoken to the old man about Michael, and that he might know the whereabouts of his son? There was only one way he might find out.

Jacky sat with pen poised contemplating the beginning, the middle, and the end. If the letter ever reached Fred Humphries, then what reason would he have to read it? Who'd read a letter from an old con let alone bother to reply? Unless, of course, he told the old man the real reason that he needed to see Jay again.

It was the first letter he had ever written. Labouring day and night, he painstakingly penned the story.

*January 2014*

*Dear Mr Humphries,*

I am writing to you about a man called LJ Lovell. He shared a cell with me at HMP Ranbury. While he was here everybody simply called him Jay. That's what I called him and still do. He left Ranbury at the end of April and was transferred to Sudbury open prison from which he earned his release on the first of July. He always told me that he had not been responsible for the robbery at your house, and I have never had reason to disbelieve him.

He wrote to me fortnightly from Sudbury and then the letters stopped. The last letter I received from him was dated the thirtieth of June. He promised me he would write to me with an address, but I have heard nothing from him for over six months. I worry about him. Jay never breaks his promises. I fear that something may have happened to him. He told me in his last letter that he would be going back to Bartonford to pay his respects to his late wife, Jess, and Sally, his daughter. He always spoke of you with fondness and regret that you might think badly of him, and so it occurred to me that he would not return to Bartonford without trying to put the record straight with you.

Maybe he is with you now or you know where he is?

If he is with you or you know of his whereabouts, you may well be thinking that he is better off having nothing to do with a 'jailbird'. You would probably be right except for the fact that he is also family to me although he does not know it. It is a long story, but maybe if I give you the bare bones of it, you will understand why I am so anxious to contact him, and hopefully meet up with him again when I get my early release in October later this year.

Jay is my son-in-law. The lass he married was my daughter, Jess, and the little girl would have been my granddaughter. I could not bring myself to admit my relationship to him because of how I treated

162

*Jess as a child and in her teenage years. Jay knows about the father who took his fists to his daughter. I hit her often but never as badly as that time when I found out about her liaison with Jay – the gypsy, as I called him then. I took my belt to her. Her brother, Michael, rescued her from my clutches – stabbed me and then took off with Jess. Although I suspected it at the time, I learned only recently from Jay that Michael, my son, had taken her to the gypsy encampment. The rest is history as they say.*

*They say that a leopard never changes its spots, but I hope that I have. I have had many years to think about the evil I inflicted on Jess, and her brother to some extent, and to regret every single moment of it. I have looked long and hard in the mirror at my life and the consequences of what I did, and I would pay a king's ransom to take it all back.*

*I had a long time in hospital to think about my life and the dreadful way I had treated them so, when I was recovered, I tried to find both Jess and Michael. I guessed that they had left with the gypsy band. Naively I thought that I could put things right, but I never found them. In desperation, I took to the bottle, gambled away my business and my home, and eventually turned to stealing to buy more liquor. In the end, I was caught, charged, and sentenced to three years' imprisonment.*

*Jay and I became close in the few months we shared this prison cell and he told me about Jess and showed me a photograph of the granddaughter that I was never to see. It broke my heart. I never did tell him that I was Jess's father. I was too ashamed. Instead, I did everything I could to help Jay, and to get him moved to an open prison. I have promised myself that if ever he and I meet again I will tell him the full story and hope that he will find it in his heart to forgive me. Otherwise, I will walk away and leave him in peace. That is why I need to know where he is and see him again.*

*I know that my son, Michael, is probably lost to me. I have never forgotten the look in his eyes when he took that knife to me and I have long since forgiven him for his actions. If the tables had been turned, I would have done the same. I would dearly love to meet up with him just the once to beg his forgiveness. I fear it will never happen.*

*Jay told me before he left Ranbury that he had doubts that the fire that killed Jess and Sally was accidental and that worries me. He told me that Jess would never have lit that wood stove. So, either somebody else did or it was never lit in the first place. I have made a promise to myself that if there is a vestige of truth in Jay's doubts, then I will get to the bottom of it.*

*I have just under another nine months to serve before I can even start to try to rectify all the wrongs that I have listed in this letter.*

*If you have heard from Jay or seen him or know of his whereabouts, I beg you to write to me at HMP Ranbury and let me know.*

*Yours very sincerely*
*Jacky Walmsley*
*HMP Ranbury*
*Retford Nottingham DN22 8EU*

# Twenty-Four

She was feeling her age. Now in her seventieth year, Wanda still had not been able to shed herself of her Bartonford Parish Council responsibilities. Neither cajoling, pleading nor extolling the virtues of the role had worked; no one in the village wanted to do it. It wasn't so much the paperwork, the liaison with the District Council, the monthly newsletters, or the monthly Parish Council meetings that she couldn't handle, it was the petty squabbling in the village that exhausted her. Whenever there was an issue, the cry 'Talk to Wanda' went up, and she was tired of it. It was getting worse, not better. The village seemed to have divided into two factions, those who wanted everything to remain the same as it had been for centuries and those who wanted change, or as they liked to call it, progress. Once she had been firmly rooted in the camp that wanted everything to stay the same, but now she wasn't so sure.

There had been a time, and not so long ago, when the village had been a real community, and everyone had been happy to make their contribution to village life, but now it was an uphill slog. No one volunteered for anything. It was now February and for the second year running, the once popular Valentine's Day dinner and dance had been cancelled for lack of interest.

It didn't help either that the age profile in the village was increasing year on year – before long the pavements would be crowded with mobility scooters. At one time there had been a reasonable turnover in properties and younger people had come to live in the village, but since the incident with the gypsies, it seemed that nobody, especially the younger brigade, wanted to live in Bartonford, let alone buy a property there. Those few houses that did sell fetched prices way below their market value.

She often wondered how different things might have been had the gypsies not arrived; the local and county press had had a field day. It had been far worse after the fire. It was never written but the implication was always there – the residents could not be absolved from some measure of responsibility.

It was just over a year since that fateful meeting in the village hall. She had learned to live with her conscience. She had done only what was expected of her as chair of the Parish Council; she had not over-reacted. Who could have foreseen the chain of events that followed? With hindsight she could see that they had won the battle, but, sadly, lost the war.

Wanda looked out of her kitchen window at the bleak grey skies of a cold February day. The rain was sheeting sideways, and the wind rocked the trees. It was a lonely existence; once they had all looked out for each other, but those days now seemed a figment of her imagination from the dim and distant past. In the past few weeks, her life had changed beyond recognition. It had started with a flurry of unwelcome visitors.

She had not slept for days. Night after night she lay awake listening to small feet scurrying around the house. It was something that she could never admit to the neighbours; she had rats. She had done everything she could think of to deter them: cleaned the cottage from top to bottom; emptied the larder and the fridge of food; emptied the food waste into tightly sealed bags and deposited the whole lot into the wheelie bin, and finally taped all bins closed with gaffer tape. There was not a crumb left in the house; both she and Mollie, her cat, had gone hungry. But still, they came.

She had driven thirty miles to buy rat poison in bulk. If she had shopped closer to home, word would have been around the village in no time. Passing a cattery on the way, she booked Mollie in for an open-ended stay.

She placed small boxes of rat poison in every cupboard in the house. She read the instructions on the box and decided to ignore most of them. The rat poison disappeared overnight. Her jubilation was short-lived. The following day she woke once more to the scurry of small feet. In the darkening shadows of the afternoon, she picked up the telephone and rang for help.

They arrived the following morning and lined up outside her house, not one van but three, each emblazoned with the name 'Rats Out'; no one could mistake their purpose. Despite their promise that their visit would be discrete, it was not.

She watched as they took the kitchen cupboards apart and the floorboards up. All possible entry and exit routes had to be found, examined, and dealt with. All dead and dying creatures had to be found and removed. At the end of two weeks, most of her savings had gone but at least she heard no more scurrying feet.

With everything finally back to normal, Wanda picked Mollie up from the cattery, baked fresh scones, and cake, and picked up the telephone to invite her small circle of friends to afternoon tea. Strangely they had full diaries; none of them could, or would, make time to visit her.

Finally, she accepted the truth. Nobody wanted to come calling on her. Rats gathered where there was dirt and Wanda had been caught napping on the job.

Drying her eyes, she put the scones and the cake into tightly sealed tins and put the empty milk bottle out on the doorstep. In the failing light of the day, she failed to notice the tiny posy of white heather that lay on the doorstep.

# Twenty-Five

"We're closed, can't you read?" Fred shouted, as he put the last of the morning's delivery of milk into the fridge. Cartons with a sell-by date of thirteenth February at the front, cartons with later sell-by dates at the back, he reminded himself. It was more than his life was worth to get it wrong. The village shop committee would have his guts for garters.

"It's one minute to nine, Fred. Don't be such a miserable old sod. Open the shop. I haven't got all day – I need milk and bread for the kids' breakfast."

He knew that voice. It was none other than Council Mouth Chrissy. They were all made from the same mould and a law unto themselves especially when it came to expecting the shop to be open all hours.

"You can bloody well wait a minute," Fred muttered under his breath, stretching out his arm to grab hold of one of the shelves to heave himself back up on his feet before shuffling toward the door. "We're open now," he said, turning the key in the lock and flipping the Closed sign over to Open.

"It's freezing me bits off out here, Fred. Who's taking over from you this morning?" Chrissy asked, bouncing in through the door.

"No one. You've all got to put up with me for the next two hours. I've better things to do, make no mistake. Maybe you're not aware that half the volunteers have dropped out. Are you offering to stand in? It's Wanda's shift, but she's gone ratty. Get it? Ratty?" Fred chortled.

"You'll cut yourself with that tongue one of these days, Fred," Chrissy laughed, nudging Fred in the ribs before he had time to step back. They'd all had a good laugh about the Pied Piper.

Fred looked up as the bell sounded to announce yet another unwanted customer, and it was only one minute past nine. Why on God's earth couldn't all these people either stay in bed or go to church? Of all the people that he could have done without seeing on a Sunday morning, it was Mrs La-Di-Da Franklin – or Ursula, as she preferred to be called.

"Good morning, Frederick. I've just popped in for my *Telegraph* and *Times* and then I'm going to make a nice cup of coffee and spend the rest of the morning checking out what's happening in the world, and more important still what's happening in the social circles. I can honestly say that there has never been a Sunday when one or more of my old school chums hasn't been mentioned by one of the columnists," Ursula said, picking up her papers from the shelves. "It's all voucher payments – no cash for you today, Frederick."

"Hi, Urs." Bread and milk in hand, Chrissy stood by the counter jangling coins in her hand. "You'll never guess what, Urs? Guess who I had an email from this morning? Go on, guess."

"I'm not into guessing games, Chrissy, and I have the feeling that you are going to tell me anyway."

"It's that Miriam, that's who," Chrissy continued. "Listen to this. She's moving to the Algarve permanent like. Selling the cottage. Not coming back. Would you credit it?"

"And why should I be surprised by that?" Ursula said.

"Well, she said that she was going out there for three months. I got the impression she wasn't that keen on the place. Never thought she'd stay there."

"It belonged to her parents. The family used to go there several times a year. Then she stopped going with them. Something happened a long time ago, but I never did get to the bottom of it. Miriam didn't go there again. So, it is rather surprising that she has decided to make it her home."

"She hasn't written to me for over a year now and it's me who does for her and makes sure that that cottage of hers is looked after. I know what you're about to say – she does pay me to do it, but it's not enough, you know. Twenty quid a month wouldn't keep a sparrow in birdseed. Here, you can read the email for yourself." Chrissy held out her phone to Ursula. "Read the last bit, Urs," Chrissy said, pointing to the last paragraph. "Sounds like she's been spending a lot of money on the place. She's got a couple of outbuildings as she calls them on her property, and she's converting them into holiday lets. And she's building a swimming pool. Going to advertise it online, she is. She must be getting a bit short of a bob or two by now – I don't think her old mum and dad left her that much cash."

"Well, I wish her well," Ursula said, "and a great deal of luck in selling that cottage. It won't be easy. No time for gossip. My coffee awaits. Good day, Frederick, and I hope that you will treat the rest of your customers with a little more respect. A good morning or even good day never goes amiss."

Fred stuck out his tongue as the door closed behind her. "You forgotten that you've got hungry kids back at home waiting for their breakfast?" Fred said and held out his hand for the money. "Good day to you, Chrissy."

"Miriam, strange woman," Fred muttered to himself. "Good for her." He hadn't forgotten that Miriam was the only other person who had stood up for the gypsies at that village meeting. She was alright, was Miriam.

Fred put the closed sign up and made himself a cup of coffee.

# Twenty-Six

Michael was determined to succeed. Every day was an uphill struggle but every day that passed carried him one step nearer to achieving his goal. There were those who had told him that he would never do it. Others encouraged him and said that there was nothing he couldn't achieve if he set his mind to it. In his early years, he had hidden his light under a bushel. He had battled with his homework by torchlight and it had paid dividends. He had never told his father or mother that he had achieved eight GCSEs with five A and three B grades – the highest achiever of his year. On the last day of term, he had packed his books and walked out of the school gates. He had returned once and that had been to collect his GCSE certificate. He would have liked to stay on – take his A levels – but there was Jess to think about. It was he who had put her in hospital, and it would be he who would look after her and keep her safe for as long as need be.

Since parting from Byron and the family, he had spent five months cramming for the A levels he needed to get a place at university. Few had ever achieved such success in such a short space of time. Few were as determined and focused as Michael; Birmingham University accepted his application unconditionally.

Tired after sitting through lectures from nine until five, worn out after serving pizza to ill-mannered morons from six to eleven in the evening, he wanted nothing more than to drop on the bed, close his eyes and go to sleep, but that was a luxury he never allowed himself. He had study to do and a paper to turn in at the university the following day.

It was past midnight when he picked up the letter and other circulars from the small stand in the communal entrance to the flats. Discarding the junk mail, Michael turned his attention to the one handwritten envelope. Immediately he recognised the spidery but legible handwriting as that of Fred Humphries who had taken to dropping him short notes from time to time. Inside the envelope a pink Post-it was attached to a handwritten letter:

> *By good fortune (or not, as you may say when you have read it), this letter found its way to me back in January. I have sat on it for weeks undecided whether to send it on to you. It contains information regarding LJ which is of concern to both of us. Pour yourself a stiff drink and read it for yourself, and then let me know what you think. Ring me. Best, Fred.*

Michael pulled the Post-it away and glanced at the signature at the end of the letter. An icy shiver ran down his spine and his hands shook as he dropped the letter onto his desk. It was the very last person that he had ever expected to hear from. If anybody had told him that he was being evicted from the tiny flat that he rented, he would not have understood but would have taken it in his stride and found somewhere else to live. If anybody had told him that he would never come up to the mark and achieve the law degree that he had set his heart on, he would have been distraught but taken it in his stride and considered the alternatives. If anybody had told him that he was being given the sack by the pizza parlour where he worked five hours every evening and ten hours most Saturdays and Sundays, he would have taken it in his stride, probably rejoiced, and found another job. This was something altogether different.

It was nothing short of mind-blowing. Michael reached out and grabbed the bottle of Jameson whiskey that had sat unopened on the shelf from the day he had been given it. It was covered in dust. Normally he never touched the stuff. He had watched his father drink himself into oblivion and turn into a monster too many times to go down the same road. Fred was correct in writing that he would need a stiff drink; Michael reached for a mug, poured a large slug of the whiskey, and started reading.

So, the old bastard was alive. He didn't know whether to laugh or cry. All those years of believing that he had killed his father, all those years of looking over his shoulder expecting to be arrested at any moment, and all those years of crucifying himself on the fear that one day, when he least expected it, his past would catch up with him. He wished him dead; he wished him alive. He deserved to have died that day. On the bright side, if there was one, the man had lived to tell the tale which meant that the one obstacle that might have prevented him from taking the bar had been removed.

The letter had been written from HMP Ranbury. Michael read quickly to the end of the letter. His father claimed to be repentant. Finally, too late, he was admitting the beast he had been. That he and LJ had shared a cell at Ranbury was the ultimate irony.

How could he believe a word the man wrote? A man who had lied, cheated, physically and mentally abused his children, a man who had never had a kind word to say to a living soul, a man who knew nothing about love, empathy, kindness, respect or consideration for others, a man who didn't have a decent bone in his body? And, reading between the lines, the man even had the audacity to think that he and LJ might exonerate him from his sins.

Briefly, he wondered what his father would think if he knew that his only son was reading his letter. What was his game?

Michael emptied the tumbler of whiskey and poured himself a second. It burned his throat and burned his stomach. He made a mental note to throw what was left of the bottle down the sink. If there was one thing that the man had got right it was that his son was lost to him forever – not probably, but certainly.

Memories from his childhood tumbled one over another as if they could not escape fast enough from that place deep inside where they had lain buried for so many years: the endless evenings he had undressed himself, laid his clothes carefully on the small chair beside his bed, picked up a cushion, climbed under the blanket, placed the cushion under the blanket, and then pulled the blanket back over his body – the cushion that had protected him from his father's cruel fingers; the hours, days, weeks, months and years he had been imprisoned in that playpen, made to 'hang on' for hours on end, hoping that his mother would notice his predicament before his father smelt the urine, and left red welts on his arms and legs; the long, lonely days at school when he had been bullied and singled out as a weirdo simply because he didn't know how to play; the long, hard days when he toiled out in the fields digging, sowing, picking, without ever a word of thanks, and last but never forgotten, his father's cruelty towards his sister, a young girl unable to protect herself. Somehow both of them had survived their childhood, but it had left indelible scars on both of them.

Michael sat back and took a deep breath; he hated the man with every bone of his body. There were two things, however, and two things only that were of any interest to him in the letter. First, that LJ had promised to write to his father regularly but had not done so for the past seven months. On account that he, Michael, had never once known LJ to break a promise, that was of concern, how serious he was not sure. Second, that LJ seemingly shared his own belief that Jess's death was not accidental, at least not as the result of a spark from a wood-burning fire.

It was over a year since he had watched LJ taken down after the trial, and Michael's conscience troubled him. The closest thing to a brother he had ever had, he had set his priorities firmly on his studies and let their friendship drift. LJ had seemingly disappeared off the face of the earth; it was not like him unless, of course, he had caught up with Byron and the family. It was past time that he found out. Michael tore the letter into shreds, dropped them in the wastepaper basket and checked his diary.

# Twenty-Seven

The months had flown by. It was March, almost eight months since LJ had first stepped foot on Cold Comfort land.

He was grateful to Peter. How could he not be? The man had given him food and shelter and even work. He hardly recognised himself – he had new clothes, warm cords, shirts and sweatshirts, and boots and gloves for working outdoors. He had casual clothes into which he was expected to change before sitting down for the evening meal. He slept soundly at night in a comfortable bed and had put on weight.

It was a comfortable house that belied its name of Cold Comfort Farm. It had a woman's touch to it. The sitting room was cosy, a fire burned in the inglenook fireplace, shiny brasses either side. Pictures of hunting scenes adorned the walls and complemented the almost threadbare red-and-brown carpet. Two chintzy armchairs were arranged either side of the fireplace. The kitchen was simple but equally welcoming. A scrubbed pine dresser bedecked with willow china stood opposite the back door with a scrubbed pine table taking the lion's share of the space. The shared bathroom was basic but functional and his bedroom huge in comparison to the cramped space of the vardo and the prison cells he had occupied. There was no TV or radio in the house; LJ missed neither – they had never been part of his life.

He could find no fault with his employer's generosity. Although he received no wages, he was never hungry or cold. Peter was a patient and helpful teacher and not a day passed when he had not learned something new which would stand him in good stead for the future. LJ enjoyed the peace afforded by the nursery and the opportunity to nurture the shrubs and trees and watch them grow. Deep down in his heart, he still harboured the thought that one day he might work as a nurseryman on a large estate, and eventually have a small business of his own, but something told him that these were not words that Peter would want to hear. He would need to pick his moment.

Each day had its own routine. Out in the fields and glasshouses from seven until six, a half-hour break for lunch, supper on their return. After supper, Peter retreated to his study to write his journal and complete the day's paperwork. When he returned to the sitting room, they sat in companionable silence and read. Each fortnight LJ wrote a short letter to Jacky in Ranbury and Peter posted it for him. In his letters he described his luck at having a roof over his head and a job. In his letters he voiced his reservations about the man whose house he shared.

There were few house rules as such. He was welcome to go where he liked in the house except for the study which was for Peter's sole use, and Peter's bedroom. He was welcome to roam the estate, but he was not to step foot on a small area of land that had been fenced off to the rear of the house. This, so Peter told him, was contaminated land. The contamination had been cleared when he had bought the property, but it would be five to ten years before the land would be entirely risk-free. Neither was he to enter the small greenhouse down past the copse; the one with the brown sliding door. That was Peter's domain where he experimented with crosspollinating shrubs and saplings. None of those rules bothered him, but the rule that he was not allowed to leave the confines of Cold Comfort did. More than anything he would have liked to visit Jess in the churchyard and saw no good reason why he should not be allowed to do so. He also wanted to visit Fred Humphries to explain in person that he had not been responsible for the theft. Peter denied him both visits. Peter's arguments that he might be recognised, LJ found fatuous. Arguing that his appearance was so changed that nobody would recognise him, cut no cloth with his employer. Callously, Peter had said that Jess was going nowhere, and neither was Fred Humphries; he had passed on several months ago. "Then I'll go and visit both of them in the churchyard. You can't stop me, Peter," he had said, "I'm a free man." In that moment LJ had been tempted to pack his bags and leave once and for all.

That evening, glassy-eyed, Peter had apologised for his words and had asked him to wait a while longer before venturing down to the village. Peter was concerned for his safety. Peter needed him at Cold Comfort. With a misguided sense of loyalty, LJ had acquiesced to Peter's wish.

There were times when LJ felt as though he knew Peter well, and other times when he wondered if he knew the man at all. For a man, competent in seemingly everything and comfortable in his own skin there remained an aura of mystery around him. It was something that LJ could not put his finger on. Right from the outset Peter had encouraged him to talk about his family, had professed deep interest in the ways of the Roma, and listened patiently as he answered his questions. At times LJ wondered if his friend's interest in the family and the Roma was not an unhealthy interest, particularly for a man who had made his opinion about gypsies abundantly clear the moment he had first stepped foot on Cold Comfort land. Always the conversation ended with the same question, "And are you thinking about going back to them?" His answer to Peter was always an emphatic 'no'; it was the right answer.

Peter encouraged him to read and selected books out of the bookcase for him. At first, he had welcomed Peter's selections and enjoyed the novels of crime fiction writers like Ruth Rendell and Jeffrey Archer. It was some weeks later that Peter had offered him a different author; the story had given him nightmares.

One evening, quite unexpectedly and completely out of character, Peter had asked him to fetch a book for him from his study. Flattered that for the first time he was being allowed to enter the hallowed ground, he had been happy to do so. The book was called *The Angel of Death* by Holly Cefrey; he would find it on the top shelf of the bookcase. In the study, LJ's eyes traversed the spines of Peter's book collection seeking out the title he had been asked to find. Pulling it out, he glanced at the cover and flicked through the contents; it was gruesome. The books lined up either side of it were even more gruesome: *The Nazi Doctors* by Robert Jay Lifton; *Children of the Flames: The Untold Story of the Twins of Auschwitz* by Lucette Matalon Lagnado; *Mengele – The Complete Story* by Gerald L Posner and John Ware; *Doctors from Hell* by Vivien Spitz; *Echoes from Auschwitz* by Eva and Miriam Mozes, and last but not least a book entitled *The Roma and the Holocaust of World War II Victims, Then and Now* by Julia Hajdu.

Drawn like a magnet to the book entitled *The Roma and the Holocaust of World War II, Then and Now*, LJ pulled it out and quickly flipped through it – horrific images filled page after page and made his blood run cold. He recalled small snatches of conversation between his father and his uncles about the plight of some of their relatives during the Second World War when, fleeing Hungary, they had been captured by the Nazis and sent to concentration camps, treated as badly if not worse than the Jews, and eventually accompanied them to the gas chambers. Replacing the book where he had found it, he returned to the sitting room and put *The Angel of Death* down on the coffee table beside Peter. Peter smiled and nodded his thanks.

That night LJ lay awake until the early hours wondering why any sane human being would fill his library with such filth. That night he decided it was time to start making fresh plans for his future. He would not rush into any decision. While he was getting free board and lodging and learning his skill, he would bide his time while watching his back.

# Twenty-Eight

"Did you see that?" Chrissy shouted, her nose pressed hard to the glass in the shop door.

"What?" Wanda asked absentmindedly, wiping a cloth over the counter for the hundredth time that morning.

"That Oswald Billericay – out there taking pictures," Chrissy said. "He's squatting down with that phone of his and pointing it straight at my Poppy. What's he up to? Always did think there was something odd about that man. Do you think he's entering a competition or something? You'd think he'd got enough dogs of his own without singling out my Poppy. I know she's a good looker, but she ain't going to win no competitions."

"Really, dear, it's a free world you know," Wanda said with total disinterest. It was of no consequence to her whatsoever whether Oswald took pictures of Chrissy's black-and-white mongrel or of naked women. She couldn't care less anymore. Once upon a time, she would have wanted to know the answer, but now she simply wasn't interested. Life hadn't been the same since the visitation by her small furry friends. It had been a steep learning curve; she had soon found out who her real friends were. Those ladies whom she had thought of as her best friends were now no more than distant acquaintances and often passed her in the street without so much as a by-your-leave. Her only social contact in the village came from the

181

few hours that she spent behind the village shop counter, and even then, she could see it in their eyes – Wanda and the Pied Piper, the Pied Piper and Wanda. She would never live it down; they wouldn't let her live it down.

"What's your game?" Chrissy flung open the door and shouted at Oswald. "Haven't you got enough dogs of your own?"

Oswald's head shot up at the ear-piercing screech that came from nowhere. Perched precariously on his haunches, his whole being focused on the mongrel that was eyeing him suspiciously, the woman had taken him by surprise. Water flew up into the air as his foot caught the dog's drinking bowl which in turn somersaulted in the air and proceeded to drown him from head to foot. The mongrel grinned. Oswald eyeballed the dog with hatred. He had seen those eyes before; he was sure of it.

"Plenty," Oswald snarled, rummaging around for his hand-kerchief before wiping off his glasses. "All pedigrees, the lot of them. Never bloody mongrels like this one."

"Not what I heard," Chrissy said.

"Then you heard wrong, and it's time you learned to mind your own business before somebody does it for you." How could he explain to her that he was on a quest – a quest to establish the identity of the culprit? That someone in the village was responsible for his current circumstances was to his mind beyond any shadow of a doubt, and that person was going to be made to pay for it.

"No one calls my Poppy a bloody mongrel and that includes you Mr High and Mighty Oswald Billericay. I'll have you know that she is very sensitive and very particular about who she allows to take her photograph."

"She?" Oswald's head shot up. "You said that mongrel's a she?"

"Well, she could be LGBT, but we haven't had that conversation recently. We're just waiting until she's a bit older when she knows her own mind before we ask her," Chrissy replied, keeping a straight face. "Of course, Poppy's a she, you silly old duffer. Do you want me to upend her so that you can see for yourself? What's it to you anyway?"

Oswald reddened. In his quest to find the offending mongrel he had momentarily overlooked the obvious. "A case of mistaken identity, that's all," he replied, hastily stowing his phone back in his pocket and hoisting himself to his feet. "They'll not get away with it," he muttered as he went on his way.

"Another one who's lost the plot, if I'm not much mistaken," Chrissy said, returning to the shop. "This village is full of them these days."

"Is there anything else I can get you?" Wanda asked pointedly. She might have to serve this woman in the shop, but she didn't have to put up with being insulted as well.

Oswald took off his wet clothes and sat in his underpants and vest, swinging first right and then left in his office chair, his eyes scanning the rogues' gallery that he had pinned up on his office wall. There were twenty photographs so far – all of which he believed to be male; twenty black-and-white mongrels which, other than size and shape, looked almost identical – those same 'come love me' deep brown eyes, those same floppy ears, those same shiny coats, those same droopy tails, and those same wet noses. One of them was the culprit, but which one?

All around silence reigned. Even Tsar, his champion Afghan, had decided that discretion was the better part of valour and refrained from waking the neighbourhood with his constant baying for attention. Neither had he heard a peep from Madame Pompadour, the cocky, standoffish little Cavapoo which had finally accepted that she was, quite literally, in the doghouse.

How had it come to this, he thought? Oswaldian Towers, the finest canine breeding institution in the country, established over thirty years ago, and the most luxurious of boarding kennels affordable by only the richest in the land, silenced. Oswald's eyes glazed over as he looked across the yard at the unoccupied five-star luxury doggie hotel that had cost him his every last penny to build and upon which his reputation had been founded. No luxury had been spared. It was the height of luxury, the place to board the family pet whilst their owners took off on their yachts or popped over to Nevis for a cocktail. Fickle, that's what they were – every single one of his clients. The Kennel Club had a lot to answer for. He had tried to explain that none of it was his fault, that he had taken every possible precaution to prevent anything like this from happening, but would they listen? No they would not. Overnight he had been blackballed. Innocent or guilty, it didn't matter; the word was out. The owners had formed a queue at the imposing gates to Oswaldian Towers, and one by one had removed their precious dogs from his care and refused to pay their bills. Within hours the office phone that in the past had never stopped ringing, fell silent. The staff walked out in disgust after he had accused them one by one of sabotaging his business.

And now Petunia, his wife, was busy packing her bags, her flight ticket to Geneva sitting on the dressing table. She was leaving for an extended visit to see her brother, or so she said. She would return when he had sorted out the mess. He wasn't that bothered one way or the other He could well do without Petunia on his case from morning until night.

How had the Tsar managed to leave it too late? How could the Tsar, his pride and joy and the best sire he had ever had, stand back and let another dog, and a mongrel and that, clear his pitch? The visiting Tsarina, a prize bitch had got pregnant alright, and much backslapping there had been when the news was relayed to her owners. It was not until two months later when the Tsarina's proud owners had travelled three hundred miles to watch their precious give birth to her prize-winning puppies that the truth came out.

The Tsarina, who had been boarded at Oswaldian Towers for the full period of her confinement, dropped her puppies at the precise moment and on the precise date that he had predicted.

At one pm the first of the puppies was born into the world, a long-haired, long-legged, black-and-white puppy with deep brown eyes and floppy ears. It bore as much resemblance to an Afghan hound as a thoroughbred Arabian stallion to a donkey. There followed seven more of the same, one by one finding their way to the Tsarina's regal teats. Dismay and disbelief gave way to anger and threats from her owners as the puppies one by one blindly cosied up to their mother. It had cost him, both his reputation and his pocket.

How in God's name had it happened? The three-acre paddock was securely fenced and each day he made it his business to walk the boundary looking for signs of holes that the dogs might have dug around the perimeter. Those he found were filled immediately. Bitches on heat were carefully segregated from other dogs. He knew his business. He took no chances, so how in hell…? If the gypsies hadn't moved on, then he would have known instantly where to find the culprit.

It might not have been the end of the world except for Madam Pompadour, the Cavapoo bitch. She was perfect; she was a money maker, but she was also a tart. The more he thought about it, the more convinced he was about it. She just couldn't wait. Just one more day and her sire would have given her what she wanted, but no, she chose to make it with a mongrel, and if he were right, the very same mongrel that had sired the Tsarina. Madame Pompadour's three puppies bore no resemblance to either a Cavalier King Charles spaniel or to a poodle.

And for the past five weeks, to add insult to injury, his wife, Petunia, had taken it into her head to take the Tsarina and Madame Pompadour and all their puppies under her wing and bring the whole damned caboodle into their house until the puppies had been fully weaned – all eleven of them.

Personally, he would have liked to drown the whole lot of them. Much as he loved dogs, he hated those mongrel pups, each of which revelled in following him around the house nipping at his feet and trousers and tripping him up at every conceivable opportunity. He had put up with it for seven whole days after which he moved out of the house and into one of the five-star luxury doggy suites in the barn.

No longer could he look at the Tsar or at Madame Pompadour without wishing to wring both of their necks, and it was a blessed relief when he found new homes for both of them. The puppies weaned, the Tsarina had been sent home in disgrace. Petunia worked tirelessly and found homes for all eleven puppies.

Unshaven and dishevelled and dressed in his vest and pants, Oswald peered out from his five-star luxury doggy suite to see his wife's suitcases being loaded into the boot of a car. Picking up a small bunch of white heather that had blown in on the breeze, he put it in the bin without a second thought.

# Twenty-Nine

Feet up on his desk, legs crossed, Peter reached for his journal. Devoid of entries up until the thirtieth of August 2013, each following page was a record of daily events and his own observations. He smiled as he read the very first entry, the day the journey had begun:

*13th August 2013*

*This was a momentous day. Today a gypsy arrived unannounced at Cold Comfort Farm – the young gypsy who, on the same day almost eight months ago, received a six-month sentence for theft and carelessly lost his wife and child as a result of a fire. He had returned to Bartonford, so he told me, to pay his respects to both – how very commendable.*

*He will make a perfect specimen for my work – pure Roma, young, fit, vulnerable and, I believe, infinitely malleable. My end objective is to eradicate his gypsy genes one by one and thus transform him from the despicable gypsy that he is into a man. To do so this, I shall need to establish those elements of his genes that are present in the male gypsy species. I shall have to get into his mind and under his skin and examine his past life in detail. My friend and mentor, Mengele, experimented on their bodies, I shall work on the mind.*

187

Flipping the pages, one by one, he paused at several entries:

*2nd September 2013*

*Several days ago, we talked at length about Roma culture. I learned about 'women's work' and understood from what he said that men would not demean themselves to do it. The following day I assigned him his daily household duties including washing the dishes three times a day, emptying bins, sweeping and cleaning the kitchen floor and organising and managing the washing – all of which I knew to be women's work in his previous life. Initially he recoiled from my directive. I did not back down. Grudgingly he did as I asked and has continued to do so each day without my intervention. The quality of his work does not matter. If his aversion to women's work was in his genes, it is no longer.*

*3rd October 2013*

*When I question him or challenge him, he has a propensity to commence his sentences with: "Jess would have…" no matter the subject of discussion. This I have referred to several times earlier in the journal. Today I asked him what we should do about the browning of the leaves on two of the cordylines; a form of fluoride toxicity, I happen to know. "Burn the two plants, discard the soil and sterilise the pots," he said. That he proffered the correct answer was highly commendable but of more interest to me was that for the first time there was no mention of Jess or anybody else. I believe that this might be a turning point; he is thinking for himself. I believe that it may be in his genes to seek reassurance from others, and that he may have an inferiority complex which comes as no surprise. I shall work on building his confidence.*

*12th October 2013*

*I know what he has been looking for since he arrived; he will not find it. It may have escaped my eagle eye, but I do believe that he has given up the pursuit for the photograph. This is a clear indicator that they are assuming less importance in his life. Family is perhaps of less importance to a gypsy than I had believed.*

*4th November 2013*

*Today the gypsy asked me for dispensation to leave the confines of Cold Comfort Farm to visit his wife's grave and his friend, Fred Humphries, in the village. Naturally I declined his wish. He was distraught when I told him that the man had died not long after he had started his prison sentence. It surprised me that he should be so upset about it. I told him that I needed him right here. Little did he know how much I need him. He is also trusting of my word.*

*21st November 2013*

*It is a well-known fact that gypsies are violent by nature – it is in their genes. I know this to my cost. So far, he has exhibited no form of violence, but I always felt sure that it was lurking beneath the surface. I decided that I must find a way to test the presence of this gene and also its extremity. Fortunately, the gypsy is reasonably well educated – he can read fairly competently and writes after a fashion – indeed, he writes fortnightly to his old cellmate, Jacky. A week ago, I loaned him one of my favourite crime-thriller novels to read. The characters in the book are sadists; the chapters are packed with scenes of extreme brutality. I insisted that he read it from cover to cover. Over the week I observed his reactions to the story. I witnessed the pain on his face and watched him retch as the story unfolded. I offered to find him a similar novel to read today; he declined. He may have the gene in him, but it is weak and does not require me to work on it.*

*25th December 2013*

*After a pleasant but simple lunch today, I ventured to ask him if he was enjoying his 'new life' at Cold Comfort Farm. He answered in the affirmative. I further ventured to ask him if he had thought about returning to his family and his old way of life. "No," he said, but he averted his eyes from mine as he spoke. Gypsies are inherently dishonest. I will need to work on this area.*

*7th February 2014*

*Yesterday I had good reason to confine the gypsy to the house. He broke house rules – I cannot let such acts of defiance pass without punishment. For two days now he has not left the house – I locked the doors, front and back, each time I left the house and pocketed the key. It was an excellent opportunity for me to observe how he reacts to loss of open space and the outdoors. No gypsy that I have ever come across likes to be confined for lengthy periods of time. He was anxious and fractious at first, pacing the floor. This evening when I returned from the fields, he was quite calm and collected. If the outdoors is in his genes, then I believe that gene can be modified.*

*4th March 2014*

*This evening I asked him to bring me a book from the library in my study. The book I selected was called Dr Josef Mengele – The Angel of Death. I placed several bookmarks in it in the sure knowledge that he would not be able to resist opening the book to those pages. When he brought me the book, the bookmarks had been displaced. He will have seen pictures depicting the experiments that Mengele carried out on the Jews; he will have read the headlines that when Mengele ran out of Jews, he used Roma. I noticed that LJ had also thumbed through that most excellent book, The Roma and the Holocaust of World War II, Then and Now. My aim was to establish the presence of the gene related to loyalty. I observed no adverse reaction from him. I had expected it to be strong. Perhaps loyalty is of less importance to gypsies than I had assumed. It would be vain of me to believe at this early stage that he had switched his allegiance from the Roma to me.*

Peter closed the journal and leaned back in his chair. In deep thought, he reviewed the progress he had so far made. It was still inconclusive but without doubt LJ was showing far fewer gypsy traits than he had when he had first arrived. Time was on his side; an experiment of this nature could never be hurried. For the time being he would watch and wait.

# Thirty

It was a balmy summer evening. Fred stretched his legs out in front of him and ran his hand over the smooth, silky wood of the bench, the very same bench where he and LJ had sat and put the world to rights. Barny lay sprawled across his feet in the June evening sun. Gently he nudged him aside and wiggled his toes to get the circulation going again. But overall, he wasn't doing badly for an eighty-one-, going on eighty-two-year-old. Where had eighty-one years gone? One moment you were the school prankster, forever in trouble, and the next you were leaning on a stick, and doing your best to keep everything ticking over. Fred chuckled to himself. What he had got up to in his boyhood was nobody's business. There had been no one more imaginative or devious than he when it came to playing pranks on teachers and schoolmates. If they needed to be taken down a peg or two, then he was the one to do it, and he had rarely been caught. And neither had he lost his touch. Fred grinned to himself, closed his eyes, and drifted off.

Waking with a start, Fred slapped his hands over his ears. "What is it Barny? You make enough noise to wake the dead, do you know that?" Barny was the latest addition to the family, a mongrel, and a stray, as mischievous as his owner. Barny barked again. "I'm not deaf you know, Barny. I know it's the bloody phone ringing. Just takes me a bit longer to work it out than you. I'm on it, alright?"

"Hello," he said. His face lit up as he recognised the voice at the other end of the line. "I wondered when you might ring. How many months is it since I wrote to you? Going on four, if I remember rightly. I was beginning to think that you'd fallen off the end of the earth, Michael. What've you been doing all this time?"

"Working, Fred."

"How's the course going?"

"Hard work but good. They told me the two-year course would be intensive; that was the understatement of the year. Nearing the end of year one. My tutors say the LLB is in the bag if I keep it up. Done a bit of work experience as well – that paid off. The firm even asked me to think about joining then when I qualify. It's uni work from nine till five then pizza work from six to eleven, weekends included. I finish up for the year in a few days, then off until mid-September to start the final year."

"All that pizza will do you no good at all, pack the pounds on," Fred chuckled. He was a big lad the last time he had seen him. He didn't need any more padding.

"Funny you should say that Fred, but I've lost over three stone in the last eighteen months. No time to eat and I cycle to uni every day. You wouldn't recognise me."

"Don't tell me you've got long hair and grown a beard? Typical bloody student."

"Yep, both. Saves on trips to the barbers and time spent shaving. I quite like the new me."

"I'll be the judge of that next time I see you, whenever that might be." Fred hesitated and got back to the question that had been burning in his head for the past four months. "I was beginning to worry that I'd upset you by sending you that letter. Didn't know what else to do."

"No, you did the right thing, Fred. It took me a while to get my head around it."

"It was just the LJ thing. It still bugs me. I like the lad, you know

193

that. Don't like to think of him as missing. He had a rough time in more ways than one. I wouldn't like to see any harm come to him."

"Nor me, Fred. I should have written to him when he was inside, but I didn't. The road is paved with good intentions, isn't that what they say? Some brother-in-law I've turned out to be."

"He'll have found his way back to Byron, surely? Have you been in touch with him?"

"Not that easy, Fred. Byron and mobile phones are like oil and water. He uses a pay-as-you-go but he never remembers to put any money on it. I've tried ringing him several times over the last year, but it always rings out."

"So, he hasn't rung you either?"

"He doesn't know my number. I left my mobile with Jess when we went to court. It went up in smoke like the rest of it. I got a new phone and a new number after I left Bartonford."

"So, that's that then?" Fred said despondently.

"Not entirely. Not long after I got your letter, I got in the car and tracked Byron and the family down at the Hereford winter camp. LJ wasn't there. Byron hadn't seen hide nor hair of him, and neither had anybody else."

"A wasted journey then?"

"In part. Byron's now got my mobile number. He'll call me if LJ shows up. Nathan and Buckland have rejoined the family, complete with respectable Roma wives in tow."

"Who?" Fred asked.

"Byron's nephews. The two that Byron was convinced were responsible for your robbery. They upped and left the camp in Bartonford the same day that Jess died but not before Byron had taught them a lesson that they'd never forget. I'm amazed that they ever dared show their faces again, but it seems that they've convinced Byron that they were not responsible, swore their innocence on the Bible."

"All I know is that it wasn't LJ, Michael."

194

"We both know that Fred."

"I thought he might come back here, but I haven't seen him. I'd have heard if anybody else had. I'm keeping my eyes and ears open as you asked, but there's nothing worth mentioning."

"According to the old man's letter, LJ's got his suspicions about the fire too," Michael said.

"Sounds like it," Fred agreed.

"The police aren't going to open up the files just because we have our suspicions. You know and I know that they wanted that case closed even before it opened."

"Your dad was a bit of a bastard by the sound of it."

"Rotten to the core, Fred."

"Sounds like he's trying to make amends in his own way," Fred said, testing the water.

"That's not going to happen, Fred. He made his bed and he'll have to lie in it. We're all of us best shot of him. He can rot in hell for all I care."

"Then we'll say no more about it." It was no more than he had expected Michael to say; he had his answer. "I've got a new friend. Picked him up four months ago. You'll have to meet him if ever you get back down my way. He's called Barny, a black and white mongrel. He likes the ladies."

"Send me a photograph," Michael said. "You make me laugh and there's little enough in the world to laugh about right now. You keep me sane, restore my faith in humanity. Thanks, Fred."

"I'll do that, Michael. You're always welcome here if you need a break. You can't burn the candle at both ends, it's not good for you."

"You know what I'd like, Fred? I'd like to go abroad for a week. I've never been abroad. I've got a passport now. Maybe I'll stick a pin in a map or just go online and see what's going cheap."

Fred hesitated.

"Are you still there, Fred, or have I lost you?"

"No, you've not lost me," Fred said, trying to recall exactly what he had heard. "I was just thinking, something I heard in the shop not so many months ago…I've got it. Miriam, that's her name. Used to live in Bartonford and shipped out to live at her mum and dad's old place in the Algarve. If I've got this right, she was building a couple of holiday lets on the property. It's an old farmhouse, Villa Casa Messines. Could be that they're finished by now. Maybe worth a call or dropping her an email? A bit of sea and sand and a good book would do you good."

"Sounds interesting," Michael said. "Can you send her email address?"

"I'll do that, put it in the post in a day or so. If you get hold of her, best not mention anything about Bartonford or the family, hey? She's made a new life for herself it seems, clean break and all that. I think she was going to advertise it on the internet. Try that as well. If all else fails, come and visit your Uncle Fred."

"Sorry to have left it so long, Fred. Late for my shift at the pizza parlour. I'll call again soon." Michael hung up.

Fred and Barny sat up to the early hours talking through the problem. Michael was too young to understand. Fred might not get on that well himself with his daughter, but he always knew that if ever he needed her badly enough, then she'd be there for him. Not so for Jacky. With one daughter dead and a son who hated his guts, who'd look out for him in his old age? What would he do, where would he go when he was released? It was a sorry state of affairs and whichever way he looked at it, he couldn't see that Michael would ever change his mind.

"What shall we do, Barny?" Fred stroked his beloved mongrel. "Wag once for yes, and wag twice for no."

Barny wagged his tail. "You've more intelligence than the lot of them put together," Fred said. "Looks like you've settled the matter."

Fred picked up his pen and wrote a brief reply to Jacky's letter. In it, he wrote that he hadn't heard from LJ and neither had anybody else. After two minutes he signed the letter 'Fred Humphries, No 4, Pettifer Close, Bartonford', and wrote a postscript: 'Your son, Michael is studying law and, I have no doubt, will make a brilliant lawyer. Please don't ask me how I know this or where he is since it wouldn't be right for me to tell you…Maybe one day. If you need a roof over your head in October when you come out, you have my address."

Had he done the right thing? Only time would tell.

"Walkies," he said to Barny. "Let's get this letter in the postbox before I change my mind."

# Thirty-One

Self-appointed vigilante Ursula Trenchard, a long-term resident of Bartonford, lived in a picture-postcard cottage next door to the village pub and directly across the road from a small relatively new development. Ursula had led the battle and fought tooth and nail to prevent it being built, but in the end, the offer from the developers to build a small shop on the complex and to rent it to the village at a peppercorn rent had won the day. In a way she didn't resent it any longer; the shop had been a major asset to the village and the people who owned the houses in the new development were a never-ending source of fodder for Ursula's infinite counselling skills.

Ursula prided herself on being the most intelligent and know-ledgeable woman in the village – a match for any man. With a network of contacts that stretched from Land's End to John o' Groats, she was, she claimed, known and respected by politicians, lawyers, the police force, corporations and newspapers alike. She had an opinion on everything and relished the opportunity to share it with everybody far and wide. She majored in two subjects: deteriorating morals and wasters; wasters being loosely defined as anyone on benefits, anyone who made little or no contribution towards society, and those who simply scrounged off the state's honest men and women. Gypsies were more than fair game, especially when they had had the nerve to take up residence close to a decent village like Bartonford.

She had rejoiced out loud when the gypsies had finally left, taking with them their tatty caravans and their scrawny horse. She prided herself that she had played her part in ridding Bartonford of them.

Other than the debacle at the summer garden party, which had been a quite shameful affair in Ursula's opinion, Wanda's most unfortunate infestation of rats, and Oswald wandering endlessly around the village taking photographs of dogs, it had been a relatively uneventful interval.

A church warden, a member of the Parish Council and shop committee, fundraiser par excellence, the chairperson of the unfortunately now defunct Bartonford Ladies Group, she kept herself busy with good deeds, and no one escaped. It was of no concern to her that at times she was less than popular in the village.

Ursula was probably the most disliked individual in the whole of the village, but there were few if any who had the nerve to cross her; her reputation went before her. Long-term residents were used to her high-handed manner and opinions and tolerated her. Newcomers were less tolerant and unbeknown to her, frankly, champing at the bit to put her in her place once and for all.

It was September and the leaves of the chestnut trees that lined the road had already started to take on their autumn hue. Ursula looked through the window and tut-tutted to herself as she saw the postman pull up in his van outside the cottage. A never-ending source of annoyance, she had repeatedly written and complained to the post office about the late delivery of mail. It was past time, she wrote, that the Royal Mail got up a bit earlier in the mornings. So far, her words had fallen on deaf ears. Ursula despaired of them all, bent down, and picked the post up from the doormat.

Junk mail, which included appeals from charities, holiday catalogues, two for one offers, and anything else that looked vaguely as if it contained a sales pitch, was immediately consigned to the recycle bin. Utility bills were carefully scrutinised for errors of which there were always several, and the rest of the mail stacked in a neat pile ready for her attention at such time as she had made her coffee and sat down. Ursula liked routine and order.

A large white envelope with a London postmark caught her eye. Ursula turned it over for more clues, but there were none. It was certainly a good quality envelope and therefore worth opening. Slitting open the envelope with her silver paper knife, Ursula withdrew the contents, a single sheet addressed to her in person and signed by a chief executive, obviously a person of some importance, and read on.

*5 September 2014*

*Dear Miss Trenchard,*

*It is my pleasure to inform you that you have been nominated for an Exceptional Contribution to the Community Award (ECCA). This is a new award that is sponsored by several organisations including DEFRA and the Rural Development Programme for England.*

*I am not at liberty to disclose the name of the person who has forwarded this nomination to us. I am, however, delighted to tell you that those placed first, second and third will be invited to a lunch to be held at the Grosvenor House Hotel, Mayfair, London WC1 2NF on 25 October hosted by our patron, HRH The Duchess of Cornwall. The winners will be photographed with our patron and interviewed by several society magazines.*

*Enclosed with this letter you will find a short application form which confirms that you wish your nomination to be taken further. Please return this form by 12 September. Once we have received completed forms from all of our nominees, we will move to the second stage of the process. This will involve circulating a short questionnaire to a representative group of households in your postcode area seeking their feedback on your contributions to the community. The forms will be sent out on 16 September with a return by date of 3 October. Each feedback sheet will then be scored by our panel of judges and a total score given. Your total score will then be compared with those of the other shortlisted nominees.*

*The judges' decision will be made final on 10 October and thereafter you will receive a letter notifying you of the winners, together with a summary of the feedback that we have received from residents in your postcode. We wish you every success with your nomination and look forward to receiving your completed application form in the enclosed stamped addressed envelope.*

*Yours sincerely,*
*Becca McIntyre*
*Chief Executive, Exceptional Contribution to the Community Awards.*

Ursula kissed the letter and hugged it to her breast. Fame, at last, she thought to herself, but no more than she deserved. Her campaign strategy already taking shape in her mind, Ursula completed the form and popped it into the postbox. There was no time to waste. In ten days, the feedback forms would be flooding through the letterboxes of her revered friends and neighbours in the village; she had work to do.

Restraining herself as she had never, ever done in her entire life, she kept quiet about the nomination. Instead, she smiled her way through each day of the following weeks. Complimenting parents on the exemplary behaviour of their children, gardeners on the excellence of their gardens whether she believed them to be so or not, shop volunteers on their unfailing commitment to the village shop, dog owners on the bright eyes and shiny coats of their dogs, and motorists on their compliance with the village speed limits, Ursula kept a smile fixed on her face from morning until night. There were those in the village who were seriously concerned about her welfare and those who conjectured that her behaviour could only be put down to the fact that she was taking happy pills.

On the third of October, late in the afternoon, Ursula closed the front door behind her and heaved a sigh of relief. Never before had she realised how exhausting it was to be nice to people twenty-four seven, and she was completely worn out.

The following day she happily reverted to type. She berated three residents whose grass had not been cut for several weeks and others for litter on the pathways outside their houses. She chastised several volunteers for turning up late to open the village shop and spoke seriously to several parents of teenagers who were letting their children run wild.

On the twelfth of October, she received the letter she had been waiting for. Her hands shook as she bent down and picked up the large white envelope. She could feel success in her bones – it could only be good news, and in less than two weeks she would be hopping on the train to London, first-class, of course, taking a taxi from Marylebone to Pall Mall and conversing one to one with HRH The Duchess of Cornwall.

Ursula poured herself a small glass of sweet sherry. It was really far too early in the day, but she was determined to savour the moment. Sitting back in her armchair, she carefully slit the envelope open and pulled out a spiral-bound file to which was paper clipped a letter from Becca McIntyre. As she read the letter, her face dropped.

*11 October 2014*

*Dear Miss Trenchard,*

*It is with regret that on this occasion you have not been placed in the ECCA Awards. We do hope that you will be nominated next year and have more success. We enclose, for your information, a summary*

*of the feedback that we received from households within your postcode*
*area.*

> *Yours very sincerely,*
> *Becca McIntyre*
> *Chief Executive*
> *Exceptional Contribution to the Community Awards*

Her face a picture of misery, she turned to the folder and started to read the summary of feedback from the villagers: a busybody who has nobody's interests at heart except her own; a prying old woman whose deeds do more harm than good; a snooty self-opinionated woman who sees herself as a cut above everyone else; a meddler in other people's affairs, totally unable to empathise with anyone because she never listens; a bossy breeches, my way or the highway is her motto; Lady Muck who preaches morals to everybody but has none herself; an interfering old bitch, always the first to criticise; the village clown – struts around the village as if she owns it; a woman who makes up the rules as she goes along to suit her own purposes; a racially prejudiced bigot, dangerous, especially to gypsies – ask the gypsy who was sent to prison and ask his dead wife and the little girl at the same time.

The list went on and on. Shock and horror turned to anger. Ursula simply could not believe her eyes and that was only the first page. "Two-faced, small-minded, bloody hypocrites," she yelled at the portrait of herself that hung on the wall.

Ursula turned the file over so that she did not have to look at it again.

Hours later, self-pity oozing from her pores, Ursula reflected on the words of her so-called friends and neighbours. The sherry that she had poured that morning remained untouched. Slowly her anger subsided and was replaced with a measure of acceptance combined with deep melancholy. Finally, she admitted to herself that there was more than a modicum of truth in what had been written about her. She had indeed spent a good part of her life taking pleasure from everybody's misery. She had not seen it coming; it had simply crept up on her.

So enveloped was she in her own misery, she failed to notice the tiny drawing of a small posy of white heather on the envelope. Neither did she spot the heather that lay crushed and broken deep in the bottom of the brown paper envelope.

# Thirty-Two

Elizabeth Goodge's tutors were not impressed with her choice of subject, but she had made up her mind. Her dissertation was going to be on the health and welfare of gypsies. "Why?" they had asked. Because, she had replied, it related to her chosen degree course of population and geography, and nobody else, as far as she could establish, had ever worked on a similar dissertation.

It was early September, two weeks before uni started again, when she decided that it was past time that she stopped thinking about it and got on with it. Eyes glued to her computer screen, Elizabeth called up endless websites and scanned one set of statistics after another. Two days later, she had made little progress. Each set of statistics she found – of which there were few – conflicted with the next set. There was little if anything from which she could draw any conclusions. Disillusioned, she closed down her laptop, intending the following day to draw up an alternative shortlist of subjects for her dissertation.

The idea occurred to her in the night just as she felt her eyelids closing. The following day, Elizabeth googled 'permanent gypsy sites Worcestershire, Herefordshire and Gloucestershire', all counties within easy reach of her flat. Refining her search further, she selected three towns that she would visit in person. Her criteria for selection: first, that there had been a permanent Traveller or gypsy site within or near the town in the past twelve years, and second, that the town had a long-established funeral director's business. Hereford, Great Malvern and Gloucester all met both criteria.

The following week, Elizabeth set off to her first port of call. By ten forty-five she was parked in Berrington Street car park less than a five-minute walk away from Morse and Son, Funeral Directors, Hereford, established 1964.

Elizabeth looked in the window and grimaced. A huge vase of white plastic lilies, which appeared not to have been dusted for the past twenty years, sat alongside an array of urns and a selection of granite and marble headstones. Briefly, it crossed her mind that whoever had bothered to inscribe the words, funeral directors, on the window might have saved their time and effort; it could be none other than that of a funeral director.

Spot on time, Elizabeth opened the door and walked in. Her appointment was for eleven with Mr Morse. During her brief conversation with him on the telephone, she had tried to explain the purpose of her call, but her words had fallen on deaf ears.

"Good morning, Mr Morse. My name's Elizabeth Goodge. I made an appointment?"

She was met by a short, rotund man, his half-moon glasses perched on the end of a shiny nose. Dressed in black and white from tip to toe, he held out his hand to her and put on his serious face. "Elizabeth, ah yes. It's right here in the diary. I am so sorry about your loss."

"As it happens, Mr Morse, I haven't lost anybody, at least not yet."

"So, you're here on your own account. Good for you. I like youngsters who plan well ahead. Do take a seat, my dear, and I'll take some details."

"No, not that either, Mr Morse. I did try to explain it on the phone. You see I am a university student, and I am doing a dissertation on gypsies," Elizabeth started.

"A disserwhat?" Mr Morse interrupted.

"It's a thesis. We have to write one in our final year at uni – kind of a long well-researched essay. Mine is going to be about the health and welfare of gypsies, focusing on the most prevalent causes of death in gypsy communities. I've taken the internet apart and there's just nothing for me to go on, so that's why I am here. It occurred to me, and you probably think it a stupid thought, that funeral directors might have the information that I need. I am guessing that you keep records of the cause of death of most of your clients, if that is the right word for them, and you'd know if they had been gypsies or not." Elizabeth sat back and frowned. Now that she had said it out loud, she was not at all sure about the logic of her thinking.

"I see. Well, I think I see. But why, my dear, why don't you just check the statistics from death certificates or pop into a few doctor's surgeries?"

"Simple," Elizabeth replied. "The cause of death is on a death certificate, but there's no indication whatsoever about ethnic origin of the deceased. I dismissed going to see doctors because I know they can't release any patient information to me about anyone – dead or alive."

"Interesting. This is a first. It so happens that I've got a cancellation. My next appointment isn't until one this afternoon. Tell me more." Mr Morse leaned forward, his arms folded on the desk, and listened with interest.

"I think I'm right in thinking that there's a permanent Traveller site just outside of town?" Elizabeth began.

Mr Morse nodded. "Correct, my dear."

"And I see that you're the only long-established funeral director in the town, so I thought that you might keep records."

"Naturally, my dear. We are, and have been, the only funeral director in town these past sixty years – father and son business, you know. What isn't in the files is up here." Mr Morse tapped his head. "I never forget a gypsy funeral –some of them low key, some of them just like those you see on TV. You should see the size of some of the coffins – big enough for three bodies, but you see gypsies like to take a lot of their possessions with them. Poor as tinkers, if you'll excuse the pun, but when it comes to a funeral they dig deep. Nothing is too much expense or trouble. I've even been asked to put tea and sandwiches in a coffin before, would you credit it? They nearly always start from the camp – gypsies don't like to die in the hospital so when their time is near, they are taken 'home' by their families. You never forget a gypsy funeral and I've done quite a few."

Elizabeth's eyes sparkled. "So, you'll help me?"

"If I can, I will, but you must remember that I too have to consider patient confidentiality – dead or alive it still applies. But there is nothing to prevent me speaking with you in general terms if that would help. So, ask away. I am all ears."

"Do you have any idea how many people live on the permanent site?"

"Probably a hundred during the summer and the camp is packed to the gunnels during the winter – maybe two to two hundred and fifty people. They come here to winter, as they call it."

"And is there a transient population as well?"

"There is indeed. I've no idea how many but you often see the old Romany wagons on the road or parked up alongside the road. Rarely the same ones so I think the answer is a definite yes. Ask me another."

"This is the big ask, Mr Morse. Can you find me some statistics? How many gypsy funerals you conducted between 2000 and 2012, and the cause of death of each of them? And I don't mean Travellers."

"Precise, very precise. That's twelve years, my dear. Are you serious?" Mr Morse asked wide-eyed.

"Deadly," Elizabeth replied hopefully. "You're my very best hope."

Mr Morse drummed his immaculate manicured nails on the table and grinned. "Well, I hope you're not in a hurry, my dear.

This could take a while. It so happens that you have come to the right place. I keep meticulous records and not just on that damned computer. Wait a moment and I'll go and check my files. I'll organise a cup of coffee for you while you wait."

Elizabeth smiled and sat back, perfectly happy to wait as long as it took. "Thank you," she said.

Her coffee drained, she checked her watch. Still plenty of time to get to her next appointment on time.

"You gave me quite a job there." Mr Morse returned, dropping a pile of folders down on the desk between them. "I kept a teeny-weeny bit of information back from you earlier. You see, I've got another gypsy funeral coming up in two weeks and unusually they asked me if I would plan everything for them. I had just started to look back over my files of similar funerals, so I didn't have to look far for them." Mr Morse picked up a piece of paper from on top of the pile. "I think it's all here. No names, you understand?"

Elizabeth nodded. "No names."

"There were about forty deaths between 2000 and 2012. You understand that I can't be precise about all of the causes of death, but I'll not be far wrong. I have a very good memory."

"So, over twelve years that would be about three to four a year?" Elizabeth calculated. "Is that usual?"

"Well, Elizabeth, here's the thing. Up until 2004 there were no more than one each year, and then it seems we had a few bumper years between 2005 and 2007." Mr Morse adjusted his glasses and looked at his notes. "In 2005, three died in accidents and seven of natural causes. In 2006 eight died in accidents and two of natural causes, and in 2007 there were six more poor souls who died in accidents and four from natural causes. The strange thing is that it drops right off in 2008. We're back to about one a year. It's most odd now I come to think about it. It's even more of a coincidence that most of them were Roma – yes, my dear, I do know the difference between Romanies and Travellers. They were terrible accidents if I remember correctly – families, you know. There was a big fire, and several motoring accidents, not a dry eye in the house. Tragic really. The rest died from natural causes – pneumonia, heart conditions, bronchitis, childbirth, et cetera. I've written it all down.

"They don't live as long as us, you know," Mr Morse continued. "It's a well-known fact – living conditions, reluctance to get help from outside and chest conditions tend to take them before their time. If they only got themselves off to the doctor's sooner, then a whole lot more of them would survive, but that's a personal opinion. Mind you, not all doctors are as obliging as others. Some of them don't like going out to the camps, and I have to say, my dear, I'm not that keen on going visiting the camps either, but so far, I've come out of all my meetings totally unscathed and mostly with a sprig of lucky heather in my lapel.

"I do remember most of those accidents, though. Dr Boscombe attended them all. He was a good man. He was exceedingly kind to the families and even came to the funerals to pay his respects. Come to think of it, Boscombe signed off nearly all the death certificates. When was it he moved on? Probably early 2008. Everyone missed him when he left. He was a real asset to the community," Mr Morse said, gathering up the files on the desk. "Here, my dear, you can take this summary with you. You'll not go far wrong. I hope I've been of some help. If you want any more information, then you know where I am."

Elizabeth reached out and took Mr Morse's note and put her iPad back in her bag. She had tried to take note of everything he had said just in case she needed to refer back to it. "I can't thank you enough."

"It's been a pleasure, my dear." Mr Morse opened the door and waved as she walked back to the car park. "Don't forget, I'm here to help you any time you need me."

*

By early afternoon she had found a car parking space nearby the theatre in Malvern. Apostle & Sons, Funeral Directors, occupied the ground floor of a three-story red-brick Victorian building two minutes' walk away.

"I'm one of the sons. Ronald's the name," a cheerful voice said the moment she opened the door. "You must be Elizabeth, right?"

Elizabeth nodded. His smile was utterly infectious. Tall and slim and in his thirties, she guessed, Ronald wore a well-tailored, dark, navy, pin-striped suit, white shirt and black tie. She returned his smile and held out her hand. She was beginning to like funeral directors.

"You're the one doing the degree in population and geography, right? Can't profess to understand what that entails, but it sounds impressive, Elizabeth. Come in, take a pew. Now, enlighten me. Quite how can Apostle and Son be of any possible help to you? Something to do with gypsies, you said?"

"Well, Ronald, as I mentioned on the phone, I'm trying to establish the most prevalent causes of death in the gypsy population, not Travellers, you understand. I've combed the web for information and hit one brick wall after another. If any of the statisticians could agree on how many gypsies actually live in the UK, then that would be a good start. And then there seems to be no way of establishing the cause of death by ethnic minorities, because it isn't recorded on the death certificate. Do you see where I am going?"

"Give me another clue, Elizabeth," he said with a smile.

"I kind of figured out that funeral directors would know. After all, you bury them, and I guess that you know what most of them have died from," Elizabeth replied, wishing again that she had explained it better. "I gather there's a big permanent site out at Dutton."

"There was, but it closed down back in 2012 to make room for a supermarket. But you are correct in that we would know the cause of death of our clients – it's important when you're dealing with the families. So far you're on to a winner."

"I'm interested in the years 2000 to 2012. Don't ask me why those specific years, but they are as good as any," she laughed. "I do know you can't give me names, but if you could give me numbers of deaths by year and an indication of the cause of death then I would think I had died and gone to heaven…Oh, sorry. That's probably entirely the wrong expression to use here."

"I always did enjoy a challenge, Elizabeth, and if you can occupy yourself for fifteen minutes then I think I might find you that place in heaven – short-term, at least," Ronald replied, entirely nonplussed by her request. "I'll be back soon. There are some magazines on the table. Make yourself at home. Help yourself."

Elizabeth glanced at the magazines, *Funeral Director Monthly, The Funeral Service Journal,* and decided that she would happily give them a miss.

"Here we are. Be prepared. That's always been my father's motto. It's what you have to be in this business – death isn't choosy about who it takes or when it decides our time has come. Take a look and see if this is what you were looking for," Ronald said, handing her two sheets of paper. "Excel, spreadsheets, love them," he said. "My father is the brawn, and I am the brain, if I say so myself."

Elizabeth let her eyes wander down through the columns – year of death, age of deceased, sex, and cause of death. "Gosh, 2009, 10 and 11 were pretty bad years for them. Ten in 2009, nine in 2010, and another eight in 2011. And then just the odd one a year in preceding years," Elizabeth said. "And quite a lot of them motor accidents."

"There are some bad roads around here, Elizabeth. They come in for the winter, hare around the Malvern hills, and are surprised when the brakes fail. They're all warned," Ronald replied.

"And the rest of them? Pneumonia, bronchitis, heart failure, childbirth…I've seen a list like this before," Elizabeth replied.

"Yes. Those are the most typical things that they die from. Looking at this now, I'm quite surprised to see how many natural-cause deaths there were in those years. They were all very mild winters. You expect it when we have harsh winters but not when they were mild. If it weren't for Dr Boscombe, I'm quite sure that there would have been a lot more."

"Dr Boscombe?" Elizabeth narrowed her eyes.

"Yes, one of the local doctors and an exceedingly popular chap he was too. A giant of a man, but as gentle as a lamb. I do believe he came to town in 2008 and moved on late 2011. No idea where he went. Is anything troubling you, my dear?" Ronald asked.

"No, not at all. It's just that I've heard that name before. Coincidence. There must be dozens of them around," Elizabeth replied, pushing it to the back of her mind. "You have been amazing, Ronald. Can I take this sheet with me? I must be going now, but thank you so much. You run a really good ship."

"At your service, young lady. Just remember where we are if you ever need our service – Apostle and Sons is the company and Ronald is my name. Good luck with the dissertation."


It was late afternoon by the time she had completed her third and final visit of the day, to Gloucester. The trip had not been a waste of time.

# Thirty-Three

The email was from Mr Michael Walmsley writing that he had seen the Villa Casa Messines holiday let on the web. He described himself as a mature law student who was in desperate need of a break away from his studies, to read and relax and enjoy a little sunshine – the sort of sunshine that he knew he would find in the Algarve. If possible, he wrote, he would like to rent the accommodation for a week at the beginning of September. House-trained and self-sufficient, a self-contained apartment would meet his requirements perfectly. He would be more than happy to make an electronic bank transfer in respect of the rental of the accommodation.

"Guess what, Joanna? We've got ourselves our first paying guest and he's coming in two weeks. He has specifically said that he is coming here to read and relax so you, young lady, might have to keep your distance just a little bit – at least until we get to know him, and then we'll see," Miriam said.

"How old is he?" Joanna narrowed her eyes suspiciously. "If he's really old he won't be much fun."

"I have no idea, dear. He says he's a mature student so that could mean that he might be in his early twenties or his late sixties. It'll be a surprise."

Miriam replied to the email that same day informing him that he would be the first guest in the new accommodation and so she could not guarantee that everything would be perfect. If he had no objections then she would be happy to treat the week as a 'dry run for her new venture' and would be pleased to offer him the week at fifty per cent of the normal asking price, and that she would be happy to take cash on arrival. Adding a footnote to let him know how much a taxi from the airport should cost, she wrote the address and her telephone number. She would look forward to seeing him on the second of September.

Quietly Miriam hoped that her first paying guest would want to do just a little more than read and relax. It would be such a shame for him not to spend time in Silves and Messines, and it would be so much fun if he might accept her as his guide. It was a very long time since she had had the company of a man, let alone an intelligent man who was studying law.

Michael did not know what to expect, but it was not a slim, elegant woman in her late thirties, glowing with health and exuding happiness. Tanned by the sun, she wore a loose white linen short-sleeved shirt and a multi-coloured floral skirt that reached down to her ankles. Around her head she wore a bandana that matched the skirt. Around her neck she wore strands of brightly coloured beads that complemented her outfit. By her side, holding her hand, was a child, quite tall, her eyes blue, her cheeks high-boned and angular. Both were redheads and wore their hair in the same bobbed style.

"You must be Michael. I'm Miriam and I'd like you to meet my daughter, Joanna. Joanna – say hello to the gentleman." Miriam smiled. He was, she guessed in his late twenties, early thirties, tall, slim, and broad-shouldered. His hair was shoulder length, his beard well-trimmed. He looked exceptionally fit.

Joanna held both sides of the bottom of her skirt out wide and curtsied. "I am very pleased to make your acquaintance," she said slowly and clearly.

Miriam laughed and glanced proudly down at Joanna. "She does it with everyone when she meets them for the first time. This little madam is five going on fifteen. I hope you won't mind, but she has been pestering me for ever that she should be the one to introduce you to the accommodation and show you around. I've made her promise to keep it short."

"I am delighted to meet you, Joanna," Michael said, turning back to Miriam. "She is a credit to you – and so pretty. She has the same confidence as a child I used to know."

"I've taken the liberty of preparing some supper in the main house for all of us this evening. It was a little presumptuous of me, but I thought you might be tired after your long journey. Is that okay with you? Please do say if it's not. I'm not easily offended. Dinner will be at six – sorry it's so early, but this little one has to be in bed by seven."

"You're both spoiling me, and thank you, that is most generous of you." Michael picked up his suitcase. "Lead the way, Joanna."

The accommodation was lovely – fresh and new and tastefully decorated. Joanna's guided tour was amazingly informative – a bright child if ever he had met one. Michael took a quick shower, changed his shirt, and combed his hair.

The meal was superb. Miriam was a brilliant cook, and he could see that she was enjoying entertaining him. Joanna chattered nonstop throughout the meal about all the places that she was going to take him, quite forgetting that her mother had said that the gentleman was to be left to read and relax.

He ate with the family every evening and during the day the three of them either frequented the beach, swam in the swimming pool, or toured the tiny streets in the local towns of Silves and Messines, stopping only for frequent ice creams for Joanna and glasses of the local wine for themselves. On the third evening, he stayed overnight in the main house. That she was ten years older than he did not deter him in the least. Miriam had the energy of an eighteen-year-old and the intelligence and knowledge of a mature woman. They had both laughed the following morning when Joanna had asked in all innocence whether her mother's bed was more comfortable than the one in the holiday let. Yes, he had replied, I think it is.

Within days he had been promoted from Michael to Uncle Michael which had touched something deep down inside him. On more than one occasion he had come close to asking Miriam about her previous life in Bartonford, but each time he had stopped himself. Fred had said 'best left'. Besides, he had come for a holiday, not to be reminded of sad times. They rarely spoke about anything but the here and now. Miriam spoke only of her life with Joanna in Portugal and Michael of his life in the small flat close to the university that he was renting for the duration of his studies.

All too soon the week came to an end and his suitcase was packed. "I am not going to let you go, Uncle Michael, until you promise me and Mummy that you will come back and see us soon. You don't have to wait until next summer. You can come for Christmas, can't he?" Joanna said, turning to her mother. She was not going to take no for an answer.

Miriam shrugged towards Michael who returned her shrug. "It seems like we have been told, so if it alright with you, I should love to come to the Algarve for Christmas, that's if you haven't got anything else planned?" Michael winked at Joanna.

"Nothing at all. It would be my pleasure. We can't wait to see you again," Miriam replied. What would she do without Joanna? Only a child could be so direct and see how much they wanted to see each other again. "The taxi is here."

Michael kissed Miriam on the cheek and swung Joanna in the air. "You look after your mummy for me. Will you do that?"

Joanna nodded and sidled up to her mother. He could see that they were both close to tears.

Winding the window down he called out to them, "Bye-bye. Bye-bye."

Joanna stared back at him and frowned.

# Thirty-Four

Peter sighed. It was time to make the preparations for LJ's ultimate test. Sliding open the brown door to the greenhouse, he walked in and gazed at his collection. They were his prize possessions, the datura of all datura, the king of the species, and most definitely not for resale. The long greenhouse that he preferred to call his studio lay beyond the copse and out of sight of the main house. This was where he experimented with cross-pollinating shrubs and the place where he grew a small number of very rare and deadly plants. Strictly temperature-controlled; it was also virus-free to protect the plants from harm. He wore protective clothes whenever he spent time there.

Datura fascinated him. It came in many varieties: hell's bells, devil's trumpets, angel's trumpets, henbane, moonflowers, jimson weed and thorn-apple. Each name conjured something vastly different and equally macabre in the imagination. It had been a remarkably good year for them. Over the weeks he had watched the buds burst open and the huge trumpets emerge. With impatience, he had watched those same trumpets wither and die before being replaced by the green spiky seed pods. At last, they were ready for harvesting.

There was datura – and datura. Those he grew in this greenhouse were specimens that could not be purchased from garden centres or nurseries. They had been imported from Colombia in South America. These were the plants that produced the most toxic seed pods of all, the seeds from which the drug scopalomine was manufactured. That was what made them special. Scopolamine was the drug that was prescribed to prevent motion sickness and the tremors of Parkinson's disease. He had no interest whatsoever in curing diseases or mitigating their effects on sufferers, but the datura seed had properties that were of far more interest to him. When ground to a powder, the seed formed the basis for a truth serum, the serum that Josef Mengele was purported to have used in his experiments on Jews and on Roma throughout the Second World War.

Mengele was his all-time hero whose abilities and achievements had, in his opinion, been sorely underrated. The war had provided Mengele with the perfect opportunity to experiment with live subjects, but with the end of the war and the need to flee the country, his experiments had been curtailed, cut off in their prime.

Peter shook the small bottle, held it up to the light and nodded in satisfaction. It was a perfect job. Lying at the bottom of the bottle were the pills that he had produced from the powder, the pills that, at the right time, he would use to assess the progress of his project. With the power to alter the mind to the point where the gypsy was incapable of lying, it would be the ultimate test.

It was just over a year since the gypsy had arrived. He had grown quite accustomed to having him around the house and the farm. Over time, he had noted a progressive change in him and was not without hope of success. He had worked hard to keep the gypsy at the farm sensing from time to time that the man's thoughts were elsewhere, and that there was the danger that he might fly the nest. The gypsy was receptive and keen to learn. Time after time he had dangled the carrot that the more he learnt the business, the greater his chances of success in the future. Was he truly a changed man or was he still the gypsy, secretly champing at the bit to return to his old ways? There was only one way that he would know for sure.

As if by divine intervention, the opportunity to conduct the ultimate test presented itself the following morning. Returning from his fortnightly trip to deliver plants to his clients, he had found LJ sitting by the front door nursing his head. "Can't take my eyes off you for two seconds," he remarked. "What have you done this time?"

LJ dropped his head; a patch of matted blond hair hid a nasty gash to his head. "One of the metal hoops – it broke. I was bending down, and the hoop broke loose and sprang up. It caught me on the top of the head. I've repaired the hoop – it won't get loose again. It's just a headache now. Nothing to worry about."

"Looks nasty – may need the odd stitch or I might be able to tape it together. Let's get it done," Peter replied, waving his arm towards the front door. A smile crept across his face. A stitch, some tape, and a regular dose of aspirin…

"You'll live," Peter said, wiping the last of the blood away from the gash. "Just a bit of tape now and it'll soon mend. Take these. They're painkillers."

LJ took the tablets from Peter's hand and washed them down with a glass of water. They tasted bitter, but he thought nothing more of it.

"Now rest. Lie on the sofa. Put your feet up and your head back on the cushion," Peter said. Pulling a stool close by the sofa, he watched and waited until LJ's eyes started to roll around in their sockets. The time had come. Peter pulled his notebook and his pen out of his pocket.

"Listen to me, LJ. I'm nobody other than a voice in your mind – your subconscious. When you least expect it, I pop up and we talk together. We are always honest with each other. We can't hurt each other because we are one and the same. You are part of me, and I am part of you. I would never tell you anything but the truth." Peter smiled. "I will ask the questions and you will answer my questions honestly. Are you happy with your life, LJ?"

"No."

Peter frowned and hesitated. "What is it about your life that you would change at this moment?"

"Leave. Go."

"Leave where?"

"This place."

"Cold Comfort, you mean? Why do you want to leave?

"Evil."

"What is evil?"

"Peter."

"Why is Peter evil?"

"Watching. Watching all the time."

"Maybe he is watching over you, LJ. That's different. Maybe he cares for you. Maybe he loves you like a son. You don't need to be afraid of him."

Peter straightened his back and gathered his thoughts. Reminding himself that he had not set out to win the gypsy's heart, he refocused his mind on the goal he had set for himself. "Let's talk about Jess. She is in your past. A past you don't need anymore. Am I right, LJ?"

"Jess!" LJ sat bolt upright and pointed towards the corner of the room. "Jess, she's here. Desperate to tell me something. Jess..."

"You're hallucinating, LJ. There is no Jess. There is no one in the room with us. If it helps, then you can tell me what you think she is saying."

"I didn't light the fire. I didn't light the fire."

"Calm down, LJ. There is no fire, LJ. There is no Jess. Lay back and rest."

Studying the man lying on the bed, Peter drew breath. The exchange was far from that he had expected. It was disappointing that LJ thought him evil and that Jess lingered on in his mind. He knew that it was decision time. He knew that his patience would not last forever. He needed either encouragement to pursue his project or a reason to curtail it. The all-important question had to be asked.

"Are you a gypsy?"

"Yes. Roma and proud. Always." LJ replied.

"Close your eyes and sleep tight," Peter said wearily.

Putting his notebook back in his pocket, Peter removed the stool, retired to his study and wrote another entry in his journal:

> *The truth serum works. Thank you, Mengele, for steering me in that direction. You have saved me a great deal of time and effort. It has been an invaluable learning experience and an interesting experiment. I appear to have made far less progress with this subject than I had thought. It is disappointing. Outwardly he bears little evidence of his gypsy roots; inwardly he remains a gypsy with the genes of a gypsy. Strangely, Mengele, I am extremely disappointed. You would see this as a weakness in me, but I have grown quite fond of him. Had this experiment succeeded, I had even thought of adopting him as my own son, the one that I could never have. I now know that one day soon he would have walked away. I cannot allow that to happen. While he sleeps, I shall move him to his new home. It is the perfect place for him to end his days.*

# Thirty-Five

It was late autumn, verging on winter. Black clouds raced across the sky waiting to dump their load on those brave enough to step foot outdoors. He had been soaked three times already and Barny had not been in the least bit impressed either. He wouldn't be without him for the world but having to take him out for walks in all weather was something Fred had not entirely bargained for. He made a mental note to get the back garden fenced in as soon as he could afford it. On days like this, Barny could then do his business closer to home.

"Quiet, Barny. It's going right through my head and I know there's somebody at the front door. I've told you before, I'm not deaf," Fred shouted.

Fred opened the door and looked at the man standing under the porch carrying a small hold-all. He was unmistakable – the same features, the same build, the same height. This was Michael's father. When he had issued the invitation, he had thought it unlikely that the man would ever turn up on the doorstep but here he was, large as life, against all the odds.

"Fred Humphries?" the man said, rain dripping off his coat.

"Jacky, I presume?"

"That's me. Sorry to turn up like this unannounced. I got your letter."

"You'd better come in then," Fred said. "Don't mind Barny. His bark is worse than his bite. He thinks the world revolves around him. In your bed," he said, pointing towards the kitchen. Barny sniffed at the stranger's feet, jumped up and put his front paws on his knees, and stopped barking.

"You must have the magic touch – he's never like that with strangers. They do say that dogs know who to trust and who not to. Looks like he approves. I'll put the kettle on and make some tea. Hang your coat up and leave your bag there. Get yourself warm and dry by the fire." Fred pointed towards the small sitting room where the log fire burned brightly.

"I haven't seen one of those for years," Jacky said, pointing at the old brown teapot on the tray.

"It's the only way to make a good cup of tea. What's the point of jumping up and down when you want a second one?" Fred poured the tea into matching brown mugs. "When did they let you out?"

"This morning. The doors were thrown open at seven-thirty and I was through the process including the paperwork in record time – standing outside waiting for a bus at ten. I caught a coach from Nottingham to Evesham and then buses to get here. Still, can't complain. HMP paid my fare, forty-six pounds it cost. Cost a lot less to travel when I went in. They call it a prison release grant – a joke really. Fortunately, I haven't been idle for the past year and I've saved some money – not a lot, but enough for a few weeks and until I can get a proper job," Jacky said. Even as a man of the world, as he liked to think of himself, the day had been a harrowing experience. It was inconceivable just how much had changed in the outside world in three years.

Fred studied his visitor: he was shabbily dressed but clean-shaven. His eyes were clear and bright, his speech was slow but clear, and there was no sign of him having drunk alcohol.

"So, what plans have you got?"

"To find LJ, that is, unless you've already found him," Jacky replied.

224

Fred shook his head. "Not yet."

"I somehow doubted it. And Michael? Do you know if Michael has seen him?" Jacky tested the water.

"He hasn't seen or heard of him either. He's been out looking."

"So, you're in touch with Michael? Sorry, that wasn't a trick question earlier. I just thought that you might be." Jacky frowned. It was not an auspicious start.

"We're in touch," Fred replied. "He doesn't want to see you. He's doing well. Making a life for himself."

"No more than I expected. It's hard, but I'll respect his wishes," Jacky said quietly. "Good cuppa, Fred. Thanks." Jacky drained his mug and got up. "I'd better be on my way. Just thought I'd look you up. It was good of you to write."

"Sit down, man." Fred pointed to the chair and poured him a second mug. "When I gave you my address, I didn't mean just drop in for a cup of tea. If it's a bed you need for a day or two then it's here for you."

"A day or two would be much appreciated. Thanks."

"When you've got that down you, you'd better put that bag upstairs. First on the left. The bed's made up. It's a bit cramped, but you'll get used to it. Right now, I've got to take this little devil out for his last walk of the day, and I'm not looking forward to it." Fred got up and started towards the hall.

"I'll do that. My coat's still wet and I'm thinking that Barny and I need to get to know one another."

Barny sat down at Jacky's feet and waited for the lead to be attached to his collar. "Well, I'll be damned, he never does that for me," Fred said, opening the door for them. "If anyone asks, you're my brother come for a visit."

"Cocoa," Fred shouted, the moment he heard the front door open and close. "Hang that coat up again. If we get a puddle on the floor, then we'll mop it up later." While Jacky had been out, he'd been

225

mulling things over. The man seemed a decent fellow, with a lot to answer for, and a lot of putting right to do, but a decent fellow all the same. He would be quite happy to extend his invitation of a couple of days to a week, and then maybe a week to a month, and then…Who knows? He missed company, which was not a word that he would ever have used to describe Sam, his son-in-law. It was all very well having fun and games but when you had nobody to share it with…

Fred settled back in his chair, put his feet up on the footstool, cradled his cocoa between his hands, and regaled Jacky with stories of his latest escapades. Jacky roared with laughter. In all his years, even in prison, he had never met anybody with such a mischievous, cunning mind; Fred took the biscuit.

"Would I be right in thinking that you played some small part in the bins business?" Jacky asked.

"You could say that. Had to do a bit of moonlight visiting. Just moved a few bins around after everybody was safely tucked up in bed. And I've still got some of that weed killer in the shed – works a treat on hedges," Fred replied chortling to himself. "I must dispose of it safely sometime. We wouldn't want anybody to get the wrong idea, would we? I know he was my son-in-law, but he was a pain in the backside. Went too far when he got LJ arrested," Fred said. "And Ursula Trenchard, well, I managed to take her down a peg or two. Tricky one that. I had to call on a few favours around the village, but they were all up for it." Fred chuckled at the memory. "If it's stopped raining, I've got something else to show you. Follow me. It won't take long."

It was pitch-black outside. Fred switched the torch on and pointed the light. "What do you think about them?" he said.

"Not what I think, are they?" Jacky asked.

"They are," Fred said proudly. "Rats – beauties aren't they? I just bought too many of them. That pompous old bag, Wanda, you know the one I told you about who called the Parish Council meeting to get rid of the gypsies, well she's got a new nickname these days – the Pied Piper. Sorted her out I did, good and proper. I helped a few of them through her letterbox and, blow me down, they did the rest for themselves. I'll tell you about the squire and more about Lady Ursula tomorrow. Those stories will make you laugh too. And this one's no innocent either, let me tell you." Fred stroked Barny's head. "Yes, you, old son, like the ladies, don't you?"

"You mean Barny's your partner in crime?" Jacky shook his head. Tears of laughter ran down his face. It wouldn't do to get on the wrong side of Fred.

"He went out on the town one night just like dogs do. Did I tell you about Oswald Billericay? Nasty piece of work. Said all manner of nasty things about the gypsies. Breeds dogs, he does. Posh kennel up the road. So, this little friend of mine visited the kennels one night and had a whale of a time. He might have had a bit of help from me, but I would never admit that. And guess what happened then?" Fred chortled.

"I hate to think, Fred."

"Oswald, breeder extraordinaire of world-famous pedigree dogs, found himself saddled with a load of black-and-white mongrel puppies. There was hell to pay. He's gone a bit funny in the head now. Wanders around taking photographs of dogs, trying to spot the culprit. Tried to pin it on Barny, he did, but I told him that my Barny never goes out on his own, and never without me." Fred grinned. "Gone out of business, he has. Shame."

Jacky shook his head. "You amaze me, Fred, my friend. A perfectly planned vendetta. If the stories about the squire and Lady Ursula are half as good, then I can't wait for the morning. Thank you, Fred. I appreciate what you've done. I'll not get on the wrong side of you."

"We've not quite finished yet, and this is where I might need your help. There's one more that needs to get his comeuppance. I've got an idea, but I need someone to bounce it off, and if it looks like it might work, then I need a gofer. Reckon you'll have to stay for a week at least," Fred said.

"Count me in!" Jacky replied without hesitation. Whatever it was that Fred had in mind then he wanted to be in on it.

"I'm not a vindictive man, Jacky, but they all deserved what they got. One day this village will be run by real people again – people like you and me – and not the pompous know-it-alls who think themselves a cut above the rest," Fred pronounced, nodding his head. "Now, I'll say goodnight."

# Thirty-Six

"Good morning. My name is Elizabeth Goodge and I am ringing to report the suspicious death of eighty or more gypsies," Elizabeth said, rolling her eyes as she listened to the response from the other end of the line. "I'm twenty years old, a student and as sane as you are...No, I have not been drinking. In case you hadn't noticed, it is eight o clock in the morning, and I don't do drugs either...You want me to repeat that? I want to report the suspicious deaths of eighty or more gypsies...Another crank, did I just hear you say? You really should put your hand over the receiver if you are going to make remarks like that... What evidence do I have? Plenty, well maybe not evidence but a great deal of information that points towards it being a strong possibility...Stay calm, you say...If you put that phone down on me then I promise you that I shall go straight to *The Courier* and share my story with them and believe you me, you and your colleagues will never live it down...Nine o'clock? Yes, that's fine. I'll be there." Elizabeth cut off the call, drained her coffee and gathered her papers together.

Elizabeth marched up to the front desk. "I rang earlier. Elizabeth Goodge. I have an appointment to talk to somebody at nine o'clock."

The duty officer covered his mouth with his hand and yawned. "Take a seat, Miss Goodge, and I'll let DI Roberts know that you've arrived."

"Miss Goodge?" a voice called. Elizabeth looked up to see a man walking towards her. He was not what she had expected, not her stereotype of a detective. Tall and dark-haired, he wore denim jeans and a worn brown leather bomber jacket over a white T-shirt. In his early thirties, she guessed. Tanned, he had either spent a great deal of time under a sunbed or recently returned from a holiday in the sun. Whichever, it suited him; he was extremely attractive.

"Detective Inspector Gary Roberts. Let's go through to my office and you can tell me all about it. Coffee?" he asked as he opened the door and pointed to a black leather office chair opposite his own.

Returning with two steaming mugs of coffee, he dropped the formalities. "Elizabeth isn't it? Call me Gary. I'm all ears."

Elizabeth took a sip of her coffee, composed her thoughts, and laid a sheet of paper on the table. Summarise and keep it simple, she reminded herself. "By way of background, I am a student studying for my BSc in population and geography and I decided to do my dissertation on age at death and cause of death of gypsies – not Travellers, gypsies. There is a difference you know." Elizabeth paused and looked up; so far so good, his eyes had not glazed over, and neither was he doodling on the pad in front of him – he was listening.

"Do you know that there is no record of ethnicity recorded on a death certificate, so consequently there are no statistics of death by ethnic community? Well, that's not entirely true –I gather that in Scotland they've started to collect that information, but I think it's pretty ad hoc." Elizabeth listened to her own words. "Apologies, I told myself that I would get straight to the point and not wander off the subject. It's just that the whole thing makes me angry."

"Take your time. I'm in no rush," Gary said, eyeing the pile of files on his desk and trying hard to ignore the constant ping of his mobile. "Sorry, can't turn it off. Goes with the territory."

"I will try to get the point. Since I couldn't get any meaningful or consistent information from the web, I decided to go and visit a few funeral directors operating in towns that had permanent gypsy sites either within or on the outskirts of the town. I wanted to get a feel for the death rate and cause of death. I thought that if anybody might know it would be them, and I was right. They're a mine of information, long-established and they keep good records," Elizabeth explained.

"Good thinking. I'll add that one to my list." Gary smiled.

"I thought that I would just dip my toe in the water initially and look at a twelve-year window, 2000 to 2012. Five weeks ago, I went to visit funeral directors in Hereford, in Malvern, and in Gloucester – three towns in three different counties. There are permanent authorised traveller sites in or close to all three towns."

"Can you remember the precise date, Elizabeth – for the record?" Gary picked up his pen.

"It was the tenth of September," she replied, checking her notes. "To be honest with you I chose those towns because they were all fairly close to home. I'm not keen on driving long distances."

"Carry on."

"My first visit was to Morse and Sons in Hereford. I explained what information I was looking for. Mr Morse, a lovely elderly gentleman, went off to check his files. Now, listen to this. He told me that he had conducted a whopping thirty gypsy funerals between 2005 and 2007. Seventeen died in accidents and thirteen from natural causes."

"Is that significant?" Gary asked.

"In itself, maybe not. But before 2005, there had been an average of one death a year. After 2007, the death toll dropped right back to the same average of one a year. Bear with me…" Elizabeth got into her stride.

"My next port of call was in Great Malvern, Apostle and Sons. I talked to the son, Ronald, a real brainbox if ever I met one, a whiz with a computer – you know, everything filed away in the right place, statistics to help plan the business, figures for the taxman. It took him no more than fifteen minutes to fish out the information I was looking for – deaths in the local gypsy community between 2000 and 2012. And wait for this – there were twenty-seven deaths between 2009 and 2011, sixteen from accidents, eleven from natural causes. The average number of deaths before 2009 was one a year. After 2011, the average deaths fell right back to one a year." Elizabeth hesitated. "Are you following me?"

"Not entirely, Elizabeth." Gary put his pen down and sat back in his chair. "I assume there's more?"

"You will when I tell you this," Elizabeth spoke slowly. "There is a common denominator between the deaths in Hereford and the deaths around Malvern. The man's name is Dr Boscombe. He arrives in a town, and the following year there is a huge increase in deaths. He arrived in Hereford in early 2004 according to Mr Morse. He left Hereford in 2008, and rocks up in Dutton, not far from Malvern, just before the next spate of deaths. He leaves the Malvern area at the end of 2011, and bingo, the death toll drops right back again."

"Most likely a coincidence, Elizabeth. These things happen. Gypsies don't live long and live a pretty reckless life for the most part," said Gary, explaining away her theory.

"I don't think it is a coincidence, Gary. After Hereford and Great Malvern, I went to Gloucester, and guess what?"

"I'm not in the guessing game, Elizabeth."

"The same pattern – the gypsy death rate goes sky high between 2001 and 2003: twelve in 2001, eight in 2002, and ten in 2003. Our man, Boscombe, arrives in the year 2000 and leaves in 2004 on his way to Hereford. Three different counties, all neighbouring, three different towns, all approximately fifty miles away from one another, and incidentally approximately fifty miles away from where we are sitting right now. Coincidence?"

"Could be," Gary replied, looking at his notepad. "You said eighty or more suspicious deaths. My maths isn't the best, but you've just mentioned eighty-seven deaths."

"Well, I was giving the good Dr Boscombe the benefit of the doubt. Some of the deaths could have been from true natural causes. I didn't want to exaggerate."

"The good Dr Boscombe? Strange thing to say about a man you suspect of having killed eighty or more gypsies," Gary said.

"Mr Morse spoke highly of him as a doctor. Even Ronald commented on how much he had been liked within the community. And Mr Oliver – that's Mr Oliver of Oliver Funerals, Gloucester – couldn't speak highly enough of him. He can't be good and bad at the same time, can he?"

"A Jekyll and Hyde, you mean?"

Elizabeth thought about it. "Sounds unlikely, doesn't it?"

"Have you told anybody else about this, Elizabeth?"

"No. It's taken me weeks to build up the courage to come down here and tell you. The more I thought about it the less likely it seemed, but the more I thought about it, the more sleepless nights I had. At least I've been able to offload my concerns onto you. Thanks for listening, Gary. So, what are we going to do about it?"

Gary laughed. "We, Elizabeth are going to do nothing about it. If there's anything in it then it's a police matter."

"Okay, correction. Are you going to follow it up or do you still think I'm a crank?"

"I never said that. Give me some credit. The facts and figures make for interesting reading, but there's nothing conclusive in what you have told me. The accidents would have been properly investigated at the time. If the police concluded that they were accidental deaths, then that's what they were, and we can't go digging up bodies all over the country on a whim."

"But they didn't spot the pattern – three different counties, two different police forces. Wouldn't it have been easy for them to miss the link?"

"Possibly," Gary conceded. "And don't forget that I operate out of Warwickshire and as far as I know nothing like this has happened in this county in the last few years."

"That's it then, is it?" Elizabeth picked up her notes from the table and started to put them in her bag.

"You can leave those notes with me if you don't mind." Gary brushed his hand against hers. "I can't promise anything, but I'll make some enquiries. It won't happen overnight."

"Will you let me know if you find anything more?" Elizabeth asked hopefully.

"I'll keep you informed, best I can," Gary said. "And, Elizabeth, if I were you then I'd find a different subject for my dissertation. Better safe than sorry. Call me any time you want to," he said, handing her his card.

Right at that moment, he had a full case load – an attempted murder, a major theft from a local upmarket jewellery store, a stalker, and a missing woman, but there was something about Elizabeth's story backed up by the facts and figures, rough as they were, that told him that he should not dismiss it entirely. Gary placed Elizabeth's spreadsheet in a file that he marked Suspicious Gypsy Deaths and made a mental note to make some further enquiries.

# Thirty-Seven

Keith Ingrams wanted nothing more than to be shot of it. The development planned for the land that had once housed the old garage and workshop and the greenhouses beyond had been jinxed right from the beginning. In the first place it had been a no-brainer; the land he had picked up for next to nothing, property prices were high. That was before the gypsies arrived. After which property prices plummeted and Bartonford was no longer a sought-after village. Had he not been constantly barraged by the Parish Council to get on with it, he would happily have left it as the eyesore it was. On the eighth of October, the bulldozers and lorries convoyed through the village leaving their muddy footprints on the tarmacked roads and turned into the site. Work was about to begin.

"You'd better put that old lumberjack shirt of mine over your sweater and put my old brown bobble hat on as well. You don't want to go in there looking like something out of Savile Row. No one down there is going to recognise you, don't worry," Fred said. "And muddy up those boots as well."

"I'll never get that shirt on. Look at the two of us!" Jacky replied, sidling up to Fred who hardly reached his shoulder.

"I bought it three sizes too big. You'll get in it alright. Good luck," Fred said. "Off you go."

"Foreman about?" Jacky asked the flagman who was busy directing heavy traffic in and out of the site. "Who wants to know?" he asked. "Bob. Looking for a bit of casual work for a few weeks. Need a few folding ones in the pocket, if you know what I mean. Saw the site. So here I am," Jacky replied, winking at the man.

"You may be in luck, mate. One of the labourers hasn't turned up. Man in the yellow hardhat and reflective jacket with Foreman written on the back. Down there," the flagman replied, pointing to the far end of the site.

"Thanks, mate," Jacky replied, turned, and strolled slowly away.

"Flagman at the gate told me you're the foreman. I'm strong as an ox, argue with nobody, get on with the job, keep me head down, and happy to be paid cash. Could you do with a labourer?" Jacky asked.

The foreman looked up from the plan in his hand and eyed the newcomer suspiciously. He'd been caught out before with men who walked in from the street looking for work. "What experience have you got?" he asked, playing for time while he sized him up.

"Three years for aggravated assault, three years working on building projects in Ranbury prison – all manual jobs that kept me fit. I just need some cash to keep me going." Jacky grinned. An ex-con was the least likely casual to go shouting foul to the authorities.

"Eight pounds per hour cash. Any problems and you're out on your ear. Tell that fellow over there that I sent you," he said turning back to the plan.

Jacky smiled. Too easy, he thought. By the end of the day, he had sworn to himself that he would never use that phrase again. It had been back-breaking work and he wasn't as fit as he had thought he was, but he had kept his head down and his shovel in the trench clearing the earth the digger left behind.

He was the last to leave. "See you tomorrow," he called to the flagman who was directing the last of the traffic out of the site before securing it for the night. Jacky hung around outside the gate and fiddled with his boots. "Bugger these bloody boots. If I've cleared stones out of them once, then I've done it a hundred effing times today. Need some new ones."

By the time he had taken his boot off, inspected it inside and out, and started to put it back on his foot, the man had taken a set of keys out of his pocket and was fastening a padlock on the gates. Jacky watched and grinned to himself – a piece of cake. There was no other security – no dogs and no cameras.

That same evening Jacky reported back to Fred and both agreed that it was best to get the job done and out the way so that Jacky could make a speedy exit from his short-lived career as a labourer. At ten pm Fred put his jacket on and reached for his coat. Barny sat expectantly by the door eyeing his lead.

"Not tonight, Barny. Me and Jacky have work to do – men's work."

"Wait." Jacky bent down and whispered in Fred's ear, "I thought I saw a torch somewhere on the other side of the road." Fred cupped his hands around his eyes and looked around. "Your imagination, Jacky. Let's get on with it."

"Okay, you're on lookout Fred, and stay well out of sight. You know the signal. Do it again."

Somewhere close by an owl hooted – once, twice, three times. "How's that? Been practising all week." Fred grinned.

Jacky moved silently through the shadows to the gate, extracted a length of wire from his pocket, lingered by the gate, turned, and gave Fred the thumbs up. Picking up an old golf bag and a shovel from the ground beside his feet, he carefully swung one of the gates open and closed it behind him. What he had to do would take less than a matter of minutes.

Fred watched as Jacky disappeared deep into the churned-up expanse beyond and out of sight.

Using the dim light of a torch to light his way, he stepped warily across the field. The bag was heavy. The last thing he needed was to trip and wake up the following morning in one of the trenches himself. The one he had chosen had been freshly dug earlier that day; the labourers had not yet been down to clear the loose earth. The following day he and a few other men would be getting on with the job. Climbing down into the trench, Jacky pounded the shovel into the ground below. After weeks of light rain, the ground was easy to work. After twenty minutes he had dug a hole one foot in depth and five foot in length. Unzipping the golf bag, he tipped the contents into the trench, and covered them with earth. Careful to cover all signs of disturbance within the trench, he zipped up the bag again, scrambled up the bank, and set off back to the gate.

Fred heard the snap of a padlock and nodded in satisfaction; the whole job had taken half an hour and in all that time there had been no passing traffic. On the gate he hung a small bundle of white heather.

Jacky heaved himself out of bed and dressed ready for another day's work. His back ached; he had found muscles that he never knew existed. It was noon before the gang moved on to the third trench. Stretching, he stood back and let two other members of the gang drop down into the trench before him. "My bloody back," he said out loud. "I'll be right down."

As he spoke, he heard the magic words from down in the trench. "Effing hell. We've got ourselves a body, boys – and maybe more than one at that. Jacky, go get the foreman."

"You sure?" Jacky called.

"Nope, but I'll tell you what, you'd be hard pushed to find as many bones as these in an effing graveyard," the man called back.

Jacky trudged across the field; the foreman was halfway through a mug of tea. "I'm sent to tell you that there's a problem in trench three. Looks like bones and a lot of them."

238

Swearing under his breath, the foreman followed Jacky back to the trench. If it were bones, he'd have two options – either suggest that the men made the bones disappear or call in the police.

"Downed tools, have we? We've got the concrete coming in tomorrow," he shouted at the men standing around the trench. "You want to get paid or not?"

"Looks like a battlefield down there, boss, and whatever's down there has had its head chopped off." The gang leader frowned and scratched his head. "This field – it's right near where that woman and her kiddie died. Sorry, boss but I ain't working down here and neither is anybody else."

One by one the gang picked up their spades and trudged slowly back to the Portacabin, Jacky in their wake. Shortly afterward, two police cars and two unmarked cars arrived. A tent was erected around the trench and the men were laid off until further notice. Jacky walked home.

Three days later Jacky was still in recovery. Walking around like an old man, he spent most of the day trying to get comfortable in one of the armchairs while Fred went out for the papers and then served him endless cups of tea.

"I hope you are not laughing at me, old son," Jacky said, as Fred plonked the paper down on his lap.

Fred grinned; it had been all he could do to keep a straight face when he had heard the news in the shop. "You're never going to believe this, but Ingrams has walked away from the site. Said he never wanted to build there in the first place and for all he cares it can stay like that for the next hundred years or until some other mug wants to buy it. He's quit. A gypsy curse on the place, he says. And he doesn't care what sort of bones they find. He's had a bellyful."

"Maybe we didn't go in hard enough, Fred."

"But you haven't heard the best yet, Jacky. Someone's made an offer for the land and Ingrams has only gone and accepted it. Don't you want to know who?"

"Spit it out, Fred. You're going to tell me anyway."

"The Parish Council, that's who. Picked it up for a song. And guess what they're going to do with it? They're going to get it levelled again, turf it and make it into a playing field for the kiddies in the village. What better memorial to Jess and Sally?"

# Thirty-Eight

Chief Inspector Farquhar looked up from his pile of papers. "Enter. Good afternoon, Gary. Good Christmas?"

Gary nodded. Christmas was not a time of year that he enjoyed – the annual trip back to his parents on Christmas Eve, the annual reunion with his brother and his unruly family, Christmas lunch which inevitably arrived late afternoon after much cursing and swearing by his mother, and finally Boxing Day, eating the leftovers and going for a walk down by the Avon. He could well do without it. "Yes, Chief. Thanks for asking."

"So, what's the news on the fire?"

"Arson, Chief. SOCOs have just reported back – a gypsy family, parked up on a layby just outside of Balsall Common. Accelerant, petrol," Gary replied.

"Gypsies?" Farquhar looked up from his desk and removed his glasses. "I don't like this sort of thing on my patch, Gary."

"Gypsies," Gary confirmed. "Two dead from burns and smoke inhalation and a third – a woman – holding her own in hospital. One of our lads is at her bedside waiting to get a statement from her when she comes around."

"Any witnesses?" Farquhar asked brusquely.

Gary fumbled with the file in his hand and laid it flat on the desk in front of him. "No witnesses as such, Chief. The police constable reported that when they arrived at the scene, a doctor was already present. Claims that he was passing by on his way home when he saw the flames. He called the fire brigade. According to the constable, the doctor said that he had tried to get near the caravan, but the heat was too intense. The woman was stumbling around and then eventually passed out, which was when he gave her CPR. The police and paras arrived shortly afterwards. When the constable looked for the doctor, he had gone and so had his car."

"Lucky he was passing, at least for her," Farquhar said. "Not so bloody lucky for the other poor bastards. Appeals for witnesses – other road users, walkers…?"

"In hand, Chief."

"Talk to the doctor again."

"Wish we could, Chief. Sounds like it was all pretty chaotic there. The constable got his name but nothing else. The car, he remembered, was an old Rover, four by four."

"These things happen…Shouldn't be difficult to trace him."

"Mind if I pull up a chair, Chief? This could be a long one." Gary sat down in the soft leather chair opposite Farquhar and composed himself. "The man – that is the doctor – gave his name as Boscombe, Dr Boscombe."

"Get to the point, Gary. I've got an appointment with the super in half an hour," Farquhar snapped.

Gary took a deep breath and slowly exhaled. "I think Boscombe might be a serial killer of gypsies, and more likely than not, set the fire himself."

"A doctor? Serial? What are you talking about, man?"

"If I'm right, I think he may have helped eighty, maybe more, gypsies to an early grave," Gary started.

"This better be good, Gary." Farquhar sat back in his chair and folded his arms across his chest. "I'm waiting."

Gary opened the file and pulled out Elizabeth's spreadsheet. "A local girl, a university student, Elizabeth Goodge, came into the station a couple of months ago. I talked to her. To cut a long story short, she'd been doing some research into the cause of death of gypsies for her dissertation. Bright girl, she visited Hereford, Malvern and Gloucester, figuring that if anybody might be able to give her the information she needed, then it would be funeral directors. They're all towns that have, or had, a permanent gypsy site and quite sizeable transient populations of gypsies. Hereford was her first port of call. Talking to the one and only long-established funeral director in town, she uncovered that the death rate amongst the resident population of gypsies sky-rocketed over a three year period between 2005 and 2007. There were thirty deaths, some natural causes and the rest as a result of accidents of one kind or another. Before 2005, the average annual death rate was one. After 2007 it fell back to one and has remained at that level since."

"Fascinating. They don't live that long, you know. Get on with it," Farquhar said, beginning to show his impatience.

"She then went to Malvern – there used to be a big site just outside of Malvern at Dutton. Same story. In the three years spanning 2009 and 2011, twenty-seven gypsies died. Again, the average death rate was negligible before 2009 and dropped right back down again after 2011. She then went to Gloucester. Same thing. Thirty gypsies died between 2001 and 2003." Gary looked up and checked that he still had the Chief's attention.

"Don't tell me. Average death rate before 2001 virtually nil. Average death rate after 2003 nil again."

"Spot on, Chief."

"Suspicious deaths?"

"Not that we are aware of. According to medical records the verdicts were all natural causes or accidental death. But there is a common denominator – Boscombe. He practised medicine in each of those towns during the peak of those deaths. The same Dr Boscombe signed off all the death certificates. Maybe the same Dr Boscombe who stopped by the fire at Balsall Common?"

"Let me get this quite clear, Gary. Are you suggesting that a doctor has been touring around the country systematically killing gypsies?"

Gary nodded. "Yes, Chief."

"I don't recall seeing any report of this from you, Gary. I presume you followed up on this girl's story."

"Not personally, Chief. None of the incidents were in Warwickshire, so I passed the information on to West Mercia and Gloucestershire and asked them to make some enquiries. Mercia spoke to Boscombe's partner in Hereford, and his partner in Dutton, near Malvern. They both spoke highly of Boscombe – hardworking, committed, always willing to go the extra mile, especially with helping the gypsies. Sorry to see him move on. Gloucester checked him out with a Dr Howard. Much the same, glowing feedback, nothing too much trouble for him, excellent bedside manner, a special rapport with the gypsies. With everyone giving him a clean bill of health and nothing in the medical records to suggest that the deaths were anything other than accidental or natural, I parked the enquiry. I had an attempted murder, a major theft from a local upmarket jewellery store, a stalker, and a missing woman…" Gary tried to justify his actions.

"And now this Dr Boscombe rocks up on our patch. Is that what you're telling me? Common enough name, Boscombe…"

"As you say, Chief," Gary interrupted, "a common enough name. When I heard it again after this morning's incident, I made some more enquiries for my own peace of mind. I checked him out with the General Medical Council. I should have done it before." Gary ran his fingers through his hair. It was the moment he had been dreading for the past hour. "The thing is, Chief, that there is no Dr Boscombe. There never has been. There's no one by that name registered with the GMC. They've no record of anyone by that name ever qualifying as a GP."

"Impossible." Farquhar jolted his head back and stared long and hard at Gary. "No man can pass himself off as a doctor and get away with it, not in this digital age."

"Not quite. It's happened before and this one's clever, Chief,"

"Why? What earthly reason would he have to kill gypsies? It doesn't make sense," Farquhar raged.

"Hate? Vendetta? What earthly reason did Hitler have to send all those Jews to the gas chambers?"

"And you think he's on our patch now?" Farquhar repeated, staring out of the window towards the town.

"The man's name at the fire this morning was definitely Boscombe and he said he was a doctor. The man's description fits with that given to Mercia by his partners. Six-three, broad shoulders, heavy-set, in his sixties. The rest of the details about his appearance change depending upon who you ask."

"Photofit?"

"Working on it now, Chief."

"Family?"

"He seems to have had a wife. No one ever saw her, but he spoke of her often enough. The reason he gave for leaving each of the medical practices was that Mrs Boscombe's elderly parents needed care and that they were moving to be close to them. The same reason every time he moved on."

Chief Inspector Farquhar ground his teeth, stood up and paced the carpet. "There'll be all hell to pay upstairs when I tell the super about this. If you're right, Shipman's got nothing on this one. I'm putting you in charge of this, Gary. Don't mess up. Drop everything else. Holidays are cancelled until we've got him, and this mess has been cleaned up. I want extra patrols around every known gypsy site in the county. Put out an alert. I'll square it upstairs. You – find the bastard, and fast. And while you're about it, ring that Elizabeth Whatshername and tell her she's got a job with me anytime she wants it. High time we had a few more intelligent women on this force. I hope to God, you're wrong about this, Gary."

"Elizabeth? Gary Roberts. Sorry for not getting back to you sooner. It's been a bit manic here. You did a great job," Gary began. "Just ringing to let you know that we're throwing everything at it. Looks like he's on our patch now."

"Hi, stranger. I was beginning to wonder if I'd ever hear from you again," Elizabeth said. "I could have told you that he'd not missed Warwickshire off his list."

Gary scowled and shook his head. Was she one step ahead of him again? "There's no record of any suspicious deaths involving gypsies in Warwickshire in the past twenty years, Elizabeth. I've checked. Maybe you've got your facts wrong this time."

"Did you know that there was a fire on the edge of a small village called Bartonford, near Aubrey in January 2013? A young mother died in the fire and her three-and-a-half-year-old daughter was presumed dead, although her body was never recovered. Are you still there?"

"What's that got to do with gypsies, Elizabeth?"

"The fire was on a gypsy encampment, but the woman who died, Jess Lovell, was no more of a gypsy than you or I. She was married to one, yes, but she wasn't a gypsy. Maybe that's why you didn't find it in your records."

"And your source of information, Elizabeth?"

"I've been out and about talking to the gypsies. Everyone knows everybody else's business, Gary. There are some things that you won't get from your wonderful computer databases unless you know what you are looking for."

"I'll look into it. Thank you, Elizabeth." Gary slammed the phone down. "Fuck,'" he yelled at the computer screen as he called up the details of the Bartonford fire.

# Thirty-Nine

Darkness had fallen several hours earlier. Three or four, he wasn't sure which. Some days he kept count of the minutes and the hours. Other days his mind wandered off to distance places and he lost count. When day came, a glimmer of light filtered through the door and cast shadows throughout the dungeon. He knew the winter had drawn in. The days were shorter and gloomier, the nights long with sub-zero temperatures. LJ lifted his head and looked down at the irons around his wrists and ankles which anchored him to the bench. He had not given up. He would not give up. Twisting and pulling at the restraints, he winced with the pain where the irons had cut into his flesh. One day, he told himself, the chains would break, and he would be free. His ears rang as his head crashed back on the bench and he fought to control his breathing. The cold and damp had taken its toll, his chest was congested, his breathing shallow.

It was that time of day. In moments his tormentor would arrive as he did each evening and would goad him and laugh at him before feeding him morsels. LJ closed his eyes to calm his mind and muster what little strength that he had left.

"Doesn't time fly, LJ? Can it really be almost sixteen months since we met on this very same spot? Did you enjoy Christmas, LJ?" LJ felt movement in the air and then the man's breath on his face. Turning his face away, LJ ground his teeth and waited silently. Peter gripped LJ's chin and jerked his head towards him. "Look at me when I speak to you." LJ stared defiantly into Peter's eyes. "It was Christmas Day two days ago. I had turkey and all the trimmings. It's all over for another year. Nothing to say for yourself today. You never were much of a conversationalist."

"Bastard," LJ muttered, as he fought to control the cough that was trying to tear him apart.

Leaning forward, Peter rested his elbows on his knees. "How long is it that you've been in your new home? Almost one hundred days according to my journal. You must have become quite fond of your little hideaway by now. I didn't know it existed when I bought Cold Comfort. It's almost invisible from the outside, covered in weeds and grass. I only noticed it that day when I found you standing and looking down the hill. It's probably not been used since the last war. It was once a bunker, you know. And you're still alive – that's pretty impressive. It must be the way I have looked after you. You've been lucky. It's much warmer underground, isn't it? Otherwise, I'm guessing that you would be dead by now."

"I've plenty of time today, LJ. All the time in the world. Sorry state isn't it, but there's no one to blame but yourself. You know that, don't you? I tried with you, tried so hard, but what did you do? I'll tell you, shall I? You pretended that you were happy and content in your new body and mind, but you lied to me. The truth will out, LJ, and it did. You'll have to forgive me if I repeat myself today, but I promise you that you will not be hearing my stories again. My word is my honour."

LJ shook his head and laughed. "You don't know the meaning of the word."

"You were my very own little specimen, you know. My friend and inspiration, Mengele, spent days, months, years even, experimenting on Jews until he ran out of them and turned to Romanies. It was he who gave me the idea. He was quite obsessed with trying to find out what made Jews the way they were, what it was in their genes. He had this theory that if he could establish what those elements were, then it had to be possible to eradicate those genes one by one. He played with their minds, he played with their bodies. His aim was that one day there'd be no Jews left – those that didn't end up in the chambers could be dealt with scientifically. If it might work for Jews, it might work for gypsies, I thought. It was a crying shame that his life's work was so cruelly terminated with the defeat of Germany.

Do you know they nicknamed him the Angel of Death? And then you came along. I couldn't believe it. My very own Roma specimen walked right in through the door, so to speak."

"Did you bring the gas with you? Is that your game? Your very own holocaust? Sadist," LJ said. His voice was weak, but his words were clear. "They'll get you. They'll string you up or, better still, they'll send you to the gas chamber."

"No one has caught me yet and it will remain that way. Did I tell you that you stink? This place stinks as well – just like a pigsty. That's worse than anything for you, isn't it? I used to watch you washing your hands all the time, scrubbing your hair and your body. You made me smile. I noticed the looks of disapproval that you gave me when I washed my underpants in the washing-up bowl. It was deliberate, it was all part of the experiment, you know. I wanted to see how long it would take before you started to turn a blind eye, before you forgot that you were a gypsy. But you didn't, did you? Now look at you: filthy, dirty, and lying in your own excrement. I gave you everything you needed – shelter, work, food, companionship, and consideration. There was nothing more you needed. I gave you the opportunity of a new life, free from the shackles of your previous existence."

LJ watched on as Peter jangled a bunch of keys in front of his face. "Are these want you want?" he said, as he threw the keys on the floor. "Get them and set yourself free. Be my guest." LJs slowly turned his head and blinked. His vision was clouded. He could not see the keys, but he knew they were near, taunting him.

"Do you remember that day when that metal hoop sprang back and made a gash in your head? Do you remember that I patched you up and prescribed aspirins for the headache? Well, LJ, they were not aspirins – they were the crushed seed pods of datura – a truth drug. It was used in the concentration camps. Mengele swore by it. And then you lay back on my sofa and told me all I needed to know – that you were still proud to be Roma, and after everything that I had done for you. It was the wrong answer, LJ. I wanted you to tell me that you were a man, that you had put your past behind you."

"Never."

"I hate gypsies, every last one of you. I've made it my life's work to rid the country of them. You are all loathsome, detestable creatures with no respect for anybody or anything, and dirty inside and out, whatever you may claim. You have no place in this world. One day you will be wiped out completely. Do you want to know why I hate you all so much? No, why should you? But you have a right to know. I can see it in your eyes that you don't really care, but I am going to tell you. Are you listening to me?" Peter shouted.

Somewhere in the recesses of his mind, he knew he was staring a murderer in the face. His eyelids drooped – he wanted to sleep. He wanted to put his hands over his ears to block out the man's words. He wanted to close his eyes and never wake up. And then from afar he heard her voice. "Fight, LJ. Fight." In that moment he knew that he was not alone. Jess was with him giving him strength. He was not ready to die.

"I wouldn't share this particular secret with just anybody, but it's safe with you. You won't live long enough to tell another living soul." Peter sat back and relaxed. "I was sixteen at the time, and a normal teenager – big for my age, and although I say it myself, quite handsome. She was tall and slim but voluptuous for her age.

She was fifteen, she told me. She was a gypsy, a Roma. She came on to me like they all do, like a bitch on heat. Oh, I know what you are going to tell me – that Roma girls are good and pure. But this one was not. Time and time again I walked away, ignored her taunts. She was always there, on every street corner. And then one day, in my passion, I took her long and hard and then I saw her for what she really was. A whore. Nothing but a dirty whore. She disgusted me. I was angry. I lost my temper. I beat her until she was almost unrecognisable. You see, I had to make sure that nobody would ever look at her again. I suppose she could have gone to the police and reported me, but that's not what gypsies do, is it? They look after their own, don't they? Four of them came for me, not one but four. Do you know what they did? Three of them pinned me down and stuffed a filthy dirty rag into my mouth. The fourth tore my trousers and pants off. He put rubber gloves on his hands and took out a knife. You can imagine what happened next. Suffice to say that there would be no children in my life."

LJ laughed. "That was one blessing."

"You may laugh now, but I shall have the last laugh. In that moment God gave me my mission in life – to rid the world of gypsies. I waited patiently for my time to come and during that time I read a great deal. I taught myself all about medicine. Ten years on, I reinvented myself as a doctor, LJ. It was too easy. All I needed was a suit, to be able to talk the talk, to carry a black leather bag. No one questioned my qualifications. Yes, there were obstacles to overcome, but never any that prevented me from practising my art. I made it my business to take special care of gypsies. Wherever the gypsies set up camp, Dr Boscombe was never far behind. I was good to them. I never refused to visit the sick. I was everything a doctor should be. I listened to their tales of woe. I was kind and considerate. I gave them my time but maybe I didn't give them the medical advice or medicines that might have saved their lives. I knew what I was doing. I knew your Uncle Silas,

LJ. He was an objectionable man – arrogant and argumentative. He was suffering from flu and then it developed into pneumonia. There was nothing I could do for him, of course."

"I studied mechanics in my spare time. Summer months could be lean, with few illnesses in the camps. During those periods, I had to find other ways to further my mission. Let's just say that accidents happen, shall we?"

"I looked after gypsies for almost thirty years. Many perished at my hands, possibly hundreds, I don't recall now. I would have to refer back to my journals. I should have had years more in medical practice, but it was not to be. The warning signs were there, and it was time for me to bow out. That's when I decided to retire and move to Bartonford. You won't remember my wife, will you? She was before your time. She wasn't a demanding woman at all. She came here with me, but it didn't work out."

"I couldn't believe my luck when I saw you and your little family roll into town. You see, already I was missing my mission. I knew it was an omen. I watched you all for hour upon hour. The binoculars that hang in the hall up at the house – they're ten by fifty – powerful. She was a pretty little thing that wife of yours. Pity that she was a cripple. I watched all your comings and goings. I knew where you went and what you did by day and where you sat and with whom you passed your time by night. You were careless, you were all careless – to leave a young girl and her child on their own. Yes, it was me who set fire to your vardo. It was too good an opportunity to miss – two gypsies less to procreate. It was a shame that it had to end the way it did."

"You monster." LJ yelled. His eyes wild, his head shot up as he yanked once more at his restraints. Pain racked his body. More than anything he wanted to kill this man with his bare hands, but he knew that his strength was failing, and it was now beyond his power. "What kind of a man are you?" he whispered.

"Is that a rhetorical question, LJ? I am clever. I am determined.

I rarely fail. Let me try to cheer you up a bit. Would you be surprised to know that I too have weakness? I always wanted a son, but those gypsies put paid to that. At one point when I began to believe I could make a man out of you, I went so far as to make a will, leaving the house and the farm to you – the son that I would never have. A moment of weakness, I know. I've missed you and I've missed my work but I had a most interesting morning today. It wasn't planned, it was fate. Two more gypsies perished in an unfortunate fire – it should have been three. Strangely, I didn't get the same satisfaction from it as I have in the past. I think it's because I've moved on – from the body to the mind. The mind fascinates me. I think you might be the last, LJ, but only time will tell. I shall speak to Mengele about it, he will guide me."

LJ summoned his last reserve of energy, lifted his head, and spat at the man sitting beside him.

"That wasn't very nice, LJ. In that action, you have sounded your own death knell. It is time to let you go. No more water. No more food. In my experience, your vital organs will soon start to close down. It will be a slow death but it will be interesting to watch. I'll look in on you. My life's work is recorded in my journals. One day it will be published, and I'll be as famous as Mengele. I thought we should have this conversation today before you lose your faculties completely. I wanted you to go to your grave a happy man. Goodbye, LJ."

Listening, he heard the jangle of keys as Peter picked them up from the floor, and then the click of a padlock. There was nothing more he could do. Shedding a tear for Jess and Sally, LJ closed his eyes.

# Forty

Fred boiled the kettle and poured the water into the old brown teapot, swirled it around, emptied it, and added three good spoonsful of tea; teabags were unheard of at Pettifer Close. Rapping on the kitchen window, he chuckled to himself. Come rain or shine, Jacky was out there finding something that needed to be done, with Barny never far away.

Jacky had become a true friend and companion. If Fred had known how useful it would be to have another man around the house, he'd have had a lodger years ago. In the space of just over two months, Jacky had rebuilt the fence around the small back garden so that Barny could run freely, the gutters had been cleaned front and back, the small porch over the front door repaired, the flower beds weeded and dug, and the garden furniture varnished. Now, up to his ankles in mud, Jacky was busy digging a vegetable patch. For a man who, by how own admission, had hated physical work not so many years ago, he was indefatigable. You don't appreciate it until you haven't got it, he often said.

Fred couldn't help but admire him. He worked hard, never complained, and not once had he touched a drop of hard liquor. Occasionally of an evening, they shared a bottle of beer, the second was never opened. He was quietly optimistic that Jacky was a truly reformed character, but only time would tell.

He had just had the best Christmas that he could remember for a long time. He had had peace of mind – no Sam or Marie regimenting his day; no Sam or Marie watching eagle-eyed as he pushed his half-eaten, unappetising Christmas lunch to one side of his plate; no Sam or Marie nudging him to wake up the moment he dozed off. Intuitively, he had kept Christmas a low-key affair for both his and Jacky's sakes. In the event, they had enjoyed a good wholesome Christmas lunch and forsaken the forced merriment. He had bought a warm leather jacket from a local charity shop and a pair of green wellington boots for Jacky. Jacky had artfully crafted him a new walking stick from a length of timber that he had found in the shed. Both were well pleased with their Christmas gifts. Neither of them was sorry that Christmas was nearly over. On Boxing day evening, they ate leftovers on trays on their laps. Fred sat watching *The Man with the Golden Gun,* Barny at his feet. Eyes half-closed, Jacky sat back and turned his mind to something that had been niggling him.

"You happen to know who owns that field opposite the Ingrams development?" Jacky asked out of the blue.

"Why do you want to know?" Fred looked up, pausing the film.

"Curiosity."

"He's a recluse, reckon that's the word, and a nasty piece of work. If I remember rightly, he calls himself Peter Boston. Word has it that he runs a business up there, a nursery up there or some such thing but nobody seems to know much about him. Been there a few years. Never comes down to the village. Nobody sees him. Likes to keep himself to himself," Fred replied.

"You met him?"

"Once. Went up there to pay my respects when he first moved in. He pointed at a no trespassers sign and told me to get lost. One look at him was enough – huge fellow, broad-shouldered, mean look about him. Stay away from there if you take my advice."

"Does he have a dog?" Jacky asked.

"Not that I know of, but I do know he's none too fond of them," Fred laughed. "Young Chrissy will bear witness to that. Her little Poppy once got under the fence down by the main road and bolted up the field. She called him back and luckily, he came bounding back to her, but not before she'd seen this giant up on the hill pointing a rifle at the dog. She won't be doing that again."

"A rifle?" Jacky enquired, "What do you need a rifle for around here?"

"Pass," Fred said. "But I checked him out with the local coppers – he's got a licence."

"Nice bloke," Jacky said, as his thoughts returned to the light on the hill.

Jacky went over it in his mind again. It was bugging him. Who in their right mind would take a walk down a steep hill in the pitch-black, stop for a few minutes and then walk back up the hill, and with nothing but a torch to light their way? And who would do the same thing for four nights in a row?

It was four nights ago when he had taken Barny out for his last walk that he had first noticed the light. Two ash trees outside of the gates to the old garage and workshop had been felled and made for a perfect resting spot. He'd sat down and lit a cigarette, his last remaining vice. It was then that he had seen the torchlight for the first time. He'd thought little of it at the time – probably another dog walker.

He'd taken the same walk the following night and sat on the same fallen ash. No more than a few feet from where Jess had taken her last breath. He had felt her presence strongly. Lost in his own thoughts about all the things he had not been able to say to her in life, he had almost missed the same light descending the hill and, minutes later, receding back up the hill.

The following evening there had been a full moon, and, against the shadow of the moon, he had seen the outline of a tall broad-shouldered man walking sure-footed down the hill, torch in one hand, a bag in the other.

The same on the fourth evening. The man could be no other than the recluse that Fred had spoken about, the man who owned the land, and saw visitors off at gunpoint. No one but he would walk that land in the dead of night.

Fred had long since fallen asleep, and Barny whimpered and stirred. It was time for their late-night walk. Jacky picked up a torch from the kitchen and went out to the shed. In the moonlight of an earlier evening, he had seen the glint of a chain-link fence on the far side of the brambles that divided the road from the recluse's land. Slipping a pair of bolt cutters and leather gloves into his pocket, he picked up a sickle. Barny lay quietly waiting as Jacky pushed his feet into his wellington boots and tucked his trousers in. "You're my eyes and ears, tonight, Barny," he whispered, stroking the dog's head. "If you hear anything or see anything you let me know, otherwise it's silence, understand?"

For the fifth night running, Jacky sat on the fallen ash. He checked his watch. It was eight pm. He'd make his move after the torchlight had come and gone. Taking a cigarette from the pack and his lighter out of his pocket, Jacky looked at them and returned them to his jacket. It was a dark night, and a lit cigarette would be visible for miles. Barny lay down at his feet and closed his eyes.

With time to kill, Jacky let his thoughts drift back to Michael. 'Your son, Michael,' Fred had written, 'is studying law and, I have no doubt will make a brilliant lawyer. Please don't ask me how I know this or where he is since I will not be able to divulge this information. Maybe one day...' He had spoken little of Michael to Fred since he had arrived at Pettifer Close, too ashamed of the way he had treated his only son. If Michael didn't want to know him then there was little he could do to change his mind. If Fred knew of his whereabouts, then he would share that information in his own good time. In his heart, he knew that he had a lot to prove before that might ever happen.

Suddenly, out of the corner of his eye, he caught sight of the light descending the hill. It was too dark to see who carried it, but he knew it would be the recluse. The light went out. Jacky sat and waited, counting the minutes. On each of the previous four evenings it had been no more than a few minutes before the light reappeared. This time, almost an hour had passed. Chilled to the bone, unable to feel the tips of his toes or his fingers, Jacky rose stiffly to his feet and picked up Barny's lead. Aborting the operation seemed the only common-sense thing to do, but in that moment, he remembered something Fred had said not two hours since. "He runs a business up there, a nursery or some such thing." Jacky knew it was important. He felt it in his bones. Think, think, he told himself. And then he remembered one sentence in the last letter that he had received from Jay telling him that he had planned to revisit Bartonford to pay his respects to Jess and there was a nurseryman in the village whom he might call on for a temporary job. Jacky didn't believe in coincidences.

If he had to wait all night, he would. One way or another he was going to go up that field and find out what was going on. No sooner had he sat down again than the beam of the torch receded once more into the distance.

He waited another fifteen minutes. "It's time. Let's go, Barny," he whispered as he slipped Barny's lead and together they crept across the road and into the brambles.

Surely and steadily, he wielded the sickle left and right hacking a path through the brambles, Barny constantly at his heel. The dark of the night impeded his progress. The bramble patch was wide and dense, and the branches thick but the sickle made short work of them. Finally, he reached the chain-link fence and pulled the bolt cutters out of his pocket. Cutting a straight line down through the fence, his eyes constantly flicking back and forth to the hill ahead, he pulled the two sides of the fence apart, just wide enough for him to squeeze through.

Dropping the sickle and leaving the fence behind, Jacky felt his way one foot after another up the slope. The torch remained in his pocket. It was steeper than he had expected and even more treacherous underfoot than he had anticipated but he could not afford the convenience of the torchlight. Twice he turned his ankles in the runoff trenches, and twice he stumbled over unseen mounds.

He rested – his knees hurt and he was out of breath. Looking back down the hill to the road, he judged that he had now covered just about the right distance. Barny whimpered and scampered ahead. Jacky froze and strained his eyes in the dark. He could see nothing. Barny returned and whimpered again. "Show me," Jacky said.

Hauling himself back on his feet, he used his ears to follow Barny. Barny pawed the ground. Almost invisible to the naked eye, covered by grass, were steps leading down into even denser darkness.

Jacky held his breath and glanced up the hill. There were no lights, no movement. From his jacket, he withdrew the torch and pointed it down the steps. At the bottom of the steps, there was an old wooden door locked with a padlock and chain. The steps were slippery, the stench from below made him gag but he was not going to be deterred. Barny jumped up and clawed at the door. Jacky pulled the bolt cutters out of his pocket. The chain was old and rusty. The sound of the chain breaking echoed across the night.

He pushed the door open, one hand flying to cover his nose, the other gripped tight around the handle of his torch. The blood drained from his face as he shone the dim light on a figure lying lifeless on a bench, chained by his ankles and wrists to metal rings set into the concrete bench. The man had struggled to free himself; there were flesh wounds around his ankles and wrists. He was skin and bone. He had been left to die if he was not already dead. Jacky swallowed hard as he shone the torch on the man's face. It was gaunt, its eyes were sunk back into the face, its skin had a deathly pallor.

259

Wide-eyed, unable to speak, Jacky stumbled backwards. "My God," he whispered to himself as he put his fingers on the man's neck. There was a pulse, only just, but it was there. He was unconscious, his shallow breath coming in rasps. Hastily Jacky pulled the bolt cutters out of his pocket and severed the chains.

The man weighed nothing – there was hardly an ounce of flesh left on him. His head lolled back as Jacky picked him up and manoeuvred the both of them carefully and inch by inch back up the steps and out into the night. Glancing back up the hill, he could see nothing but the dark of the night. Speed was of the essence; the man did not have long to live, and the recluse's rifle was too close for comfort. Jacky hoisted the lifeless figure over his shoulder in a firefighter's lift, and throwing caution to the wind used the torch to navigate his way safely back down the hill, Barny at his heel. Through the chain-link fence, back through the bramble patch, and they reached the road again. Jacky ran as if his life depended upon it.

"Open up, Fred!" Jacky hammered on the door. "Hurry."

"I'm coming. Don't wake the whole neighbourhood, man." Fred threw open the door and took one look at Jacky and the load over his shoulder. "Oh Christ! Is he alive? Where did you find him?" he said.

"The recluse. A bunker hidden in the hill. He's breathing but only just. Get blankets and warm water. Ambulance and police," Jacky said, as he carried LJ's body into the small sitting room and laid him tenderly on the sofa.

Jacky and Fred watched as the paramedics wrapped LJ in a foil blanket and attached an oxygen mask to his face before carefully laying him on a stretcher and walking the stretcher out to the waiting ambulance. "Shall we come with him?" Jacky asked.

A girl, dressed in green overalls, no older than Jess would have been, shook her head. "I think he's stable for the moment. His physical injuries don't seem serious. They'll pump fluids into him and probably sedate him. Trust me, he'll be in good hands. If there's any change at all, they'll ring you," she said kindly, as she closed the ambulance door.

"I'll make some tea. Looks like you could both do with it." PC Gill took off his hat and headed towards the kitchen. "DI Gary Roberts is on his way right now. I just called him."

"Brown teapot, three spoonsful of tea, and make sure you warm the pot first," Fred shouted, flopping down in one of the armchairs. He turned to Jacky. "You played a blinder there, my friend. How did you know?"

"I didn't. Just knew that something wasn't right up there. He always said he wanted to come back to Bartonford to pay his respects to Jess and Sally. And then I remembered he'd mentioned a nurseryman in the village. He's been under our nose for God knows how long and we knew nothing about it." Jacky shook his head. "That poor lad."

"You couldn't have known," Fred replied. "If it weren't for you... Give me a minute, Jacky. I've got a phone call to make. It's private."

Fred opened a small drawer in the hall stand, pulled out an address book, and tapped the numbers into his phone. The call rang out. Fred left a short message: "We've found LJ. You need to be here in Bartonford. It's urgent Michael. Call me."

DI Gary Roberts reached for the phone and, half asleep, put it to his ear. "A report about a man called Lovell," the voice said. "It's down here to call you day or night if anything relating to gypsies comes in. His name is LJ Lovell. He's got a record. He's a gypsy. Seems like someone has done their level best to kill him. Pettifer Close, Bartonford. Ambulance and police on their way."

Forty-five minutes after the call, Gary walked in the door and introduced himself. "DI Gary Roberts. I hear Mr Lovell's holding his own. I'll be in charge of this investigation. Can you walk me through what happened?"

"I'll top up the pot," PC Gill said, retreating to the kitchen.

Gary pulled out his mobile phone. "It would save time later if we record this conversation," he said.

Jacky nodded his agreement; how many times in the past had he heard those same words? Wrapping his hands around his third mug of tea in the past hour, Jacky recounted the events of the past days and finally the events of that evening. Fred filled in the details about their relationship to LJ.

"The man who lives up there is a nasty piece of work. He's got a rifle," Fred added.

Gary pulled a piece of paper out of his pocket. "Do you recognise this man?"

Fred nodded. "It's him."

"Sorry to wake you, Chief." Gary put his mobile to his ear. "We've got an incident on our hands. We've found him. I'm sitting less than half a mile from where he is now. Bartonford. He's got a rifle. I'm going to need an armed response team up here pronto...I'll do a briefing up by the church. I'll wait for the team there." Gary cut off the call and turned back to Fred and Jacky. "We've been after this one for a while. You deserve a medal – both of you," he said. "Don't go out again tonight – and lock the door."

"Okay, you're the boss," Fred said.

Emotionally drained, conversation and explanations exhausted, Fred and Jacky flopped back in their armchairs, each lost in their own thoughts. In the distance, they heard rifle fire, not once but twice, closely followed by a volley of shots and then silence, broken only by the telephone ringing in the hall.

"That was Michael. He'll be here first thing in the morning," Fred said.

# Forty-One

Jackie sat slumped at the kitchen table, his eyes swollen and red, and swallowed the last dregs of his tea, long since cold. The night had been endless. He had not slept at all. Images of LJ lying prostrate, left for dead in that evil-smelling bunker, flashed before his eyes. Images of the hatred that Michael would be unable to disguise when he arrived later that morning tormented him. Images of Jess pleading for him to leave her alone stabbed his conscience. Images of little Sally playing with her toys one minute, the next her hair on fire, tore at his heart. In the early hours of the morning, he had been sorely tempted to pack his bag and run. It was only when he remembered his words written to Fred that he knew there could be no running away this time: *I know that my son, Michael, is probably lost to me. I have never forgotten the look in his eyes when he took that knife to me and I have long since forgiven him for his actions. If the tables had been turned, I would have done the same. I would dearly love to meet up with him just once more to beg his forgiveness. I fear it will never happen.* This was his chance, his only chance, to make peace with his son.

"Has Barny been out for his morning walk?" Fred interrupted his thoughts.

Jacky shook his head. "Sorry, Fred, it went right out of my mind."

"Don't apologise to me. Apologise to Barny. He's been crossing his legs for the past two hours. Fresh air will do you good. Michael won't be here for another half hour," Fred said, throwing Barny's lead at Jacky. "And stop worrying."

A car door slammed. Fred looked out of the window, took a deep breath, and headed for the front door. "Hello, Michael," he said. "Look at you. Thin as a rake. Could do with a haircut but the beard suits you. Need specs now, do we? Wouldn't have recognised you if I'd bumped into you in the street. Good to see you. Come on in. Hang up your coat and let's go through to the sitting room. There's a fire burning in the hearth."

"Is he alright?" Michael asked, as he hung his coat up. "I'd have come sooner. I didn't pick up your call until last night. I've been out in the Algarve with Miriam over Christmas."

"Have you indeed?" Fred raised his eyebrows. "In the circumstances, he's a bloody miracle. Must have good genes, those Romanies. Had a call from Warwick not two hours ago. LJ's doing well."

"I'll drive," Michael said. "The car's outside."

"Sit down, will you? And slow down. He's resting right now. The doctor has given him a sedative and prescribed a minimum of twenty-four hours of sleep to give his body time to recover. Tomorrow afternoon he'll be able to receive visitors. Not before."

"What happened? Where did you find him?" Michael asked.

"I didn't. Someone else did. Without that someone, he'd have been dead in a few days if not before," Fred said, choosing his words carefully.

"Who found him? I need to thank them…"

"Someone you know – and yes, you do need to thank him." Fred hesitated; it was time to level with Michael. "Hear me out, Michael, and don't interrupt. I haven't been entirely honest with you these last couple of months, but I'm not going to apologise for that. I thought long and hard before I made my decision. You remember the letter I sent to you? The one your father wrote? Do you remember what you said about your father?"

Michael narrowed his eyes and frowned. "Yes. I said he could rot in hell and nothing has changed."

"You did, Michael. Harsh words. I'm a lucky man, you know, Michael. I've got a nice little home, friends, and a daughter and son-in-law – not that I see much of them, but they're family all the same. I know they'll be there for me when I need them. Your father..." Fred hesitated. "He has nothing but regrets – no family to turn to when he left prison, no friends, no roof over his head. Everyone deserves a second chance, Michael, so I wrote to him and told him that he was welcome to look me up when he was released."

Michael pulled his cigarette packet out of his pocket and took a cigarette out.

"You smoke too?" Fred grinned. "So does Jacky, but only outside, and when he thinks I'm not looking."

"Jacky? What are you saying, Fred? Are you telling me...?" Michael shook his head. "I don't believe it."

"It was the back end of October when he turned up and he's been living here in this house with me ever since. I could have given him your contact details long ago, but I didn't. I wanted to know that everything he had said was genuine. I would trust him with my life. You only have my word for it, but he is a good man."

"How can you say that Fred, after what he did to Jess?" Michael's eyes blazed with anger.

"People can change, Michael. Your father has. It was your dad who saved LJ's life. Ask him about it. He'll be back from walking Barny in a few minutes," Fred said. "Go and have that cigarette before he gets back."

Fred drew back the curtain and peered out into the back garden. Michael was leaning heavily on the fence, his back to the house. Jacky stood at the side gate, his face ashen, eyes fixed on the man in the garden, Barny by his side.

"Hello, Michael," Jacky said quietly.

Michael turned and stared at the man standing by the gate. Tall, broad-shouldered, well-built but without an ounce of fat, muscular, clean-shaven, and with no signs of the red veins that had once crisscrossed his face, he wore a shirt and tie and spoke softly. "Fred tells me you saved LJ's life. I owe you."

The words wouldn't come at first. "I'm sorry. Sorry for everything. I just wanted the one chance to meet up with you again and apologise to you personally. I did terrible things, Michael. I wish I could take it all back."

Michael nodded. "I hear you."

"The tea's brewed," Fred shouted through the open window. "Nothing like a good cup of tea."

"After you, Michael," Jacky said.

"Sit down the pair of you. Take the weight off your feet. And try to be civil. I'll bring in the tea and then we talk," Fred said, taking command of the situation. So far so good – Jacky was playing it straight down the line, from the heart. Michael was stumped for words as he had hoped he would be.

"Where did you find him?" Michael asked.

"Locked away in an old underground bunker up on the hill right opposite the old garage and workshop. I'd seen some strange goings-on up on the hill over a few nights and decided to go and check it out myself. He was lying on a bench half-starved to death, unconscious and tethered by chains to the bench. We don't know how long he'd been there, but it could have been months judging from the state of him."

"How? Why?" Michael asked incredulously.

"Don't know," Fred cut in. "But I can tell you that the man who put him there probably didn't live to tell the story. A detective, DI Roberts, came around last night. Jacky told him what he knew. Then Roberts showed me a picture of someone they had been looking for. We heard him call for back-up, for an armed response team. Then half an hour later, we heard shots. I guess that they took him out."

"I still don't understand. Why would anybody incarcerate LJ and leave him for dead?" Michael persisted.

"Your guess is as good as ours, Michael. Maybe we'll get some answers from DI Roberts tomorrow. We're dropping in to see him at Warwick. He'll be taking formal statements from Jacky and me at the same time."

"And then in the afternoon we go to the hospital? I'll drive us all there," Michael said.

"I've been thinking about that. Family first. You go, Michael, and take Jacky with you. LJ thinks the world shines out of your backside and, I'm guessing, he's pretty fond of Jacky too. He'll need all the support he can get. Whatever has gone on in your past – you with your father, your father with you, it's LJ who counts right now."

Michael pulled his mobile out of his pocket. "I need to make a call. I'll go out in the garden."

"And I'm going to take Barny out for a walk – a long walk – give you two time to talk, and don't waste it," Fred said, pointing his finger first at Michael and then at Jacky.

Jacky watched as Michael went back out into the garden and lit another cigarette. "Do you think he'll give me a second chance, Fred?"

"Rome wasn't built in a day, my old friend." Fred smiled. "I'll be back later."

# Forty-Two

DI Gary Roberts slotted the second of the signed statements into the file. "Thanks, Jacky. Thanks, Fred," he said. "That's the statements done. I went to see Mr Lovell briefly earlier on this morning. He told me what he could. It's amazing he can remember anything, the state he was in."

"So, what happened the other night, Gary? We heard the shots," Fred asked.

"He was ready for us. I reckon the ambulance and police car sirens spooked him when we answered your call. Had a rifle already loaded and started firing as soon as we called him out. No one hurt but he wasn't going to give up without a fight. Let's just say that he won't be troubling anybody again in this life."

"You mean?" Jacky said.

"Yes. He's in the mortuary right now," Gary replied.

"Did you find the bunker?" Jacky asked.

Gary nodded. "We did. Pretty gruesome. According to Mr Lovell, he thinks he had been locked in there for over three months, possibly from the end of September but can't be sure. Boscombe fed him scraps and gave him water daily right up until the day before you found him. That's what you saw in the evenings, Boscombe taking down his daily rations. Enough to keep him alive but barely."

"Boscombe?" Fred frowned. "Thought his name was Boston, Peter Boston."

"That's the name he's been using since he moved to Bartonford. Before that, he was known as Dr Boscombe."

"A doctor?" Fred questioned.

"Yes. A self-appointed doctor. Never had a medical qualification in his life but somehow managed to pass himself off as a qualified doctor." Gary sighed at the very thought that anybody could get away with it.

"Not possible," Fred said.

"Depends upon how determined you are. We've traced his movements back to '74 when he started as an orderly in a big hospital in Staffordshire. Called himself Peter Boston back then so maybe that was his real name, but I doubt it. Spent ten years there and then left. The following year, our Dr Boscombe, Peter Boston as you know him, appears as a GP and starts to do his rounds. First, fifteen years in the home counties then Gloucester, Herefordshire, and Worcestershire. Finally, he comes to Warwickshire."

"You boys have been busy in the past twenty-four hours," Jacky said.

"Not that busy. Boscombe made it easy for us. Forgive me but I'm going to call him Boscombe, it's too complicated flitting between Boscombe and Boston. He kept a journal going right back to his teenage years. There was an incident when he was sixteen, recorded in the journal in gory detail. I'll not go into it. Then nothing until '84 when he turns up as a doctor – not qualified or anything, you understand."

"How did he get away with it?" Fred scratched his head.

"A black leather Gladstone bag, together with what we assume are forged papers and certificates, and a whole lot of front," Gary said. "The bag was in the hall up at the farm, full of medical supplies and surgical instruments. He never stayed in one place for more than three years. Moved on before anyone's suspicion was aroused.

I reckon he was a paranoid schizophrenic, but I don't know much about these things. Out of touch with reality, muddled, confused, delusions of grandeur – it's all there," Gary said.

"OCD?" Michael said. Fred and Jacky exchanged puzzled looks. "Obsessive Compulsive Disorder. I've just covered it in my course. I'd have my doubts that he was OCD. He'd never have held down a doctor's job as he did."

Gary nodded. "Well, whatever he had, or he didn't have, he was one nasty piece of work and obsessed for sure."

"And his obsession?" Michael asked.

Gary took a deep breath. What he had to tell them would hit hard. "Gypsies, Michael, the Roma in particular. From what little we have read of the journals so far, he had one main mission in life and that was to rid society of the Roma by any means possible. He used two ploys. First, in his guise as a doctor, misdiagnosing the ailments of the gypsy communities that he worked with, failing to prescribe adequate medicines, discouraging those in need of hospitalisation from getting the treatment they needed. More than a hundred deaths all marked down to natural causes and death certificates signed by Dr Boscombe. More than we had originally thought. From his journal entries, we can reasonably conclude that many of those gypsies could have been saved given the right care. Some may well have died of natural causes but not many. Men, women, and children, he didn't differentiate between them."

"Jesus," Fred said. "Why the hell would any man set out to kill Roma?"

"As I said earlier it seems to relate back to an incident in his teens – let's just say he had a run-in with a few Roma and didn't come out of it very well," Gary said.

"You said two ploys, Gary?" Michael said.

"That's right. Dating right back to '84 and coinciding with Dr Boscombe's residency in each of the towns, there was a spate of fatal accidents involving Roma. Motoring accidents, accidents with electric saws, and…" Gary hesitated. "Fires. All verdicts were accidental death, death certificates signed by Dr Boscombe. It's all in his journals. He was devious, clever. He planned everything down to the last detail, leaving no trace."

"Jess?" Michael paled. "The fire?"

Gary nodded. "Yes. There's an entry in his journal for January 2013. He moved into Cold Comfort Farm in late 2011, no longer Dr Boscombe but Peter Boston. It's all in the journal – how he'd been watching the camp by day and night, watching and waiting. He counted you out and counted you in. He knew when any of you so much as scratched your noses. He waited until the early evening after dark, and then crept in and set the fire. He saw his opportunity to get rid of two more gypsies and he murdered them in cold blood. Once Boscombe had LJ in the bunker, he went to great lengths to take Mr Lovell through the events of that day and several times over."

"The bastard, the bloody bastard." Jacky thumped the table. "I wish you'd kept him alive. I'd have shown him a few tricks that he wouldn't have forgotten in a long time. My daughter, my grand-daughter…"

Fred covered Jacky's hand with his own. "You wouldn't have been on your own, my friend. But we can't bring them back."

Michael put his head in his hands. They had always suspected foul play and now they had been proved right. It was no spark from a wood-burning stove that had sent Jess to her grave. It tore him apart to think that his sister had died so young and in pain, and it troubled him even more that he could not share his other knowledge with Fred and his father. He had to talk to LJ first.

"How come LJ lived to tell the story?" Fred asked, "Why didn't he just kill him too?"

"I said that Dr Boscombe had one main mission in life," Gary started. "When he moved to Bartonford, he ceased his career as a self-appointed doctor, but he never forgot his mission. He turned his hand to an even more macabre occupation. Have any of you ever heard of Josef Mengele?"

"Nazi doctor wasn't he?" Fred said. "Auschwitz, Second World War?"

"The same, Fred. A Nazi doctor who not only selected prisoners for the gas chamber but also conducted medical experiments on them. First, it was Jews, and then when he ran out of Jews, the Roma. Boscombe was obsessed with Mengele's work and set out to conduct experiments, which, in his warped mind, Mengele would have approved of. Mr Lovell walked right into the spider's web. He confirms that he came back to Bartonford to pay his last respects to Jess and Sally. He went to the church and then he went to stand up on the hill overlooking the place where they had died. It was then that he came face to face with Boscombe. He lived and worked with the man for a year but never left the premises."

"What experiments?" Michael asked.

"To analyse and modify his genes. Or to put it more simply brainwash him into leaving his gypsy past behind. To make a new man of him – acceptable, in Boscombe's opinion, to normal society. He had this crazy idea that if his experiment worked, he could repeat it on other gypsies, and thereby continue with his mission. When he thought the time was right, he needed to test his progress. He fed Mr Lovell with a truth drug, scopolamine, only to find out that his little experiment had failed miserably, so Mr Lovell had to die. That's when he put him in the bunker. He took pleasure in watching Mr Lovell's daily deterioration – he wanted to understand how much pain and humiliation a gypsy could take. You found him just in time."

"Why in God's name did he stay there for all that time?" Michael asked.

"Out of prison, wife and kiddie dead, family moved on, vulnerable, not sure what next. Boscombe offered him a roof over his head, food and work provided that he never left the premises. It gave LJ the time he needed to get to grips with the past and decide on his future plans. And he was learning on the job – Boscombe had set himself up as a nurseryman. LJ hankered to go into the same business. Too late, but he'd made up his mind to get out of there, catch up with the family and after that follow his dream." Gary said.

Michael turned to his father. "I didn't really thank you properly, Jacky – Dad – but I am now."

"Oh, Michael, if only it were that easy. If I'd been the father I should have been, Jess would have been alive today. I'll go to my grave blaming myself." A picture of abject misery, Jacky wiped the tears from his face with the back of his hand.

"She was happy, Jacky. She had some good years. And..." Michael stopped mid-sentence. He was close, so close.

"Are we finished, Gary?" Fred asked. "Don't know about anybody else, but I need another brew. Spotted a nice little tea shop around the corner and that's where I'm going. Michael and Jacky are on their way to the hospital."

"Not quite," Gary said. "Apparently, Boscombe had a wife when he moved to Bartonford. Nobody actually saw her, but she's mentioned in his journals. Mr Lovell reckons she's buried in a plot of land behind the house. The lads are digging it up right now."

"So, you've told LJ all this?" Michael asked.

"There wasn't much he didn't already know. Boscombe told him just about everything. A dead man can't talk, isn't that what they say?" Gary replied.

"Why did it take so long, Gary, if he's been systematically murdering Roma all these years? Where were you when you were needed? Was it because they were Roma – they didn't matter?" Michael asked quietly.

"We take every death seriously, Michael, Roma or not. I'm not going to make any excuses. All I can say is that there will be an exceptionally long enquiry into the whole thing and a lot of lessons learned, not least of all that the force needs to work more closely together and hand in hand with the Traveller communities and not against them," Gary said. "Off the record, it was a girl who tipped us off, a university student. She picked up on a pattern of unexplained deaths in the gypsy community. While we interviewed known associates of Boscombe to put together a photofit picture, she got off her backside and went out and talked to people in the gypsy camps. She heard about Jess Lovell and what had happened in Bartonford and rang me. When Fred's call came in, it had to be connected. And we knew Boscombe was not far away. He was up to his old tricks again."

"Does this girl have a name?" Fred asked.

Gary smiled; a faint blush crept across his face. "Yes, she does. But I'm not at liberty to divulge it."

"Well, whatever her name is, buy her some flowers from me and give her a kiss whilst you are about it," Fred said with a twinkle in his eye.

"That's what I had in mind, Fred," Gary replied.

# Forty-Three

Michael glanced in through the glass partition in the door and quietly pushed open the door. "Can I come in, LJ?"

"Michael?" LJ whispered drowsily, lifting his head an inch or two from the pillow.

"The prodigal son come to visit, that's me, LJ. I'm so sorry. I should have kept in contact. I should have come looking for you when you disappeared. Some brother-in-law I've turned out to be."

"Is that really you? You've grown a beard, you're wearing glasses, you're thin as a rake. You look worse than me." LJ gave him a weak smile and held out his hand.

Michael took LJ's hand in his. It was all skin and bone. "You've lost a few pounds yourself."

"You've heard what happened?" LJ said.

Michael nodded. "DI Roberts briefed us this morning. It'll be a bestseller if it ever gets published. You, you're okay?"

"Weak, still muzzy and not so hot on my feet. They're feeding me up and giving me physio three times a day to strengthen the muscles in my back and my legs. One day at a time, but I'm getting there slowly. I came back to Bartonford to be with Jess and Sally one last time...Jacky told me not to come back, to look to the future. I should have listened to him. He was my saviour

275

in Ranbury. Without him I wouldn't have survived. He was like a father to me," LJ rambled.

"So, this Jacky, he was a good friend?" Michael asked.

"The best. One day I hope to be able to thank him properly."

Michael stored it away. He had been sceptical when Fred had told him that his father was a changed man. He had been disbelieving of his father's words when he had apologised. Now LJ was singing the man's praises. Perhaps it was time to start believing that people could change. Maybe Jacky's ears were burning where he was sitting – not a million miles away in the hospital waiting room.

"Tell me what you've been up to, Michael."

"It would send you to sleep, LJ, but there is something I need to talk to you about. It's important and it's a long story. Are you sure you're up to it, or shall I come back tomorrow?"

LJ nodded. "I'm okay. If there's something worrying you…"

Michael hung his head and started to speak slowly and deliberately. "I met a woman last September. Her name is Miriam. She owns a property in the Algarve, and I needed a break from my studies. Fred told me about her. She used to live in Bartonford. I went out there for a week's holiday last September. We hit it off straight away. I fell in love with her and her child, a little girl called Joanna. She's so cute, so bright, so full of life. She looked just like her mother, both tall and redheads, hair cut in bobs."

"I'm pleased that you've found yourself a lady, Michael," LJ smiled.

"There were incidents," Michael pressed on. "Nothing I could put my finger on at the time. I went back to the Algarve this Christmas. Stayed three nights. We had a wonderful time until…"

"The last night I was there – two nights ago – Joanna asked me to put her to bed. She asked for a fairy story. I made one up about a little girl who lived in a gypsy caravan with her mummy and daddy." His words came tumbling back to him as he recounted the tale: "They travelled far and wide, their caravan pulled by their faithful pony. Her mummy had had a difficult life – her father

276

made her work, day and night, just like Cinderella. She swept the floors, cooked and cleaned, and worked in the fields by day, but she never complained. And then one sunny day when she was selling her flowers at the market, she met her Prince Charming and fell in love with him. Her big bad father didn't like the idea that she had found somebody to love her and tried to stop her seeing Prince Charming. Her brother loved her more than anything and was determined that she should be happy and so he helped her run away from home. Prince Charming lived in a gypsy camp with his family not far away, and under cover of darkness the brother and his sister stole out of the bad man's house and together went off to find him. Prince Charming's family took her to their hearts and treated her like a princess. They were married soon after and then a few years later they had a little girl. She was a princess. She was bubbly and clever and fun. She loved living with her mother and father in their pretty gypsy caravan. She had her own little cot, painted pink, that had been carved by her uncle. She didn't have lots of toys or smart clothes, but she was the happiest little girl in the world. On clear nights she went outside to gaze at the stars with her mummy and daddy. Her daddy knew everything there was to know about them and told her endless stories about them. Those were the nights she loved most. Each night she went to sleep with stars in her eyes."

"Jess and Sally. It's a lovely story, Michael," LJ said, his eyes welling up.

Michael shook his head. "It doesn't end there, LJ. Then Joanna turned to me and said, 'Goodnight, Uncle Michael. And next time you come to the Algarve, will you paint stars on my ceiling, just like the ceiling in the gypsy caravan?'" Michael paused.

LJ frowned. "I don't see where this is going, Michael. Maybe I'm just tired and not concentrating."

"But you see, LJ, I'd never told Joanna about the stars painted on the ceiling. There's only one little girl who would have known that. I suddenly had flashbacks – the way Joanna frowned at me when I said 'bye-bye' to her when I left in September, the child who ran barefoot on the sand, barefoot in the house, barefoot in the garden, barefoot on the pavements – the child who hated to wear shoes. The long willowy legs, the dimple on her chin, the instant bond between us..." Michael looked his brother-in-law in the eye. "LJ, in that moment I knew. Joanna is Sally, Sally is Joanna."

"Sally's dead, Michael. She died in the fire," LJ said.

"No, LJ, that's where you are wrong. Sally didn't die in the fire. She would have died in the fire if Miriam hadn't taken her away first," Michael said. "Everyone thought she had died."

LJ closed his eyes. His little girl alive? It just wasn't possible. "Taken her away? What do you mean, Michael?"

"When the truth hit me, I packed my bags and left the Algarve. I caught the next flight out. I couldn't trust myself to speak to Miriam about it. I was angry. I was confused. I was bewildered. I needed time to get my thoughts together. I needed time to go over it all again and convince myself that I had not gone mad. It was then, when I landed at Birmingham, that I picked up Fred's call telling me that you had been found. I rang Miriam early yesterday morning and confronted her with it. I told her that I was Sally's uncle, and I knew who Joanna was. I told her how I knew. She didn't deny it. She admitted that she had abducted Sally."

"How? Why?" LJ asked.

"Why? She told me about the times when Jess and Sally used to go and see her at her cottage in Bartonford. Jess never mentioned her visits to either of us, did she? They went to see Miriam the day before she was leaving Bartonford to go and live in the Algarve. Sally used to call her Auntie Miriam. She told Sally all about the seaside and Sally pleaded to go with her. They were close. Miriam's own hours-old child was stolen from her – her words, not mine – when she sixteen. Taken away and adopted. Her parents knew best. To this day she has never seen the child again. She called her Joanna Rose. I am not making excuses for what she did.

"She packed the car and locked the cottage behind her. On a whim, she stopped by the campground to drop some sweets in for Sally. It was about six, she told me. She knocked on the door. No one answered. She tried the door. It was unlocked. Jess was fast asleep on the bed. Sally heard her and said to her, 'I knew you wouldn't go away without me.' Sally slipped her hand in hers, and in a moment of madness Miriam put her in the car. By the time she got to the cross-channel tunnel she knew she'd done wrong, but she couldn't turn back. Sally slept under a blanket on the backseat. No one noticed she was there. They arrived in France and drove down to Portugal. Sally was so excited about going to the seaside. It wasn't hard for Miriam to convince herself that all she was doing was taking Sally for a holiday. She'd get her back home, sometime, somehow. And then she heard from an acquaintance in Bartonford that Jess had died, and you were locked away in jail. She told Sally that you had both gone to heaven. She was trying to protect her. Sally loved the name Joanna and soon forgot that she had ever had any other name. Auntie Miriam became Mummy."

"But didn't you recognise her? Didn't she recognise you? Surely..." LJ probed.

"A child grows up so fast, LJ. The little girl I met had red hair the colour of Miriam's. She was tall for her age, confident. She spoke fluent Portuguese. Look at me, LJ. I've changed too. Lost all that weight that I used to carry. I have long hair, I wear glasses. She wouldn't have recognised me either."

"It's difficult to take all this in, Michael. Sally is alive?"

"Yes. The bottom line is that Miriam abducted your little girl, LJ. I've told no one else. What happens next is up to you. She's ready to take her punishment."

LJ closed his eyes and turned his head away; Michael waited. "Jess was watching over her, Michael," LJ said from a distance.

"It's nothing more than a miracle that she is alive. How can I want someone who saved my daughter's life to be punished for it?"

"You don't want me to report her to the police?" Michael asked. He had readied himself to make the call. It was the moment he was dreading.

"No, no police, Michael. It's a family matter," LJ said. "Our Sally is alive. That's all that matters. You say you've told no one? Not even Byron?"

"No one. I wanted to see with my own eyes that you were okay before I spoke to Byron."

"Tell Byron that I am well. Say nothing to him about Sally for the moment," LJ said.

"But he'll want to know. He loved Sally so much."

"Do this for me, Michael."

Michael swallowed hard. LJ's generosity was overwhelming. "I will. Thank you. I can't change my feelings towards Miriam. I still love her. I would like to ask her to marry me. I think she would accept."

"You deserve to be happy, Michael. You don't need my blessing, but you have it."

"What shall I tell Miriam?"

LJ puckered his brow. For seconds he did not speak. "You can tell her that the police will not be involved. Tell her that I love my daughter more than anything in the world and I will do nothing to hurt her more than she has already been hurt. I need to think about what is best for Sally. The child should be told nothing of this for the moment. Leave it with me, Michael. Give me a couple of days to work it through in my head."

"I understand," Michael said. "Whatever you decide. You have always been the most generous man I have ever met. I'm indebted to you."

"We're brothers, aren't we? Isn't this what brothers would do for one another?"

"Thank you," Michael said. "Are you feeling strong enough to receive another visitor? There's someone you might like to meet again. He's been sitting patiently in the waiting room for the last hour. He's the one who found you and fished you out of that bunker. Remember Jacky? And you're right, he's a good man. Shall I ask him to come in?"

"Jacky, here now?" LJ's face lit up.

Michael nodded, slipped his coat on, and left.

# Forty-Four

LJ sat up in bed. It was five days since he had been rescued from the bunker and five days that he had been in hospital. He had received the very best of treatment. Physically he was stronger; mentally he was coming to terms with his experience and starting to look to the future, a future that had so nearly been stolen from him. That Sally was alive remained a miracle that he hardly dared believe to be true. That Jacky was his father-in-law had come as a shock, but not an entirely unpleasant one. He had watched a grown man break down and cry as the words had tumbled out of his mouth – disturbing, and at the same time, moving. Jess had been looking over his shoulder. He felt her presence, sensed her mood. She told him to forgive, to put it behind him, to welcome the new Jacky into the family. She reminded him that Sally now had a second grandfather, one who would love her as much as anybody could. She told him that he should tell Jacky about his granddaughter.

He had explained to his old friend that he had never forgotten his kindness and support in Ranbury and that he had written regularly as he had promised. Then he had passed a bundle of letters bound together by a thick red rubber band to his old friend; the letters that Peter Boston had never posted, and that Gary Roberts had found up at Cold Comfort House.

Fred had hardly been able to contain his impatience to meet up with LJ again, and maybe pick up on some of the conversations they had so much enjoyed almost two years since – sitting out on the wooden bench on his new patio. He had remained quietly in the background, waiting while LJ was reunited with Michael and introduced to his father-in-law, and, of course, received the news about Sally. Chuffed to bits at his part in the successful reunion of Michael with Jacky and Jacky with LJ, he was in no hurry. Everything was moving along nicely. Both he and Jacky had been dumbfounded when Michael had, in confidence, told them about Sally; he more than Jacky. Had he not by some quirk of fate passed on details of Miriam's holiday home to Michael, then Sally might well still be presumed dead. The wonder of her survival surpassed any bitterness they might have felt towards Miriam. Abducting the child had been a terrible thing to do, but it had been destiny. He gave himself another well-earned pat on the back.

LJ smiled as he heard the familiar sound of the walking stick, tip-tapping across the wooden floor.

"I've missed you," Fred said.

"I've missed you too, Fred," LJ said, holding out his hand.

"I brought this for you." Fred pulled a bunch of white heather out of a carrier bag and put it on the bedside table. "I took your advice – patio's full of it. Can't seem to stop it flowering. It's been a real godsend."

"Lucky, heather." LJ looked at the green stems and the small white flowers.

Fred narrowed his eyes and took a deep breath. "There's something I've got to get off my chest."

LJ laughed. "I'll have to buy a confessional before long. What is it, Fred?"

"I'll not rest easy until I say it to your face. I've never had the opportunity to apologise to you for being a right coward, LJ. Maybe if I'd come into court that day, you would never have been convicted and none of this would have happened. I always knew that it had nothing to do with you, but they wouldn't believe me. I've spent the last two years trying to make it up to you, in my own way." Fred hung his head in shame.

"You're the last person I ever blamed, Fred," LJ said, reaching into the small drawer beside the bed. "Do you recognise these?" Picking up a pair of cufflinks and three small silver photograph frames, he lay them on the white blanket in front of him.

"My cufflinks? My photograph frames? How?" Fred looked up at LJ. Had he been wrong all the time?

"Do you remember that day when we were sitting outside on your bench putting the world to rights and talking through the planting for your garden? It was cold, but the winter sun warmed us."

Fred nodded. "Whenever I need to clear my head, I go out and sit on that bench. I've had many a conversation with you over the past two years."

"When we were sitting there, do you remember what we saw? It was so ordinary, so day-to-day that neither of us took any notice of it, but you did mention it."

"Help me, LJ. I'll be eighty-two this year and the old memory isn't quite as sharp as it once was," Fred said, his brow puckered.

"You said, 'That's unusual, we don't often see a postman twice in the day'." LJ stopped to give his friend time to think back.

"Well, blow me, you're right. That's exactly what I said, but I'm not following you."

"Peter Boston, the owner of Cold Comfort Farm had a red postman's jacket. It hung in his hall." LJ picked up the cufflinks. "These were found in a drawer in his desk by the police when they searched the house. DI Roberts worked out their significance and brought them to me to hand back to you in person. Peter Boston was the thief. He staged the robbery, knowing I was there with you. I can only assume to point the blame at me. I know the man, I lived with him for over a year. I know what he was capable of. It was just another way to bring gypsies into disrepute, another way to get one more gypsy off the street."

"The man was unhinged, demented, crazy," Fred exclaimed loudly. "He didn't deserve a quick death. He deserved to be hung, drawn and quartered. Right under our noses. How did he do all that right under our noses? We should burn the house down to the ground, have a ceremonial burning…" Red in the face, Fred ranted on. "Hell's too good for that one."

"Don't burn the house down, Fred," LJ said, a smile crossed his face.

"Why the hell not?"

"Because, Fred, he left it to me in his will complete with the land and the business, and all his worldly wealth."

"No!" Fred exclaimed.

"Yes, Fred. I remember him telling me towards the end that he had been so convinced that his little plan would work that he had altered his will and left everything to me. He told me in what were so nearly my dying hours that he was going to change it back again. I guess he didn't have time to do so."

Wide-eyed, open-mouthed, Fred stared at LJ. "You can't possibly be thinking of going back there after everything that he did to you? No man could…You know that they found his wife buried in the garden?"

"I know. I told DI Roberts where to dig. Boston told me all about her. And in answer to your question, yes, I am thinking just that, Fred. The house is bricks and mortar, no more, no less. I once told you that my dream would be to have my own nursery or landscaping business, well, now I have. I have finished with the open road. I shall talk to Byron about it. I need to settle down – for Sally's sake."

"But Bartonford, after the way the villagers treated you? Live within that community? Are you quite sure that you're thinking straight, LJ?"

LJ nodded and smiled. "It'll take time for them to accept me, I know that. But I'll show them that having a gypsy in their midst is nothing to fear."

"Well, I'll be jiggered. If that's what you want, then I'm right behind you all the way, LJ. You won't get any trouble from them, mark my words." Fred smiled to himself. If anyone stepped out of line, then it would be his greatest pleasure to deliver a stiff dose of Fred's own medicine. "It's good to hear you so positive."

"Jacky told me about some of your adventures. He was almost rolling around the floor when he told me. I haven't laughed so much in a very long time, but maybe you were a bit harsh. And the white heather was a nice touch."

"They deserved it, the lot of them." Fred grinned. Life was going to be very quiet now that he had completed his project. "You'll want the house smartened up, won't you? I can see to that, give me and Jacky something to do. We'll clear it out, give it a fresh coat of paint, get rid of all the old memories. You won't know it when we've finished." Fred's eyes sparkled at the prospect of yet another project. "When are they going to let you out?"

"Another week and I'll be out."

"So, I'll take that as a yes, and we can get on with the job?" Fred looked thoughtful. "Maybe I'm getting ahead of myself. How's this going to work with probate and all that? Maybe you can't go back until it's all sorted?"

"I asked the solicitor who came to see me the very same thing. Seems that I am deemed to have been a tenant. I had board and lodgings in place of pay, but it adds up to the same thing. I can go back there any time."

"You've got to change the name of the place, LJ. Cold Comfort Farm gives me the creeps."

"Lying here has given me plenty of time to think, Fred. I am going to rename it White Heather Farm."

"No time to waste then. I'd better get back and get things

organised," Fred said, grabbing hold of his walking stick.

LJ extended his arm and motioned Fred to sit down again. "If you're not in a hurry, I asked you to come and see me for another reason, Fred. I want to run a few thoughts past you – someone who is not family. Did, Jacky tell you about Sally?"

Fred nodded. "I couldn't be happier for you, LJ. I'm listening. I've missed putting the world to rights." Fred sat back down and made himself comfortable.

"It's about Sally. She's just spent almost two years in the Algarve with Miriam, the person that she now sees as her mother and loves. Michael says Miriam is a wonderful mother and dotes on her. Sally is five and a half years old, and according to Michael a happy and confident child…"

"Miriam's got a lot to answer for," Fred snapped.

"Let's not go there, Fred – what's done is done. It's in the past. Miriam is the only mother Sally knows now and that is one thing that I cannot take away from her. What matters is that she is alive. I have been mulling it over in my mind and this is what I have been thinking…"

Fred took a deep breath and exhaled slowly. "You're one in a million, LJ, gypsy or no gypsy – the best."

"Thanks, Fred. That's all I need to know. I'll talk to Michael."

# Forty-Five

LJ opened the door and looked out across the farm. It was a beautiful early Spring day, the sky blue, the air cold, crisp, and clean. He took a deep breath. It felt good to be alive.

Three months since he had left hospital and returned to the farmhouse, it felt like home. Painted throughout, new curtains hung at the windows, recarpeted and refurnished, there was not a trace left of what had gone before, and he had Fred and Jacky to thank for it. While Fred had supervised the internal transformation, Jacky had put his back into working the nursery. The plants and shrubs were thriving, the ground that had been dug up by the police had been returfed, and the bunker filled in. Nobody would have known that anything untoward had ever taken place on the property.

The sign which had once repelled visitors at the end of the drive had been replaced by one that welcomed visitors: "Welcome to White Heather Farm".

It had taken ten weeks to get a passport for Sally before she could return to England. Michael had helped LJ with obtaining a copy of the birth certificate which had been destroyed in the fire. Miriam had sent photographs of Sally. When the passport had arrived at White Heather Farm, LJ had mailed it to Miriam in the Algarve.

Miriam and Sally had caught the first available flight. The name on the passport was Sally Lovell.

Finally, later that day, he would be reunited with his daughter for the first time in over two years. He had been over and over it with Michael and over and over it in his head. They had agreed that neither Michael nor Miriam would say anything to Sally about LJ other than that he was a friend of Uncle Michael who had invited them to stay. LJ would then tell his daughter as near the truth as he could. He had one chance to get it right without anybody being hurt. At two, Michael, Miriam and Sally would arrive at White Heather Farm.

He was ready and waiting for them. In the near distance, he heard the crunch of tyres on gravel and watched as an old red Ford Focus slowly made its way towards the house. Michael wound down the window and waved. There was a woman seated beside him. A head bobbed up and down from the backseat. LJ smiled and waved back. It was the moment he had been waiting for.

She was out of the car like a bolt of lightning and running towards him. She had grown so much. She was tall and lithe, her hair coloured auburn and cut in a bob, but he could never mistake her for other than Sally.

"Hello!" she called, "Thank you for inviting us to stay with you. I've always wanted to come to England. I'm so excited. Can I call you LJ? That's what Uncle Michael calls you, isn't it?"

LJ picked her up his arms and swung her round. "You can, Joanna, That's such a pretty name. Welcome to White Heather Farm. You're my first guest."

"It's colder here than in Portugal, but it's lovely. Have you got a fire in your house?" she asked, rubbing her hands together.

"A big roaring fire, all ready for you," he said. "See if you can find it."

Michael grinned. "LJ, let me introduce you to Miriam."

Miriam held back and coloured crimson before holding out her hand to him. "I don't know what to say," she whispered out of earshot of Joanna. His eyes were the same sapphire blue as Joanna's eyes, his cheekbones high and angular, his frame long and slim. The family resemblance was strong. His grip was firm but reassuring. Her hand shook, communicating her fear to LJ.

"There's nothing to say, Miriam. We both want the same thing. We both want Joanna to be a happy and secure child. You are and always will be welcome in my home." LJ nodded and smiled. He sensed her calm, the tension ebbing out of her body. Michael was right. She was a lovely woman and a natural mother.

Joanna popped her head out of the front door and ran back towards Michael. "Come on, Uncle Michael. Come on, Mummy. There's a lovely fire in the house."

"We're coming, darling," she said.

Michael steered Miriam towards the house, while LJ led the way.

Mesmorised by the flames, Joanna lay sprawled on the rug in front of the fire at Miriam's feet. Michael lounged comfortably on the sofa beside Miriam. LJ settled down into an armchair which, soon after he had moved in, had become his favourite. A book lay open on the arm of the chair, *Far From the Madding Crowd* by Thomas Hardy.

"Can I tell you a secret, LJ?" Joanna said, sidling up beside him, the flicker from the fire lighting her eyes.

Miriam glanced at Michael. Both knew that she would not be able to keep her secret for long. "Mummy and Uncle Michael are going to get married and I'm going to be their flower girl. It's the best fairy story ever."

"I know, he told me," LJ said, turning to Michael and Miriam. "I couldn't be happier for the two of you."

"Will you show me my bedroom, LJ?" Joanna asked.

LJ glanced at Michael and then at Miriam. It was the opportunity that he had been waiting for. "It would be my pleasure, Joanna. How about I ask Mummy and Uncle Michael to go in the kitchen and make us some tea and cut some cake while we're gone?"

"Sounds like a plan," Michael said, reaching out for Miriam's hand.

"It is going to be alright, isn't it? I feel so guilty," Miriam whispered.

Michael nodded reassuringly. "Trust me. Trust LJ. It'll all be fine."

It was the moment he had longed for. It was the moment he most dreaded. Had he done the right thing? LJ opened the bedroom door. "Take a look. See if you like it. I had it decorated especially for you."

Joanne caught her breath as she stepped into the room and looked around. The furniture had been painted pink. Pink flowery curtains draped the windows. A fluffy pale blue carpet covered the floor. Painted pink again, a small child's desk and a chair sat under the window. "Your Uncle Michael made the desk and the chair, Joanna. Just for you."

"It's amazing. I don't know what to say," Joanna walked around and finally settled in the chair.

"Do you know your stars, Joanna?" LJ said.

"My stars?" Joanna frowned.

"Look up above. Look at the ceiling. It's the night sky and those are all the constellations." LJ watched as, in awe, she explored every inch of the painted ceiling with her eyes.

"I think I've been here before," she whispered. "It's like something out of a fairy story."

"Do you have time for a special story before we go back and join Mummy and Uncle Michael?"

Joanna nodded.

"Let's sit on the bed together." LJ said, as he held out his hand to her. "There was once a little girl called Sally and she lived with her Mummy and Daddy in a beautiful gypsy caravan..."

*

"Mummy!" Joanna shouted, as she raced back downstairs and threw herself on the sofa beside Miriam, her eyes sparkling, "Mummy! I've got a proper, daddy! And we're all going to live together in daddy's house." The words tumbled out one after another. "My proper mummy died in a fire, but I'll always love you, Mummy and you, Uncle Michael. And I've got a grandpa, Jacky and a grandpa, John, in Ireland, and a grandma. And I've got an Uncle Byron and lots of cousins. And daddy says that I can call myself Joanna or Sally or both. You didn't tell me."

Miriam smiled and took Joanna in her arms. "We wanted it to be a surprise for you, darling," she said.

"It's the best," Joanna grinned, "Daddy explained everything. And I am going to be a flower girl as well."

# Epilogue

## *June 2015*

Who'd have thought it? Fred Humphries, chairman of the Parish Council. Well, it was me who said that the village needed to change, wasn't it? Out with the old and in with the new, if you can say that about an eighty-two-year-old. I feel younger than I have for years. The Pied Piper couldn't wait to pass the baton on to me. Mind you, I don't take any stick from the locals like she used to. They know better than to come crying to me over trivial matters.

Ursula Trenchard, 'she who must be obeyed', sold up and moved out back in February. Billericay went out of business. Oswaldian House, as he called it, has been converted to stables. Barny misses the dogs, but that's all. Don't see hide nor hair of Smytheson Hodge these days. He keeps himself to himself up at the manor house. We don't have squires around here anymore. Ingrams sold his land to the Parish Council and moved down London way. What a coup that was – we bought the land for a song. It's only taken fifty years to my knowledge to get the right land for a playing field in the village. Sam and Marie keep in touch. We get on better now that they don't live on my doorstep.

There wasn't a dry eye in the house when I chaired my first Parish Council meeting. I did away with the normal agenda and set my own. I told them about what had happened to LJ at Boston's hands (or Boscombe's, whichever you prefer) and I told them that

293

they had been wrong about him right from the beginning. He was no thief, and he had been persecuted simply because he was a gypsy. There were a few raised eyebrows when I mentioned that he had bought (maybe stretching a point but whatever) Boston's old place and business.

I told them that I wasn't going to stand for any prejudice in the village. I didn't care if people were gypsies, black, white, pink, purple, gay or lesbian – everyone was to treat everyone else with respect. It did cross my mind that I wasn't entirely innocent myself – what with Chrissy and the council house lot. I've dropped the council house tag, you'll be pleased to know.

I've got a sneaking suspicion that a few of the locals worked out that I might have had something to do with putting a few people in their place over the last couple of years, not that they've said anything to me, and of course, I'd never admit it to anyone.

Well, my words did their trick. The day after the meeting, a steady stream of visitors wended their way up to White Heather Farm to give LJ the welcome he deserved. Some probably went up there out of morbid curiosity, but most of them genuinely wanted to get to know the man. He'll not make a bad catch for somebody one day – twenty-nine years old, good-looking, with a nice house and a good business. I reckon that there's a few of the girls in the village who have got an eye on him. If I know LJ, they'll have to wait a very long time, but you never know.

So, LJ's making a grand job of the nursery business. He's a natural, and with Jacky doing the spadework, the business is thriving. Jacky is still living with me. Looks like the two of us are in it for the long haul. It suits me down to the ground and Barny wouldn't have it any other way.

Miriam's kept the Algarve for holidays – we're all going there later in the year. My first time out of the country since the war. Michael stays in Birmingham weekdays to continue his studies and comes home at weekends. He'll make a fine lawyer. LJ's financing his studies with the cash that Boston left in his will – a small fortune. From what I can gather he made his cash out of gypsies, charged them for going to visit them. Charged them, and then helped them die. The way LJ sees it is that if the cash finances Michael's studies and Michael goes on to fight for the rights of ethnic minorities, and gypsies in particular, then the cash is being returned to the right place. He wanted to pay me back the money I spent on White Heather Farm while he was in hospital, but I wasn't having any of that. I had a grand in the bank from the trial fiasco and more than enough in my own account to do it. You can't take it with you and Marie and Sam are quite comfortably off anyway.

Joanna or Sally, as she sometimes calls herself, and her father are almost joined at the hip. Talk about a bond between them. He bought her a pony a little while ago. She feeds and grooms him every morning before she goes to school and the same when she gets back in the afternoons. She called him Jocklin. Funny name, I said to her, and she said that it had just popped into her head out of the blue. Does make me wonder sometimes how much she does remember from when she was a nipper. Did I tell you that she goes to the local primary school now? She's nearly six, fluent in Portuguese and as bright as a button. She's the envy of her classmates and a star pupil. Needless to say, Jacky thinks that the sun shines out of her backside. He loves being grandpa and spends hours playing with her.

I liked Byron. It was good to see him and the family again. They came to the village just a couple of weeks after Miriam and Joanna came back. They pitched up in a paddock at the back of the nursery for a week. It was good timing, Byron and the family coming back to the village. He, Byron Jnr, Colin, David, Nathan and Buckland all worked their socks off up at the old garages and workshop to get the playing field sorted out. Byron suggested a small memorial to Jess in the play area and that we plant a couple of willow trees. I liked that. LJ told Byron that he wasn't to be a stranger, family was important to him. The family were to come any time they wanted to. LJ seems to have made himself an indispensable member of the community. I co-opted him onto the Parish Council, but he volunteered himself for shifts in the village shop. Told me just the other week that he's thinking about having a summer garden party up at White Heather in the next couple of weeks – nothing posh, just a barbecue and people to bring their own drinks.

Remember that nice DI Roberts? He came to visit me a month ago and he brought someone with him – Elizabeth, Elizabeth Goodge. She's a lovely girl. I told Gary to get a ring on her finger as soon as possible. Girls like her don't grow on trees.

And me? I spend as much time up at White Heather as I do at Pettifer these days. Just one big family.

If you enjoyed this book then you might also enjoy:

# The Silver Sting

It has been thirteen years since the elderly residents of Magnolia Court were scammed out of a comfortable existence by an unscrupulous developer who took their money and ran.

A twist of fate leads Gabby, Uncle Max and Aunt Hetty's niece, to uncover the developer's whereabouts.

Pointed in the right direction by Gabby, the residents draw on their life skills to overcome one obstacle after another in order to recover what is theirs by right.

No one should underestimate the tenacity and ingenuity of this charming and endearing bunch of senior citizens. Age and infirmity are set aside as they set out on their quest to seek retribution.

In Uncle Max's own words: "I believe that our little ruse could well go down in history as an example of what can be achieved when people, irrespective of their age, pool their skills and work together as a team. Regrettably, we cannot write the story – none of us would like to spend the rest of our days at Her Majesty's pleasure – but maybe someday someone will write it for us…"

And, the sequel:

# The Silver Dollar

When an uninvited visitor threatens the happiness of one of their own, the resourceful residents of Magnolia Court have an unholy mess to unravel.

A string of lies, deception and deceit follow the arrival of Jennifer's estranged son, Jamie.

Abused and homeless, Thomas finds sanctuary with Gerald, but is he telling the whole truth?

Lives are torn apart as the truth comes out.

# Acknowledgements

As always thanks to the SilverWood team for guiding me throughout the process, keeping me on the straight and narrow, and not being afraid to tell me when my characters stray or facts included might be subject to challenge.

Thanks to long-suffering friends, Phil, Jane, and Jan for reading through and checking various versions of this novel, and thanks to Robin for his legal advice.

If I have inadvertently left anybody out, then thanks to them as well!

Lightning Source UK Ltd.
Milton Keynes UK
UKHW030929100222
398479UK00001B/43